E X   L I B R I S

PAULINE C. MARTIN

# EPIDEMIC!

# EPIDEMIC!

FRANK G. SLAUGHTER

DOUBLEDAY & COMPANY, INC.

*Garden City, New York*

All of the characters in this book are fictitious,
and any resemblance to actual persons, living
or dead, is purely coincidental.

# Contents

# EPIDEMIC!

# 1. Saturday

ALL the long day, while the *Sally Piersol* waited in quarantine, Captain Michael Dollard had known he was going to die.

Now that the ancient tramp had reached her North River pier, now that his vertigo had subsided, he could grin at his reflection in the cabin mirror and dismiss the gnawing certainty he would cease to exist by morning. Captain Dollard had ridden out most of life's storms on luck and bulldog courage. Tonight, with yet another voyage in the logbook, he could feel the same animal confidence rise within him as he opened his locker and took out shore clothes for his reunion with Gladys.

It was true that the voyage to New York had been purest hell. Particularly the final leg, when he had seen no landfall between Cape Palmas and Ambrose Light. Yesterday, wakening with a bone-deep chill shaking his body, Michael Dollard had sensed in the depths of his Celtic soul that final retribution had overtaken him . . . The others had started the same way. It had begun when he'd taken on the four half-castes during his stopover in the Cameroons: a man was a fool to sign deck hands without medical tickets, regardless of their color. The first body had gone overside long before he could set a course for New York. Five others had followed within a fortnight, turning the *Sally Piersol* into a charnel house where death claimed victims at will.

Tonight the memory of that voyage home was vague in the captain's mind. The medical books in his cabin had been of no help in fighting the strange disease. He could not risk turning back: the Strine Shipping Company would have fired him overnight had he been late with his cargo. Having no choice, he had held course—and let the sickness burn itself out.

An iron taskmaster at sea, Michael Dollard had put down panic swiftly. A few erasures in the logbook had kept his record clean. Only yesterday (when a week had passed with no new illness) he had felt the situation was in control. When death had touched his own body with icy fingers, he had shaken off the summons. Loyalty to his ship, if not to his forecastle, had held him to the bridge until he dropped anchor in quarantine.

As always, he had taken pride in the solemn ritual of deceiving the inspectors. After they had given the *Sally Piersol* clearance, his duty to the owners was done. He had resigned the bridge to his first officer and tumbled into his berth for his wrestle with the dark angel. . . . At the time, he had not cared too much who won the contest.

Now he was on his feet again, insisting he had sweated out worse fevers. His superbly muscled body still dripped with perspiration while he fumbled into slacks and a sport shirt. Once he had stuffed a wallet in his pocket and picked up the hammered-silver bracelet he had bought for Gladys in Mombasa, he was ready to test his shore legs.

His cabin door opened to the deck abaft the bridge. Stepping into the humid August evening, Captain Dollard noted the glare of lights on the pier, the stir of men in blue. New York, he reminded himself, was in the grip of another dock strike: police had been called after the Strine Company had made a vain attempt to break the picket line with non-union stevedores. The strike meant a cold-iron watch tonight—and Dollard bewailed his luck. He had meant to put to sea again at the week's end: life was always simpler when he had dropped the last buoy astern.

At the gangway he was sure the man on watch looked at him oddly, but he held back the usual reprimand. The miseries they had brought from Africa still haunted the *Sally Piersol*, tangible as the fog that had begun to seep in from the harbor. Leaving a watchman under that evil aura tonight was punishment enough.

"I'll be ashore until morning. Pass the word to Mr. Norton."

There was a pay phone in the shed. Dollard paused to ring the cafeteria where Gladys served as night cashier. Even before he heard the familiar, husky voice a heavy pulse was thudding in his brain. As he had expected, she promised to join him within an hour and suggested he go at once to her apartment. Gladys could not have been more casually friendly had they met yesterday—and this, to Captain Dollard, was part of her charm.

He was grinning like a satyr when he left the booth, pausing just long enough to check the steel chain at his belt. A copy of his lady's latchkey hung there, along with several others. Each was an open sesame at the portal of some cheerful wanton. The memory pictures they evoked did nothing to diminish his ego.

On the curb below the West Side Highway, he showed his dock pass to the police captain in charge. A miasma that had insulted his nostrils on the pier now swept over him full force—exhaled, like the breath of an ailing giant, from an alley mouth across the way.

"What goes, Officer?"

The police captain snorted. "If you mean the perfume, ask Jon Marek. He runs the Sanitation Union."

"I thought the *dockers* were out."

"So are the garbage haulers. Their last truck rolled on Friday."

The master of the *Sally Piersol* shrugged and moved on, cutting through the longshoremen's sullen picket line to gain the far sidewalk. The follies of landlubbers—with notable female exceptions—had long ceased to trouble him. Yet he remained sharply aware of the mist of decay that hung in the alley's mouth. He had breathed that sick-sweet odor far too often in odd corners of the globe. He knew the threat it posed.

His vertigo returned briefly, forcing him to steady himself at a lamppost. While it lasted, police and picket lines were lost in a black void, along with the throb of the Saturday night traffic on the highway overhead. He could almost believe New York had expired in his absence, that he was the first to discover the corpse. He shook his head angrily to banish the image—but the breath from the alley pursued him, and it was still the odor of death.

At a warehouse entrance just beyond, he stepped into the street to avoid a pair of ragged legs sprawled on the pavement. In a way he could welcome the sight of a snoring drunk, since it proved he was not quite alone in a forsaken world. There was a mission on the corner—but he abandoned the impulse to help the derelict to a cot. Instead he pushed on to flag a taxi. Gladys had promised to join him at midnight. He had no time to waste on pity.

2.

The seaman on watch waited a prudent moment after the captain had gone ashore before checking on the sobriety of Mr. Norton. Stentorian breathing behind a cabin door convinced him that the first officer would issue no orders before daybreak. It would be safe to break out a bottle of his own.

Even though the sickness had passed him by, it had been a fearful voyage for first-class seaman Ben Vardis. Four drinks later, when he staggered under the gangway beacon again, a group of unauthorized passengers had long since left the *Sally Piersol*.

The exodus began when a pointed nose appeared at the starboard cargo hatch. Fringed with whiskers and brownish fur, it quivered as it identified the smells of land: beady eyes searched for possible enemies before the foot-long creature scampered from the hold. His companions, a baker's dozen in number, seemed almost as large as they moved stealthily topside.

One by one the stowaways gathered in the shadow of the ship's rail. Still cautious, they seemed to hang back by instinct, as though awaiting their leader's signal to follow Captain Dollard ashore.

This particular stowaway was known to science as *Rattus rattus*, though he had been called by a shorter name since the Dark Ages. He was not listed on the ship's manifest, but he was a sinister part of the cargo she had taken in the Cameroons. Tonight the leader was happy to be free of the hold—and properly fearful lest freedom prove short-lived. After a hesitant moment he lifted a paw to the gangway. A new lure had reached him, more compelling than the notes of Hamlin's piper, the scent of garbage from the water front. *Rattus rattus* forgot his caution and bolted down the gangway. His companions followed in nimble file.

On the street the leader hesitated at the sight of blue-clad legs—but the gutter was deep, and it was a simple matter to dodge through the police cordon. The longshoremen's picket line was avoided by the same route. The leader had now gained the alley, and the first of several overflowing pails. The others joined him promptly to share the unlooked-for repast.

Seen in that murky light, there was nothing to separate *Rattus rattus* from his ten million Manhattan brothers. However, these knights of the kitchen stoop had a special distinction—in this case a sinister one. The difference lay in the passengers they carried.

*Xenopsylla cheopis* was the family name of these passengers— and like the rats, their presence was unauthorized. Any child would have recognized them as fleas. Only an epidemiologist would have suspected that both flea and rat were part of a cycle that had begun its function just after they boarded the *Sally Piersol*.

The cycle started with the flea, and its genesis was too slight for the eye to grasp. Found only in the vitals of *Xenopsylla cheopis*, it could be summarized in a jingle that held more truth than poetry:

Big fleas have little fleas
Upon their backs to bite 'em
While the small fleas have other fleas
And so, *ad infinitum.*

The parasite that inhabited the digestive tract of *Xenopsylla che-opis* was as vicious as it was small in size. *Pasteurella pestis* was its Latin label; it seemed a quite ordinary germ under the microscope, a rod-shaped organism whose identity had been established before the century's turn. Known as the creator and spreader of plague (the Black Death of the Middle Ages) its activities had been curtailed sharply by modern sanitation. Yet like smallpox it had never been stamped out entirely.

Had this rod-shaped organism chosen the ideal spot to flourish, it could hardly have improved on New York's strike-bound water front this humid summer of 1965.

Captain Michael Dollard had not dreamed that his port of call in the Cameroons was rife with plague. The disease had always been endemic in Asia. In Africa its incidence had grown rarer—now that massive aid programs, financed in both America and Europe, had done much to improve the lot of the average native. Medical pioneering by the World Health Organization of the United Nations had played a similar role in cutting death rates. There were still backward regions. This part of the Cameroons was one—thanks to tribal enmities and a deep-rooted xenophobia that kept outside doctors at a distance.

Dollard had signed his extra hands at that tropical port. Aware of the risk he was taking, he had not known that each new occupant of his forecastle was a reservoir of death. From that initial error, rat, flea and plague germ had joined in their classic triad . . . The trio had claimed victims by the millions in the not too recent past. During the Atlantic crossing Dollard himself had become the last human target.

That Saturday *Pasteurella pestis* found its first host ashore a few minutes before midnight—when the rat-leader darted into the warehouse door to investigate a gently snoring rag bag that turned out to be human.

The rag bag was named Willoughby Fellowes—a man of parts in his heyday, until a fondness for rye whisky brought him to this Skid Row annex. While the rat scurried about his person, it was doubtful that he would have left his impromptu bivouac even if the creature's squeaking had wakened him. A man of his habits had slept in worse company.

The rat moved on in a moment, disdaining this inferior being—but the pause had given a score of *Xenopsylla cheopis* a golden opportunity to change domiciles. Willoughby Fellowes's body was burning hot tonight—an inevitable side-effect of the pint of liquor still unprocessed in the alimentary tract . . . It was a habitat these small invaders loved best.

In a few more moments, choosing their lodgments at will, they had completed the phenomenon that gave the bacillus access to the derelict's blood stream.

Well after midnight, with the nirvana of whisky lifting, Fellowes was suddenly aware of an itching hide. Sitting bolt upright in the warehouse door, he lifted his nose skyward and howled at the sliver of new moon above the Hudson.

The sound drew no notice whatever from longshoremen or police, still following their treadmills on the Strine Pier. These were city ears, inured to every decibel of the damned.

The wailing subsided when Fellowes's busy fingers (doing their best to ease the torment of a skin afire) touched the bottle tucked in his waistband. To his surprise it was still a quarter full. He remembered that he had saved it to combat the blue horror of morning—but this was no time for prudence. He bit out the cork, spat it defiantly at the oblivious picket line, and lifted the cure-all to his lips.

Oddly enough, the hoped-for passout eluded him—long after he had swallowed the final drop. While his pain was deepest, he tossed back his head for a second canine howl. It was the proper signature for the Walpurgis Night of Willoughby Fellowes.

Long before his sickness had run its course, the island of Manhattan would echo with other, still more anguished lamentations.

### 3.

That same night in the women's locker room at the Millway cafeteria on Forty-third Street, Gladys Schreiber lowered another bottle from her lips at the sound of the manager's step outside. She was neither drunk nor sober after an evening of nipping: there was no real danger of a reprimand. A past master at such potations, she

meant to remain in this blissful state until her shift ended and she
could hasten to her reunion with Mike Dollard.

Before the captain's phone call she had been fighting devils of her
own making, all of them familiar tormentors when she faced a Saturday alone. When Dollard had called her from the pier, she was already deep in a fog of alcohol and planning to end her evening with
a sleeping pill. Now, elated by the thought of his presence in her
apartment, she continued to drink from habit only, to keep this level
of euphoria constant.

She was still tingling at midnight, when she surrendered the cash
register to her replacement and hastened to the reckless luxury of
a taxi. Her flat was on the wrong side of the Village. Usually the
ugly street depressed her. Tonight she could ignore its near squalor
while she raced up the stair, caroling her salty Lothario's name
with a fine desregard for her neighbors.

The door was ajar. Dollard lay on the sofa in what—at first glance
—seemed complete oblivion. The place was in wild disorder. Chairs
had been upended, and a lamp leaned crazily against the bookcase:
it was evident that he had fumbled his way into the room with just
enough sense of direction to reach the only bed the flat boasted.

Once she had made sure nothing was broken, Gladys shrugged off
her resentment: Mike had earned a wingding after his months at sea.
She sat beside him and ran her fingers through his hair.

"It's me, honey," she whispered. "Try to wake up——"

His stupor was not so deep as she had feared. His eyes had opened
at her touch; now he held out his arms to her. His kiss was all she
remembered. Had she been sober she would have noted that his lips
were cracked with fever. Floating on air as she was, it hardly mattered that he had not uttered a sound, save for a gasp of protest
when she slipped from his embrace at last. This too seemed con-
vincing proof of ardor.

"Back in a jiffy, Mike," she said. "I'll get you a refill."

In her kitchen-pantry, she poured two half-tumblers of bourbon
—downing hers in a toss before she brought the other to the table
beside the sofa. Dollard was dozing again. She made no effort to
waken him while she slipped into a negligee and put out the overhead lights, leaving the kitchen bulb untouched. It was a calculated
effect: her robe was gossamer thin, and the reflected rays did the
most for her figure, leaving her face in shadow. At thirty-three,
Gladys was hardly a beauty. Below the chin, she knew she need
not take a back seat to anyone.

"Glad I'm back, sailor?"

Again he reached for her blindly—but the new tide of rapture was brief. Midway in their kiss she could feel his breath escape in a long sigh. It was an eerie, hissing sound, as though the tortured lungs could receive air no longer.

"You can't conk out *again*, Mike!"

He made no response as his head rolled crazily on his shoulders. The eyes that had burned into hers were glazed; it was a collapse that could have but one meaning. Revulsion was upon her as she freed herself—so violently that he rolled from sofa to floor. Even before he sprawled at her feet, she knew Captain Michael Dollard was dead.

There was no sign of breathing when she put a hand to his chest; she had made the gesture mechanically, without hope. In life Dollard had been a Greek god with Dublin trimmings. In death he was a massive grotesque. Already she sensed there was something queer about his passing, a threat to her own safety she dared not face squarely.

When her brain steadied, she knew she had been close to fainting. Dollard had not touched his drink. Once she had swallowed it, she felt herself rising to this emergency. Mike had died of a heart attack, she told herself: it was the traditional ending for black Irishmen at the wrong end of a debauch. It was hardly her fault that he had chosen to expire here.

Gladys Schreiber had not coped with men for twenty years without certain basic resources. Knotting the sash of her robe, she moved to the window that opened on the fire-escape. The concrete apron of the areaway was fifteen feet below. After she had dragged Dollard's body to the sill, she paused just long enough to douse his clothes in bourbon, empty his pockets, and turn them inside out. Then heaving with all of her considerable strength, she lifted him to the grille.

She heard the body strike the concrete—and held her breath. When the continued quiet below reassured her, she leaned free of the rail. Dollard had landed face up, between two refuse cans—the picture of a drunk robbed of his last copper and clubbed down for good measure.

His bridge cap lay on the floor. Noting that his name and ship were stenciled in the band, she tossed it into the areaway. When the police found the body, they would appreciate a handy identification.

Dawn was gray at the window before she could put her flat in order again. Her hands were shaking when she swallowed a double bromide, but the thud of her pulses had subsided. Being a philosopher as well as a wanton, Gladys Schreiber felt she would sleep without dreams.

Naturally she had no way of guessing that *Pasteurella pestis* had marked her for its own during those two fever-hot kisses.

# 2.  Sunday

LESS than an airline mile from Gladys Schreiber's flat the white cliffs of Manhattan Central Hospital rose sheer against the morning. High in that immaculate massif, on a terrace outside an operating theatre, a man in a long-skirted lab coat was taking his final drag on a cigarette. While he lingered, he turned thoughtful eyes toward the wedge of towers in downtown Manhattan, beginning to take form again now the mist was rising.

By ordinary standards, Dr. Eric Stowe should have had no truck with this austere scene: his horoscope, read at birth, would have marked him for the playboy's role. On his father's side he was descended from one of the richest families in New York, on his mother's from one of the oldest. For the first two decades of his existence he had run true to form. At Princeton he had won golf championships, piloted his yacht in Bermuda races, and played polo in two hemispheres. He had enjoyed these gold-spoon triumphs thoroughly —until graduation from an officer-candidate school had opened his eyes to perils outside his sheltered universe.

Like a growing number of his generation, Second Lieutenant Eric Stowe had proved himself a member of a new and healthy breed—the still young millionaire who had realized in time that wealth had its own responsibilities. Freedom from want in his own sphere, Eric decided, demanded increased service elsewhere. From the day of that revelation, he had been a true citizen of the world.

Four years of medical school at Johns Hopkins (and another three at its top-flight School of Public Health) had slowed his golf game—but it had turned him into a finely tooled instrument in the fields of immunology and bacteriology. He had moved into these branches of medicine as naturally as a minister answering his call. With no need to earn—family trust funds now enabled him to live well from the income of his income—he had found his niche in the far-flung activities of the World Health Organization.

Before he turned thirty-five Eric had fought malaria in Indo-

China, brush fever in the Amazon basin, yaws in Haiti, and the peculiarly virulent form of typhus that had brought near disaster in Korea. From the first his work had fulfilled him. The road he was taking had been blazed by other medical pioneers. If he had found no new trails so far, the results he had achieved were reward enough.

Only half aware that his name was now something of a legend, Eric Stowe considered himself no more than a technician who fought disease in the most effective fashion—by keeping it from new victims. In his own mind he was no more important than the agronomist who showed Hindu farmers how to irrigate their parched earth with a pump operated by a stationary bicycle. Or the mission teacher who spelled out the elements of birth control, and opened new skies for the illiterate with the printed word.

His presence in New York this Sunday morning in August was the aftermath of an attack of equine encephalitis, acquired while he was observing an outbreak of the disease in New Jersey. The illness had come close to ending his career. When his restless spirit had threatened to cut short convalescence much too early, his old friend Dr. Selden Grove, the medical director of Manhattan Central, had persuaded him to accept an interim appointment at that hospital. His task since June had been twofold—to update the department of pathology and to study a problem that was becoming more acute with each wonder-drug discovery: control of a rapidly increasing list of germs that seemed immune to antibiotics.

Eric's sojourn at Manhattan Central had been a true reunion. Not only was the director a colleague; Dr. Robert Trent, the newly appointed surgical chief, had been a roommate at Hopkins. In the years between their careers had taken them down divergent paths. But the three men had never lost touch, since each of them in his way shared a common dedication.

The task of retooling the pathology service had been an exacting one. Dr. Eric Stowe had attacked outworn procedures and political cabals with the same forthright energy. Using his best persuasion (and the example of his own checkbook) he had cajoled the Merton Foundation into increasing its usual philanthropies when it was time to install vitally needed equipment.

This morning he could tell himself the job was done: with his health restored, he must return to his chosen field. Tomorrow or the day after (but not much longer) he would call on his chief in the United Nations Secretariat, to pin down the rumor that field work awaited him. . . .

The immunologist moved to the terrace rail to survey the city of his birth, a city he had seldom visited during the past decade. At this height, he could see only the geometric pattern of the slum that clung like gray fungus to the hospital's southern flank. Directly below, he looked down at a rubble-strewn plain, a ten-block area where bulldozers had worked since the new year to level the walls of old-law tenements. By midsummer, blowtorches had burned away the last dark stain of poverty. Billboards proclaimed this to be the site of the Merton Project, an experiment in community living financed by the Jasper Merton Foundation, under the aegis of the hospital— and the newly expanded Housing Authority of New York.

Jasper Merton's model apartments and community center had been scheduled for unveiling on a staggered five-year schedule. To- day, save for Merton House (a gymnasium and recreation hall on the project's rim) actual construction had stalled in a maze of detail. Merton had already dismissed two sets of architects, with profane comments on their competence. An eighty-year old Croesus with prejudices all his own (and a permanent elephantiasis of the ego) he had raged like a madman when gangs from nearby streets made bonfires of his road blocks and chalked giant obscenities on the walls of Merton House.

There had been persistent hints of late that the development would be abandoned. Recalling that Merton was making one of his frequent tours of the hospital this morning, Eric breathed a prayer in Selden Grove's behalf . . . For the past few days, a more immediate problem had troubled him, a threat far more important than the tan- trums of an aged philanthropist.

From the rail of the terrace, the city's water front seemed utterly peaceful. It was hard to believe that fists and truncheons had been active there last midnight, now that the city's two wildcat strikes showed no signs of lifting. Tomorrow the situation would worsen: Ted Horgan, the transit boss, had announced that he would call a one-day sympathy walkout in subway terminal, taxi garage, and bus depot.

So far there had been no reports of outright hardship, no danger signals on the Health Department graphs recording the city's inci- dence of disease. What if the three-way impasse continued—and the always accurate fever chart should rise tomorrow?

On that peaceful Sunday, soothed by a warm sun and the sense of his impending freedom, Dr. Eric Stowe found that his thoughts re- fused to focus on implied dangers. Besides, he had come to this lofty vantage point for another reason. In a few more moments, Bob Trent would be operating in the adjacent theatre—on a casualty of the pier brawl, a dock foreman injured in last night's skirmish with the strikers.

Bob Trent's operations always drew full galleries. This morning, Bob's former roommate was waiting to join the crowd of interns who had already gathered for the surgical chief's arrival. It was motive enough for stealing an hour from the wrap-up chores that awaited him in pathology.

This Sunday there was no need to look beyond these immaculate ramparts, to imagine disasters he would never solve.

"May I join you, Doctor?"

Eric turned from the terrace rail. Eve Bronson had just emerged from the door of the operating theatre.

"You've appeared at the perfect moment," he said. "I was despairing about the future. It's a side-effect of my trade."

"Bob's finished scrubbing. They'll call us in a moment."

"Aren't you assisting?"

"I've been on night duty, so he won't allow it."

The disappointment in the girl's voice, Eric knew, was genuine. Eve Bronson was far more than an expert surgical nurse who had worked in every service at Manhattan Central, en route to her own medical degree.

"What's the diagnosis?"

"Extradural hemmorhage. Why are you looking at me so strangely?"

"It's the hermit in me. Don't give it a second thought."

So far he had been able to take refuge in badinage at such moments. Clearly this was not the place to tell Eve Bronson that she had seemed fresh as the morning while she crossed the terrace—or that he had been in love with her for all of this busy summer. He had yet to verify the general opinion in the hospital that Eve was at least half-engaged to the surgical chief. Nor had he paused to remind himself that their meetings had grown frequent since vacation schedules had kept Bob on almost constant duty . . . So far he had failed to allot Eve Bronson a place in his future. Public-health work was a calling that allowed little time for such outside interests as love, and less for thoughts of marriage.

"Can we dine tonight, Eve?"

"Bob's taking me to a movie. It's his first evening out this month." Eve accepted a cigarette and a light. Her eyes were level above the flame, but he had not missed her blush. "What's this about giving up on tomorrow?"

"Today's brooding was hardly original," said Eric. "I was only taking pride in being an American—and asking myself how long I could enjoy the luxury."

Eve was smiling now: he had used the gambit before.

"Is this your sermon on the spires of Manhattan?"

"Look at those downtown towers closely. Are they another mirage that will vanish tomorrow?"

"People asked that question twenty years ago when the first A-bomb exploded," Eve reminded him.

"I'm not thinking of enemy rockets. Cities can be destroyed from within."

Eve gestured toward the soaring panorama downtown. "Who could destroy that?"

"Don't press me. I've no actual candidate."

"It's only a theory, then?"

"Less than that: an automatic mental kickback from this rash of strikes."

"I'd heard the mayor was on his way home to settle them."

"Let's hope he isn't too late. Walkouts by dockers, sanitation, and transit could be a risky triple play."

"What are you afraid of? Sabotage? An epidemic?"

"Sometimes they go together."

"Is this your idea, Eric? Or Inspector Dalton's?"

The immunologist shrugged. "Let's say that Pete Dalton and I have similar views on *homo sapiens*—when the species lives at the bottom of the ladder. I've been going the rounds with him lately: neither of us was cheered by our findings." Detective-Inspector Dalton, who visited the hospital often in line of duty, was another friend of long standing. He had recently taken over a special patrol of Manhattan's depressed areas, for reasons he had not yet divulged.

"Does Dr. Grove endorse gloomy views?" asked Eve.

"Far from it. Your hospital director feels I've much too vivid an imagination."

"He may be right," said Eve.

"I'm *praying* he's right, my dear. After all, Selden Grove grew up in one of these backwaters. He knows what New Yorkers can take and survive."

"But you still side with the inspector?"

"I'm afraid so, Eve. I won't breathe easily until those strikes are broken. To my mind, we're sitting on a potential volcano."

"Isn't that a penalty of our century?"

"Perhaps. It's no reason why we should perch there forever." Eric turned from the rail as an orderly signaled from the doorframe. "Let's go in before you decide I'm an incurable pessimist."

2.

Operating Room Number Seven (known to the hospital staff as the Bubble, since its walls were constructed almost entirely of frosted glass) glowed with man-made radiance that Sunday forenoon. Once the doors of the observation theatre had closed on the two tardy spectators, it was a self-contained cosmos, obeying no laws but its own.

Save for the purr of its air conditioners (with their built-in ultra-violet lamps for killing obstinate germs; the tall, circular room was silent. The rows of white-clad spectators—interns and student nurses for the most part, and surgeons with free time—awaited an impending drama whose curtain-raising they knew by heart. They sat un-stirring when Dr. Robert Trent emerged from the scrub room: in this theatre, there was no applause for the star until his performance ended. The surgical chief was drying his hands on a sterile towel. It was the last ritual of the scrub room before he held out his arms for gown and gloves.

Bob Trent (who was, at this instant, absolute ruler of the kingdom he surveyed) moved briskly into the theatre. He saw at once that all was in order. His inventory, though swift, was meticulous. The present scrub nurse was well aware of this habit. When Bob turned to the patient (whose shaven skull was being painted a brilliant scarlet by resident surgeon George Peters), she heaved a faintly audible sigh. The surgical chief turned to give her the quick, reassuring nod that made him beloved by his staff, even when he drove them hardest.

While Dr. Peters was draping the section of skull where a bone-flap would be laid down to expose the brain, Bob Trent stepped closer to the microphone that hung from the shadowless operating light with its multiplaned mirrors.

"This man was slugged last night in a water front brawl," he said. "X-rays confirmed a fracture in the left temporal region. We have treated him expectantly. In this case, we were warned by the track of the fracture—which seemed dangerously close to the foramen, the passage where the middle meningeal artery enters the skull to supply lining membranes of the brain."

Bob lifted his head to study the rows of eager young faces above him. Until the operation ended, it was the last time he would notice them as individuals. "Any student not familiar with the field should consult *Gray's Anatomy* on leaving. You may find this procedure in your next exam."

George Peters stood ready with the final drape, a sheet with a rectangular window designed to cover the whole area save for the section of scarlet-tinted skull, left exposed for the incision. Bob moved to the table to help arrange the sheet.

"You may inject for a bone-flap in the left temporal area, Doctor."

The microphone, manipulated by a technician in the gallery, dropped to a spot above the table where it could pick up the surgeon's remarks more readily. Bob addressed it again while he completed the draping.

"The most dangerous complication in this type of skull injury is blood loss outside the lining membranes of the brain. It is called an extradural hemorrhage. Because of the location of the break, we were on the lookout for such a complication, and caught it promptly. Otherwise the hemorrhage might have spread, pressing upon the vital centers of respiration and heart control, with fatal results."

George Peters had finished injecting novocain in a pattern that resembled the path of a mole through dry ground, raising the scalp in a small circle. The process was completed with the injection of a full syringe into the muscles above and behind the ear. Bob Trent took the scalpel from his scrub nurse, then lifted a square of folded gauze in the other hand, to press hard against the scalp, where his assistant's syringe had outlined the proposed incision. Across the table, George Peters repeated the motion.

When the scalpel slashed to bone level, bleeding was controlled by clamping the cut edge and reversing the hemostatic forceps. So skilled were surgeon and team their progress seemed almost casual. In actual fact, the operation was a ticklish emergency, conducted as rapidly as safety permitted. Coolness under pressure and the ability to work at top speed despite adverse conditions were Bob Trent's trade-marks.

The incision was U-shaped, with the open end just above the ear. With the bone exposed for its full extent, Bob was now working with a burr-shaped drill, opening holes at two-inch intervals along the curving line. The first showed blood between the meninges and the skull, confirming his diagnosis.

When the procedure was finished, he took up a flat strip of metal with a slotted end and worked it gently into the first perforation, continuing the approach on the under side of the skull until the strip appeared in the second opening. A Gigli saw, (a flexible strand of tough, twisted steel) was hooked in the slot. While George Peters steadied the patient's head, Bob attached its handles at each end of the strip and cut through the section of bone between the openings. The process was repeated until the entire bone-flap was free, except for the solid part at the open end of the U.

"Periosteal elevator, please."

A second strip of metal came into the surgeon's hand. He worked it into one opening at the closed end of the U, while Peters paralleled the technique in the adjoining drill hole. When they exerted a steady downward pressure, the whole flap lifted as smoothly as a cellar door, folding back from the operative field with its muscle attached and exposing the brain beneath.

A rush of blood and bloodstained fluid was removed swiftly with a suction tip which Bob rotated in the depths of the wound. When the field showed clear, he swabbed it clean and surveyed the steady ooze of scarlet from the injured vessel. Again he addressed the gallery: his whole being was concentrated on the area beneath the bone-flap, and he was only half-aware of his amplified voice on the theatre radio.

"Our diagnosis is now established. With the area in complete view, we see that the tear occurred where the vessel traverses the skull through a foramen."

The silence above told that his audience was as intent as he, but Bob was unaware of the reaction. From the start, he could have identified the nature of the injury as accurately as though the patient's brain were lighted from within. The striker's blackjack, meant to stun rather than maim, had done its work too well, crushing the vessel at a spot where suture was impossible. The race to reach it had been taut enough—slowed by the elaborate prepping that had, of necessity, preceded the actual trephines. Now that the bleeder was marked beyond question, it would be a relatively simple matter to control it.

"Suction, George."

Dr. Peters inserted the tube into the foramen itself, clearing it of blood in short order. Swabbing the opening dry, Bob packed it expertly with a tiny wisp of cotton. It would take the place of the usual ligatures, and stop the flow of blood as effectively. When the emergency dike was secure, he put down the pointed thumb-forcep he had used to control the flow and stepped back to await results.

It had been a textbook demonstration. A little later, when he touched the area with a cotton pledget, it was only lightly stained. The natural retraction of the arterial wall (now it had received this outside assistance) had already controlled the flow.

"How's he doing, Hank?"

"Pulse and respiration have steadied," said Henry Proctor, the anesthetist. His report, muffled though it was by the hood of draperies separating him from the sterile operating field, rang out heartily.

"He seems to be out of danger," Bob told the gallery. "We'll wait a bit longer to be sure."

The surgeon stepped back from his work, letting his wall of concentration drop. For the first time he was truly conscious of the gallery above him. During the operation it had been only a blur. Now he could pick out faces, nod to students and doctors he recognized. He grimaced behind his mask when he saw that Eve Bronson and Eric Stowe were seated in the second row. He had expected to find them among the spectators: there was no need to question his brief spasm of anger.

Next year (when his present appointment ended) Dr. Robert Trent intended to go into private practice, to reap the rewards his long tour of duty had earned him. He had not yet asked Eve to share his future. She knew he was hers for the asking, despite the lack of spoken words; it was her privilege to hold him at arm's length until she made up her mind. Meanwhile he could hardly object if she set her cap for Eric Stowe. . . . Since they had roomed together at Hopkins, Eric had been the *beau ideal* of every girl they met: sometimes it had seemed to young Dr. Trent that he was doomed to track down dates of his own only to lose them to his friend.

Bob Trent had always been Eric's antithesis. Eric had been dowered by both God and man, a charmer from his cradle. Bob was a stocky farmer's son, with a thatch that refused to lie flat and a mastiff's jaw that defied the world. Eric had come down to medical school in Baltimore in a two-seated Hispano, trailed by a chauffeur-driven limousine bearing his more immediate wardrobe. Bob had come by day coach from Tennessee, with a single suitcase and a bank loan to cover his first year's tuition—yet the two students had liked each other instantly.

The relationship (founded on mutual respect and deeply shared interests) had ripened with the years. If it was undergoing its first real testing now, Bob felt sure it would survive.

The doctors had kept in constant touch after graduation. Bob had interned at various hospitals in the Southeast before accepting a coveted residency at Manhattan Central. Eric had gone on to embrace a practice that included—quite literally—most of the civilized world, and parts of that world that were still sketched but dimly on the maps . . . That June, when Selden Grove had informed him that Eric would reorganize the hospital's laboratory and pathology service, Bob had rejoiced wholeheartedly.

The realm of medicine (he could tell himself this, not too bitterly) had special rules. It was Eve Bronson's right to applaud his friend's achievements, to contrast them with his own solid but by no means spectacular career to date. Eve hoped for a career of her own, once she had completed her training at Manhattan Central. If she cast her lot with Eric in the far places, how could a prosaic surgeon dissuade her?

Bob Trent shook off the answer to that question. A full minute had passed since he stepped back from his patient. There was no more time for private broodings.

When he returned to the table, he could see no fresh threat from the damaged artery. In a moment more he would close the incision and end this spell of duty. He had been operating steadily since four, when he had taken the dawn shift as a fill-in for a friend on vacation. So far he had not paused to ask himself how tired he really was.

For the last time he looked up at the ranks of faces. He was obscurely pleased to note that Eric had slipped out.

"Are there any questions?"

"Could we have a summary, Doctor—for Mr. Merton?"

He recognized the voice of Selden Grove, addressing him on the spectator microphone that hung above the benches. Straining his eyes, he could make out the hospital director on the last row of seats. This morning, he thought, Grove's handsome executive's profile looked more worn than usual.

The man beside him was a wafer-thin shadow—a caricature of what he once had been, when he ruled his empire in fact as well as name. On the edge of senility, Jasper Merton was still completely alive. Bob could feel the probe of his eyes, as though an invisible ray had pierced the glass of the gallery.

"I've already told Mr. Merton this is a casualty of the strike," said Dr. Grove. "Will you take over from there?"

Bob was careful to make his presentation thorough. He had always suspected Jasper Merton despised doctors as much as he feared them, that the old man's thumping contributions to the hospital had been made for the sole purpose of bullying the recipients. So far he had not risked a gamble on Merton's ignorance.

"Won't there be gangrene from shutting off the blood?" the philanthropist demanded. His voice was vibrant: there was no hint of his eighty years in the acid query. "I'd think the brain would suffer from the lack."

"There'll be no such danger, Mr. Merton," said Bob patiently. "Whoever designed us originally was taking no chances. The brain, like the rest of one's body, has several sources to draw on."

"Did this procedure save your patient's life?"

"There's no doubt of it, sir."

"In that case, young man, I'll congratulate you on an impressive piece of work. I wish all your colleagues were as clever."

It was pure venom and Bob knew it. The spectators (who had witnessed such exchanges before) held their breath as the magnate rose, with the microphone still clutched in a blue-veined hand. When he spoke, he seemed to address the whole gallery as well as the surgeon.

"The man deserved to live: he was struck down defending private property. It's unfortunate that our urge toward self-destruction can't be cured by surgery."

Jasper Merton stalked out with the remark, his wrinkled mummy face impassive, his bearing cocky as a master sergeant's on parade. Bob felt no urge to smile at Dr. Grove's haste to stay close behind. Like every staffer in the hospital, he knew that Manhattan Central's future (to say nothing of the giant housing project outside its walls) depended, almost literally, on this ancient's nod.

"Shall I close?" asked Dr. Peters.

The surgeon turned to his assistant with a slight start. "Please do, George. I'm going to catch what sleep I can before I go off duty."

In the scrub room Bob permitted his spirits to droop for the first time. He could not deny that the exchange had shaken him. Was the grapevine right about Jasper Merton? Had he decided to withdraw his Foundation's support—both from the Project and Manhattan Central? . . . The surgical chief shook off his fear as the anesthetist joined him. This, after all, was not the first time that Merton (checking his bequests with the fussiness of a spinster counting bric-a-brac) had pushed into remote corners of the hospital. Nor was it the first time he had insulted Selden Grove by innuendo. It was part of the director's job, Bob reflected, to roll with such punches.

Once he had peeled off his operating suit—and borrowed twenty dollars from Hank Proctor to complete the financing of tonight's date with Eve—he found himself humming a snatch of tune. Incredibly, he had finished his morning schedule a whole hour before noon. Barring another emergency the resident staff could not handle, he would have glorious hours of sleep before he met Eve in the nurses' wing. He needed those hours to make himself over. Tonight, he must do his not too brilliant best to wipe out the fact that Eve had gone dancing with Eric Stowe two nights ago—and would probably be dating him tomorrow when Bob had the night-resident duty.

With Hank's twenty dollars, he could afford tickets to the off-Broadway revival of Schnitzler's *Affairs of Anatol*. Perhaps the Viennese wit of the play would atone for his own lack of humor. It was strange he had been tongue-tied so often recently in Eve's company . . . Dr. Robert Trent was an expert in human anatomy. He was not the first male to discover that love can be a leaden weight on the spirits, when the lover fears his ardor is unreturned.

3.

Dr. Selden Grove paused on the threshold of his office to watch his visitor settle in the most comfortable chair. In the anteroom his secretary gestured helplessly at a stack of unanswered correspondence that awaited him, a list of unkept appointments. He forced himself to ignore the appeal.

"I believe we've covered the ground, Mr. Merton," he said. "The rehabilitation ward, the pediatric wing, and the nurses' chapel." Try as he might, he could not soft-pedal the caustic note. "Ending with our usual visit to an operating room. Did you find the experience instructive?"

The philanthropist ignored the thrust. Jasper Merton had long since developed the habit of not hearing when deafness suited his mood.

"Why'd we skip your new laboratory?"

"Our pathology department isn't quite ready for inspection. They've still painting to do——"

"It's in use, I take it?"

"Indeed yes, Mr. Merton: it's a vital service in the hospital." The director met the old man's unwinking stare without flinching. Jasper Merton's abysmal ignorance of medicine was as trying as his rudeness—but it was evident he expected more. "In fact, Dr. Stowe is doing some special research on antibiotic-resistant organisms."

The philanthropist rose abruptly. "In that case, I'll have a look."

They swept through the anteroom together: Merton seemed always in haste when on his feet, despite a formidable capacity to dawdle over details. Dismissing a second appeal from his secretary, Selden Grove followed him to the private elevator.

The ground-floor rotunda, with its marble admissions desk, its ultramodern waiting room and glass-walled florist's booth, resembled a hotel lobby that morning, thanks to the visitors entering the private wings and the cheerful bustle of staffers off duty. The director knew they were bound for links or beach. He observed them with a certain envy: it had been a long time since he had stolen a Sunday from the hospital.

Such fits of depression were rare. Usually he reveled in the blend of luck and hard work that had lifted him from a back street in Brooklyn to his present post. Today, in Merton's gadfly presence, he would have settled for a private practice in that same drab neighborhood. The irritation deepened while he followed the magnate down a many-windowed corridor that led to the older portion of the hospital. Here there was no avoiding the demolished blocks that still awaited the cornerstones of the housing project. Across the brick-strewn plain, the silhouette of Merton House was in clear view. The youth center, the director observed, had been defaced by yet another fire—as though a giant's sooty hand had smeared its wall in passing.

The old man paused to level a finger at this newest proof of vandalism.

"D'you see that, Grove?"

"The fire was set by hoodlums, sir."

"I'm aware of that. Why should I rebuild ten square blocks of tenements to house such animals?"

"The police are sure it was an outside job."

"Who cares about the source? Where's Charles Tully? I want his opinion on this latest outrage."

"We'll find him in the lab, Mr. Merton."

Tully was a veteran social worker who served as manager of the youth center. He had become a liaison between the Merton Foundation and the hospital director during the preliminary stage of the project. Much as he disliked using the man as a buffer, Grove knew he could count on Tully to soften the philanthropist's moods.

"What business does *he* have in a laboratory?"

"Right now, he's writing a paper on disease rates in Harlem. His secretary doubles as a technician there. She's helping with the fill-in."

At the corridor's end, a service elevator dropped them to basement level: it was a convenience (and a tradition) that the realm of the pathologist adjoin the hospital morgue. Before the arrival of Eric Stowe, both departments had been dank anachronisms; today, they were models of their kind. The director led his visitor into the glow of fluorescent lighting, confident that even Merton must admit his money had been well-spent in this area.

The philanthropist halted in the doorway to stare at the rows of zinc-plated counters, where microscopes and Bunsen burners, autoclaves and racked test tubes seemed to march on forever. The long, low room was divided by glass partitions. Groups of white-coated technicians were hard at work in each.

"What are these fellows up to, Grove?"

"Diagnostic work, mostly. This is only our clearing house. The autopsy rooms are behind those glass walls. So are the morgue refrigerators—and the specimen rooms, where organs are sectioned for testing."

"Why so much space? Are autopsies that important?"

"Medical science couldn't get far without them, sir."

The old man moved cautiously among the work tables, pausing here and there to favor a technician with a special scowl; but the director (who knew those black looks by heart) saw he had been impressed at last. As they reached Eric Stowe's corner, and Merton managed a thin-lipped travesty of a grin before he held out his hand, Grove could let tired nerves unwind.

Eric had been busy over a microscope. His manner, Grove noted, was flawless: the welcome he offered the visitor was deferential, but there was no trace of awe.

"What are you studying today, Doctor?"

"A type of fungus we're bringing along in our new incubator," said the immunologist. "I wouldn't touch that slide, Mr. Merton. Since the wide use of griseofulvin-type drugs, we're getting some really bad varieties."

"D'you mean they could kill me?"

Grove suppressed a smile as he observed that the philanthropist's wide-eyed stare—like his recoil—was quite genuine.

"Definitely, Mr. Merton—if they invaded your lungs."

"Then you make germs here?"

"Let's say we encourage them to do their worst—and hope we can find ways to control them."

"Humph!" The sound would have offended most ears. To Grove's, it meant merely that the old man had recovered from his spell of unwilling admiration. "Where will we find Tully?"

"His office is on the side hall," said Eric. "Let me show you the way."

"Come with us, Doctor—by all means. Now you're under the same roof, I want a word with you both."

Aware that new storm signals were flying, the director fell into step behind Merton and Eric. The boom of the social worker's voice had already reached them when they turned into the glass-walled corridor. As always, he found its timbre vastly reassuring.

The guiding spirit of Merton House, Grove reflected, was his own best advertisement: Charles Tully was one of those fortunate men who fitted his job to perfection. Mahogany-tanned, with the build of a fullback and the velvet grace of a boxer, he was the living image of a youth counselor: the snapping blue eyes under his snow-white crew cut belied his fifty years.

Remembering how Tully had come to the hospital when the Merton Project was in its blueprint stage, Grove knew the appointment had been justified. Detached from an important post at the New Delhi branch of UNESCO to make the building program a reality, he had soon become an essential part of its social service pattern. His easy skill with Jasper Merton's tantrums was another by-product of his calling. Still another, it seemed, was an ability to turn outcasts into citizens. The intense, dark-haired girl now taking his dictation was a case in point.

Studying Irene Lusk through the open office door, Grove admitted she was still an enigma. Irene was a Polish refugee who had come to the hospital on an exchange quota. On her arrival, she had been completely withdrawn, a tireless laboratory worker who seemed to exist only for the hours she spent there. Since she had become Tully's Girl Friday, there was no mistaking her lifted spirits. Grove had heard the two were lovers; for once he was prepared to accept the gossip at face value. . . .

Ignoring the fact that the social worker was deep in dictation, Jasper Merton had already burst into his office to pump his hand. If Tully resented the brusque invasion, he gave no sign.

"This is an unexpected honor, Mr. Merton," he said. "Find yourselves chairs, gentlemen. You all know my associate Miss Lusk?"

"*I've* not had the privilege," said Merton. "Forgive an old man's candor, Tully—but you've a good eye for secretaries."

Irene Lusk got to her feet, acknowledging the compliment with an oddly formal bow. Grove wondered if there was a trace of mockery behind it.

"Take my chair, Dr. Grove," she murmured. "I won't intrude on your discussion."

"Stay where you are, Miss Lusk," said Merton. "It won't hurt Dr. Grove to stand. I'm here to ask Tully a single direct question. I'd like your reaction too—as well as Stowe's."

The social worker cast a covert look at Grove. "Fire away, Mr. Merton. You'll get honest answers."

"In your opinion, is this brainstorm called the Merton Project workable? Or am I a fool to put in another dollar?"

"If you don't mind, Mr. Merton—" Grove began.

"Keep out of this. I'm asking Tully, not you."

The director flushed, but held his tongue. Tully's bland manner was reassurance enough even before he spoke.

"I can understand your impatience, sir," he said. "But I still urge you to keep an open heart—and an open pocketbook."

"The poor will always be with us. Why should I care how they live? Isn't it bad enough they live at all?"

"Mankind *is* improving, Mr. Merton," said Tully gently. "Including the underprivileged."

"Current headlines don't bear you out," said Merton. "Speak up, Stowe. What's *your* opinion?"

"The Foundation's endorsed this building program," said the immunologist. "So has the Housing Authority—and every welfare service in the city."

"The money's mine. Why should I spend it on better kennels for mad dogs?"

Tully cut in soothingly. "Is it the gang rumbles that trouble you? Or the fact that they seem to make Merton House a target?"

"Delinquency's an inevitable by-product of substandard living," said Eric. "Give these people jobs, and decent homes—they'll become good citizens fast enough."

"I wonder, Stowe. I really do."

"Self-support is the core of the project, Mr. Merton. You might call it a living proof that democracy's more than a slogan. I won't say you've no right to abandon it. But you'll play into enemy hands if you do."

Merton ignored the words as he turned to Irene Lusk. "Well, young woman? Do you agree with these balmy idealists?"

"No, Mr. Merton," said the girl. She spoke quietly, with lowered lids, but there was nothing subservient in her tone. "To me, the poor *are* beyond hope. I have seen too many like them in my own country."

"Before the Russkis moved in, or after?"

"Poverty is older than political systems, sir. As you said yourself, it will be with us always."

The philanthropist chuckled. "Your secretary isn't just beautiful, Tully: she has brains too."

"Mr. Tully won't agree, I'm sure," said Irene Lusk. "Rebuild one more slum, if you wish. Make the work your monument. You can't cure a body of disease by healing one small sore."

The social worker cut in jovially. "Miss Lusk still recalls her own youth too vividly, Mr. Merton. Eventually, I think she'll realize that people can be taught to help themselves——"

Jasper Merton got up, gathering all eyes with the motion and making the most of the silence that followed it. "I'll take your sentiments under advisement," he said. "As of now, I agree with the lady. Come along, Grove: you can see me to my car."

On the curve of the hospital drive, the director made a final effort before he handed Merton into his limousine.

"The mayor's on his way back now, sir. He'll take a firm hand, I'm sure——"

"If he doesn't, he'll hear from me."

"Dr. Stowe plans to dine with him tonight. Would you like him to report to you later?"

"I'll get my own reports," said Merton. "Stowe's well-meaning—but he's rubbed elbows too long with the pink-cloud dwellers at UN.

So, for that matter, has my friend Tully. Next time I hope you'll provide better stooges."

He settled in his car, with the shortest of nods. The chauffeur, honking at the crowd of idlers that had clustered round his mud-guards, roared into traffic with the disdain of a minion whose employer's license is police-proof.

Grove stood at the curb until the limousine had vanished in the bright steel river of the Drive. When he turned back to a hopelessly postponed schedule, he found he had no talent left for damnation. Jasper Merton, as always, had departed with the last word—and the whip was still anchored firmly in his fist.

4.

When Charles Tully was alone with his secretary, he unlocked a drawer of his desk, took out a leather-bound diary, and sat for a moment with his pen poised above it. The social worker—a sophist well-versed in the follies of man—had made frequent entries in that diary since June, using a special language all his own. Today he closed the book without added comment, restored it to the desk, and rose from his swivel chair.

"If you'll excuse me, my dear," he said. "I think I'll visit awhile in pathology."

"Suit yourself, Charles."

Tully smiled and bent to caress Irene Lusk in a way that would have astounded Selden Grove. When he strode from cubicle to laboratory, he found that the general workroom had emptied rapidly, now the Sunday morning shift was ending. At the door to the first autopsy room, he paused in genuine surprise. Today a laboratory attendant was in the act of transferring a cadaver from cart to table. Dr. Gilbert Maynard, the handsome assistant pathologist, stood by to begin a dissection.

"What's up, Gil?" Tully asked. "I thought you were in a tournament at Rye."

Young Dr. Maynard looked up with a grimace. "So I am, worse luck: my qualifying match is at two. Thank Heaven this is my last case. It looks routine, but the police want a complete p.m."

The social worker's eyebrows lifted. One of the pathology service's duties was handling police ambulance cases. Ordinary post-mortems (hit-and-run traffic fatalities, the usual run of dead-on-arrival drunks with wet brains or broncho-pneumonia) were performed by interns in a larger room beyond the great iceboxes.

"Mind if I watch, Gil?"

"Suit yourself." Young Dr. Maynard had reached for a scalpel before his assistant could place the dead man's hands at his side. "In your place, I'd have better use for my time. I've always suspected you were a frustrated doctor."

Charles Tully moved gingerly into the room. During a long career, he had seen dead bodies in strange places, but he had yet to accustom himself to the concentrated odor of formalin and phenol that seemed to hang over all autopsy tables. It was his custom to don a conventional surgeon's mask when he entered Maynard's domain. He followed the routine now, if only to shut out the worst of that antiseptic reek. (He would recall the finicking precaution later, and bless his luck.)

The techniques of the post-mortem had always fascinated the social worker. There were no sterile gowns and instruments here. Both Maynard and the attendant wore aprons and elbow-length gloves: their approach to the dead-white presence on the slab suggested the efficient butcher rather than the man of science. So did the casual glance Maynard gave the face of Captain Michael Dollard.

"What's the story, Gil?"

The pathologist indicated the police report on the clip-board. "They found him early today, in a West Side alley. Head bruised, as though someone had sapped him." He nodded to his assistant. "I'll make the scalp incision first, Al. You can open the cranium."

Seizing Dollard's thick black hair, the assistant pulled the head forward. Tully saw that the discolored area at the back of the skull bore little resemblance to a conventional bludgeoning. Moving closer, he read the police report with care.

"Don't tell me *that* came from a blackjack, Gil."

"We'll soon find out," said the pathologist. He had already set the scalpel point well back, where the incision would not show: it was the only concession the autopsy room made to the dignity of death. When the semicircular cut was made, Maynard separated scalp and bone with a single, fluent tug. The whole top of the skull was now in clear view, like a monstrous billiard ball in the harsh bath of light.

"No sign of fracture here," said Maynard. "Maybe we'll turn you into a sawbones after all, Charlie."

With hardly a pause he took up one of the formidable autopsy knives and set it against Dollard's armpit. A single stroke cut through skin and fascia, angling across the lower chest and up to the right armpit. Maynard then grasped the edge of the skin and cut through the tissues attaching muscles to ribs, until the entire bony cage was exposed. The knife moved on, to the mid-point of that great, semi-circular incision, then cut downwards, from navel to pubic bone. Lateral dissections, done with equal skill, exposed the abdominal cavity and the front of the chest.

During this routine preparation, the assistant had been busy with an electric saw, cutting a circular design at the top of the skull. Long practice enabled him to penetrate the bone exactly without damaging the brain beneath. Maynard nodded his approval when the geometric pattern was completed.

"I'll take the abdomen first," he said.

Dropping the knife for the moment, he separated the stomach from its apron-like omentum, to expose the dark-blue mass of the liver. Tully noted that the organ was badly swollen. So was the spleen, when Maynard delivered it in turn. Tully studied the doctor intently, wondering at the extent of his knowledge. (A swollen liver, after all, was common here on Sunday mornings. It was the first organ in an alcoholic to show change.)

"Congestion of liver and spleen," said Maynard. "Could be a virus infection, Al."

"The sections will answer that one, Doctor."

Again Tully looked hard at Maynard: when the young man's eye strayed to the wall clock, he could read his mind exactly. It was an axiom of pathology that the microscope was the most accurate diagnostician. Obviously Maynard intended to waste no golfing time on a drunk who had died from unknown causes. Once he had removed the organs (and ticketed them for preservation, while awaiting sections from the laboratory) he would consider his duty done.

The scalpel bisected liver and spleen. Tully felt his excitement grow when he noticed the strange congestion of both organs. He had already observed the enlargement of glands in the groin and smiled behind his mask when Maynard gave the phenomenon no more than a cursory glance. Swellings of this sort were as routine as an alcohol-flogged liver. Most sailors who reached a morgue slab had suffered recurrent attacks of gonorrhea.

Taking Al's place at the head of the table Maynard removed the circular cap of skull, severed the brain stalk with a knife stroke, and lifted out the whole organ. Tully saw him frown at last, when the light revealed no trace of hemorrhage. Once the knife had opened the ventricles, there was no mistaking the same congestion noted in spleen and liver.

The doctor snipped portions of tissue and dropped them into a bottle of fixing fluid. A similar procedure was followed with the other organs he had delivered. Tonight they would go through microscopic preparation. When finished and stained, they would come to him for a final diagnosis.

Using a short, heavy knife, Maynard now attacked the lower or floating ribs. Once they were severed, a bone-cutter snapped the true ribs as easily as matchsticks, to expose the entire front of the chest cage, including the lungs and the dead heart lying between them in the mediastinum.

Tully choked down a gasp at the sight: the suspicion he had brought into the autopsy room was now a virtual certainty. The outer surface of both lungs was definitely inflamed. There was none of the normal spongy reaction when the pathologist's fingers probed the lower portions. A simple diagnosis suggested itself promptly, and the casually expert young doctor might well be excused for making it . . . Or would he sense the true threat in time?

The knife separated both lungs from their nexus of blood vessels and bronchial tubes. Placing them on the table beside the eviscerated body, Maynard split both organs wide. The trouble was now in clear view—a patchy consolidation of tissue.

"Note strong evidence of broncho-pneumonia, Al," said the pathologist glibly. "Probably this fellow died of it, plus the shock of being rolled. We'll take sections to cover ourselves. The lab can pin down the causative organism."

The assistant, who had been filling the brain cavity with sawdust, produced a flask of sterile broth from the test-tube rack. Working with the same easy competence, Maynard dropped in bits of the inflamed lung tissue. Then, aligning a series of culture tubes, he inoculated each of them in turn. Finally he cut blocks from the lungs and dropped them into a fixing solution for later checking under the microscope.

The entire autopsy had taken less than thirty minutes. Tully sighed inwardly as the pathologist stepped back from the table.

"That does it," said Maynard. "I've still time before I go on the first tee. Will you finish up, Al?"

"Sure thing, Doctor," said the assistant.

"See you next week for billiards, Tully?"

"It'll be a pleasure, Gil." The social worker, tearing his eyes away from those dismembered lungs, stood back to let the doctor pass, then followed him from the autopsy room with his mask still in place. He needed that square of gauze to hide the wolf grin he could suppress no longer. There was no reason to tell Dr. Gilbert Maynard that his chance of living into next week was slight indeed—if what Tully suspected was true.

In the scrub room, the social worker dropped his mask in the receptacle and cleansed his face, hands, and forearms thoroughly with isopropyl alcohol. *It's too soon to be sure,* he told himself firmly. Yet the portents in what he had just seen were unmistakable.

It was pure chance that he had witnessed an almost identical autopsy in a far corner of the globe, not too long ago; on that occasion, the diagnosis had been firm enough. It was odd, Tully reflected, that a man like himself (ignorant of the finer points of medicine) should be granted a knowledge Dr. Gilbert Maynard did not possess. It was odder still that he should make the discovery at this particular moment.

Until he was sure, the secret was well worth keeping. He would not even share it with Irene.

While the mood of exultation lasted, Charles Tully permitted his other, permanent mask to slip, however briefly. Such euphoria, he knew, was a luxury he could not afford often; the laughter that bubbled on those handsome, sensual lips, the eyes that gleamed back from a washroom mirror, were warning enough. When he heard a step outside, the fleshly carapace dropped into place instantly. Walking briskly into the corridor, he was himself again.

5.

During the last global war, when he had served with distinction on a flattop, the mayor of New York had learned the art of relaxing on the edge of battle.

This Sunday afternoon, on the last lap of his flight from Cairo, John Newman seemed utterly at ease as he listened to his secretary; but he could feel the slow burgeoning of his rage as his mind closed round Tim Egan's meaning. He had suspected the worst when he had picked up the plane-to-shore phone that noon to hear that Egan would await him at Gander.

"Don't hold back," he said. "Make this a *happy* homecoming."

Tim Egan (whose resemblance to a nervous hen was only skin deep) shut his notebook. "I think that's the whole story, Mr. Mayor. When you started this holiday, we knew trouble was in the making——"

"Isn't it always?"

"The dock strike came sooner than we expected," said the secretary. "We'd hoped to settle it before the Sanitation contract came up for renewal. If Mr. Pritchard had been a bit tougher——"

Newman and Egan exchanged an exasperated glance. Pritchard was the deputy mayor (a post that had been upgraded in the last city charter). For his second term, Newman had been forced to run on a fusion ticket, and Pritchard had been part of the package. It was hardly news that his deputy was a fence-straddler.

"If he'd asked for it, he could have had injunctions yesterday," said Egan. "He wanted the men to return on their own——"

"To hell with Pritchard," said the mayor. "Is there a health hazard, so far?"

"The hospitals still have normal admission lists. Dr. Thurlow's keeping a close check at Health——"

"Manhattan Central's the key, now it's taken over so many Bellevue functions. Did you talk to Selden Grove?"

Egan's flush had remained constant: it was an occupational hazard of the mayor's staff. "I couldn't reach him before I left, sir: he was on an inspection tour with Mr. Merton. I did contact Dr. Eric Stowe."

"Dr. Stowe will do as well. What's his opinion?"

"He seems more worried than the others. Did you know he's a red-hot operator at the W.H.O.?"

"He's an old friend, Tim—and one of the best public-health men alive. I've just inspected his handiwork in Africa. If he's worried, so am I."

"New York has lived through a hundred utility strikes, Mr. Mayor. We aren't the Congo backwoods."

"Maybe the two aren't that different," said John Newman. "Even the Congo's changed in our time. Who do I go after first?"

"Jon Marek," said the secretary firmly. "*And* his Sanitation Union, if they won't start rolling tomorrow. He's our worst offender."

"How soon can we collar him?"

"I'm afraid he's gone in hiding again."

"Won't his people talk?"

"Inspector Dalton is sure none of them know his whereabouts. Naturally, the rank and file are burning. There's talk of ending the walkout at the next meeting. In any event, the inspector hopes to bring in Marek tomorrow. He'll be at Idlewild to make his report."

"Pete Dalton's a good man," said the mayor. "He has enough on his hands at the moment. It isn't fair, asking him to do my scut-work too."

"What happens when you track Marek down, sir?"

"I'm breaking him, and he knows it. It's time he stopped ghosting for the labor bosses of the fifties."

The mayor settled in his seat, with his hat slanted above his eyes. Tim Egan, pretending to relax beside him, knew better than to disturb that surface repose. If John Newman had declared war on the Sanitation Union, the war could have but one outcome.

Newman (like Marek) had fought his way up from poverty, but he had always fought fairly. His trophies—a law degree, his terms in Congress, a blue-blood wife—had been won by a man whose genius for progress was as unerring as his vision. The son of Jewish-Irish parents, he was proud of his humble origin. Hot-blooded—but hard-headed—he had always refused to believe that New York (in this dynamic decade) must continue to lose ground to the American West. And he had always insisted that the miseries of its submerged poor could be cured by means at hand.

En route to a familiar battleground, feeling his nostrils flair at the scent of combat, Newman made the most of this last, false nap. Unaccustomed to the magic-carpet speed of jets, he could not yet believe he had spanned the Atlantic in less than three hours. Or that the towers ahead, drowned in the murk of sunset, were part of Manhattan.

The plane swung toward the customs gate at Idlewild and the inevitable knot of reporters. It was always a shock to be home again, John Newman reflected—and good to remember that Marjorie and the girls were safe in Maine. So far the current conflict seemed manageable, but there were echoes behind the man-made thunder that roused his suspicions.

He was glad that Eric Stowe had promised to dine at Gracie Mansion. The immunologist was a man who gave straight answers.

An official limousine was waiting at the plane ramp, a safe distance from the reporters' clamor. Leaving Egan to brief the Fourth Estate, Newman hurried into his car. Detective-Inspector Peter Dal-

ton, waiting in a corner of the rear seat, lifted a hand in greeting.
"You look rested, John," he said. "Was it smooth crossing?"

"It would have been smoother if you hadn't sent Tim to Gander."

"The commissioner felt it would save you time."

Newman nodded: Dalton could always be relied on to get to essentials. Once again the mayor marveled at his ability to take on protective coloration as effortlessly as a lizard. Today, in his neat suit and panama, Pete could have passed for a bookkeeper whose conscience was at rest. The fact he chose to play the mouse meant he had no significant news.

"I was hoping you'd brought in Marek, at least," said Newman.

"Surely you can break his strike without him."

"I can always ask for an injunction: it'd mean work or jail for every man in uniform. I'd prefer to make *him* suffer and spare his rank and file."

"Egan must have told you I promised delivery by tomorrow."

Newman settled in his corner of the limousine. "I hope my town's as calm as you look, Pete."

"Things are always hopping on my beat," said the detective. "August is the worst month for the junior wolf packs—don't ask me why. This is my second year on this assignment. I'm still fighting in the dark."

Youth in revolt against its age was a phenomenon John Newman understood all too clearly. So (despite his disclaimer) did Inspector Dalton. In their salad days, both men had defied their rulers, no less strenuously—but those revolts had brought results. Newman had climbed to a law degree, and his desk in City Hall. Dalton had broken free of his own blighted enclave to gain his present post—with the certainty of becoming New York's next police commissioner . . . Today's youth, thought Newman, seemed to gnaw its own heart, to exist (in its sad fashion) on a diet of self-induced despair. Perhaps this was only the legacy of its elders; the admission shed little light on the problem.

"The last time I saw Eric Stowe," he said, "he wondered if some of our wolf packs were other-directed."

"I can't afford fifty-dollar words, John."

"This is a label the social scientists have coined. Charles Tully is always using it at fund-raising banquets."

"In that case, it must be the real thing. What's it mean?"

"Sociologists claim we're molded from the cradle," said the mayor. "Obviously, all of us need some kind of shaping. The fact remains that the pattern dictates our action. If we're raised in a slum—and are strong enough—we find our way to better things. Otherwise we're apt to react against society like a cornered animal, the moment we're big enough to flip a switchblade."

"Tully's a bit too deep for me," said the detective. "Blame evil on the times, if you must—or the environment. For my money, these young bandits are simply taking orders from above."

"All of them?"

"By no means. Most of them are rebels without a cause—just as they've always been. Others are trained for a purpose—or I'll turn in my badge. Too many of the jobs they've pulled lately are out of bounds for teen-agers."

"Can you give me an example?"

"Last night a monster bonfire was set against the walls of Merton House. Army commandos couldn't have done a neater job."

"Who trains them? The underworld?"

"These teachers could come from abroad," said Pete.

"Any names on file?"

"You can pick the enemy," said the detective.

"Does Eric buy your theory?"

"Definitely. He's seen the same thing happen overseas. Pinpointed sabotage. The murder of derelicts——"

"We've had *that* problem for years, Pete."

"So we have. The rate has stepped up lately."

"Psychiatrists have checked on such killings," the mayor argued. "They claim you can't escape them in an age of anxiety, no matter how senseless they appear. They call it automatic sadism. Murder for fun, if you like——"

"It could also be part of the pattern of anarchy I spoke of. A proof that freedom isn't worth having if we can't lick poverty."

"I'm afraid you're oversimplifying, Pete."

"So are the head-shrinkers, when they use words like sadism," said the detective.

"Have you any particular wolf pack in mind?"

"I could name several. The ones I'm watching specially are the Royal Dukes. Their turf is just outside Manhattan Central."

"Any specific charges?"

"Nothing I can't hang on other gangs. It's the *way* they operate that interests me."

"What's their make-up?"

"Over ninety percent Puerto Rican. Their war-lord is an eighteen-year-old named Juan Lemayo. A bad apple since he could walk, to judge by our precinct blotter."

"No point in making arrests, I gather."

"Right now I prefer to sit tight and hope he'll slip."

Newman shook his head. "This time, I almost hope you're wrong. It's bad enough, admitting we're the breeding ground for this sort of violence. Have you *anything* to tell me that isn't supposition?"

"Only this solid thought. Jon Marek was born forty-two years ago —in Central Asia."

"So we're back to Marek?"

"Maybe we've never been away," said Pete. "His parents were medical missionaries. A special fanatic sect that wouldn't pull up stakes. Ever since the take-over, they've been living in that same mission compound, under house arrest. It seems their new landlords consider them more valuable alive than dead. Couldn't that mean Marek struck on orders—to save their lives?"

"Because this particular enemy wanted a strike?"

"Exactly—as part of the old pattern of chaos."

"It's hard to believe without proof."

"Suppose I bring you that proof tomorrow?"

"I've said I'll break him. This gives me another reason."

"And if it means his parents' death?"

The mayor stared at the car window. The limousine had already slipped into the East River Drive. His official residence was only minutes away.

"Regardless of the reason, no man has the right to strike against a city's welfare," he said slowly. "I'll grant that's a hard ruling—if what you say is true."

"You're a hard man, John Newman," said the detective.

"Not half so hard as those enemies you mentioned," said the mayor, and accepted the salute of the guard at the gate of Gracie Mansion.

Two hours later, sipping iced coffee with Eric Stowe on his veranda, Newman could still pretend that his insulation was lasting. A breeze had swept in with evening, riffling the tide in the East River. Thanks to the gilt-edged apartment buildings facing the mayor's official home, there was no hint here of the stench that hung over so much of New York. Most of these fortresses of wealth had their own incinerators.

Pete Dalton had long since returned to his thankless beat. Steeped in old times, the mayor and his visitor had held the subject of the latter's call at arm's length. . . . Newman broke the spell with an effort. Eric was one of the few friends to whom he could speak his mind without fear. The opportunity was too precious to waste.

"You know why I hurried back," he said. "What d'you make of our problem?"

"Frankly, I wouldn't care to be in your place tomorrow."

"It isn't like you to apply the needle," said the mayor. "Can't you give me a visible enemy to fight?"

The immunologist put down his glass. "Have you ever thought that such questions can't be answered any more? A generation ago we could tell friends from the other kind. Now they have a way of merging."

"Is that a sensible reply?"

"Very well, John. Call these union mavericks together, and break the strikes. Bring the gangs to heel, and persuade Jasper Merton to leave his money in the project. The enemy will still be in our midst —and there's nothing he likes better than keeping us off balance."

"Do you seriously think our troubles were planned halfway across the world?"

"Why not? The earth's a small planet."

"Where's your proof?" Newman demanded.

"I have none at the moment. Neither does Pete. It's only an uneasy instinct—but I trust it."

"If I remember correctly, you had the same theory when I left on my vacation."

"So I did, John. Enemies aren't easy to identify these days. Or did I say that once?"

The mayor hesitated, remembering Pete's tenuous lead on Marek. Uncertain whether to confide in Eric, he found himself detailing the inspector's story. Once he had sketched the background of the missionary family in the Orient, and the ambition-ridden son in America, he could ask himself if he believed a word of Dalton's theory.

"Maybe it does add up to a motive, Eric. But to my mind, it's far-fetched reasoning."

"Pete doesn't work by the rules. It might explain a great deal— if you could get Marek on the carpet."

"We'll have him in custody tomorrow, and the sanitation strike will be broken. I'll promise you that much."

"See you keep that promise," said Eric. "Until your city breathes clean air again, it's under a cloud. In more ways than one—" He broke off as a phone buzzed inside. "I've enjoyed our visit, John. Sorry I couldn't be more constructive."

The mayor sighed and turned to answer his houseman's signal.

"That will be the governor," he said. "He'll want my plans for tomorrow. I was hoping you'd give me a lead, Eric. Obviously, both you and Pete have done your best."

The two men entered the foyer of the mansion. Newman saw that his servant had left the phone extension open in the downstairs alcove. He turned toward it with a second sigh as Eric put out his hand.

"You'd better answer. It's a bit early to secede from Albany."

"I sometimes wonder."

"Good luck with the strikers tomorrow. I don't envy you that meeting."

"That's where we differ," said the mayor. "I expect to enjoy it thoroughly."

## 6.

Jon Marek, the man Pete Dalton had sworn to put on the mayor's carpet, was pacing a carpet of his own at that moment. It was the second day of his self-imposed exile, and he had begun to hate his loneliness with all his heart.

The apartment he had chosen as a hideaway was on an obscure street far uptown; its regular occupant was a clerk in the union office, absent on vacation. Before his departure, he had given Marek a duplicate key: it was one of several havens the Sanitation Department leader utilized when it seemed prudent to retreat from the well-planned chaos he had created. On previous visits Marek had posed as the tenant's brother. Only yesterday he had used the same masquerade while he visited on the stoop with neighbors—until a call from his lawyer had warned him the police were using all their resources to track him down.

He had defied the law before and won. Tonight he could not keep down a spasm of fear at the sound of each passing car. The years had brought Jon Marek success in his field, but there had been no compensating peace of mind. Alone with his thoughts, he found them increasingly dark; bereft of his usual coterie of sycophants, he could not escape the conviction he had overreached at last.

A single friendly call would have made all the difference in this hideaway, but he dared not use the phone. Just two people knew the number besides his lawyer: they were Ken Busch of the Dockers'—and the Voice he still refused to give a name. His lawyer would not ring the number again. Busch, in hiding like himself, had no valid reason to communicate. This time, at least, he could shrug off the threat of the Voice.

Calling this strike had been his own inspiration. He could not believe the man from whom he took orders would be concerned with its outcome.

Pouring another drink, Jon Marek twirled his television dial, only to cut off the program. With Dalton on his trail, it was safer to pretend that this tiny apartment (like so many other New York dwellings this summer weekend) was untenanted. The silence did little to reassure him. Because of the cloying heat, he had stripped to his shorts and was padding the carpet barefoot. At intervals, he paused at the wardrobe mirror to stare at himself in gloomy wonder.

The mirrored image was hardly inspiring. At forty-two, Marek resembled a molting rooster whose ego, like his drooping comb, was sadly in need of stiffening. The birdlike profile (complete with wattles) suggested a much older man—a cipher approaching retirement, eager to take his pension to Florida. Marek, like most leaders, needed a platform to disguise his runtiness, a burning issue to lift his heart.

Where (beyond the usual hunger for more wages, the demand for shorter hours) were the fundamental hates that had once divided the workingman from his employer? How could he make this strike call stick? What was the value of his power, if his underlings drew back from its use?

Things had seemed different a few years ago, while he had been clawing his way to the top. In those years, he could believe his success had been earned. Sometimes (when his sleep was troubled by the conscience no man can stifle entirely) he could damn his willingness to accept both policy directives and ready cash from the same enemy who had menaced his family from his birth . . . His now aging parents (who still existed in the enemy's shadow) had urged him to make the break complete when he escaped to the free world. The effort had been beyond him. Instead he had faced the American agents of their captors and made his bargain. Loyalty to one's forebears was a virtue he had not outgrown.

When the Voice that controlled him was silent, there were months on end when he could say, in all honesty, that he had fought the good fight for labor, that the gains he had won for the downtrodden had justified his sinister means. Reviewing his strategy in the present strike, insisting the city must knuckle under one more time, he felt his chest swell with the old, sure arrogance.

In that flash of pride, the cramped apartment that had seemed a prison became a bandit's cave. When the phone rang, he struck the wall with his fist, positive it was news of capitulation.

"Are you there, Marek?"

Recognizing the whisper, he scowled at the phone. It was Ken Busch, not his lawyer.

"What d'you want? I told you not to call me here."

"Did you know the mayor hit town this evening?"

Marek felt his heart plummet. Newman had warned him not to try the city's patience again. This new strike had been a desperate gamble: he had been sure that Deputy Mayor Pritchard would sign the terms he demanded.

"Who's afraid of Newman?" he demanded. "Give me a half-hour in his office; I'll get a contract."

"Stop talking nonsense, Marek," said the head of the Dockers'. "He's smoking us both out, and you know it."

"I'm standing pat," said Marek. "So are you—once you get over your jitters."

"How often must I explain a utility strike's illegal today? Even if your men hit the street tomorrow, you'll go to jail."

"Not if they can't find me."

"Have you gone mad, Marek? Or d'you think you're another Hoffa? Stop living in the past, and tell me what to do. I'll be jugged myself if the courts rule against me."

"We can both win if we sit tight."

"Not with half my locals bellowing for a compromise—and your own vice-president planning to run for shelter."

"Who told you that?"

"I have my sources," said Busch. "If you don't show by morning, he's going to City Hall and hang the blame on you."

"Get off this wire, Ken. I have to call my lawyer."

"Don't bother," said Busch. "It was Saul Gordon himself who advised it."

Once he had heard the receiver click, Marek banged up his own phone and dialed his lawyer's private number. There was no answer; for some time, he had suspected Gordon of playing both sides of the street. Replacing the phone in its cradle (with a hand that was beginning to shake violently) he was debating the wisdom of ringing his office direct when the instrument buzzed again.

"Keep this line open, Jon: I've been trying for five minutes to get you."

The new voice was ice-cold. Marek stared at the phone in despair before he addressed it through clenched teeth.

"Isn't it time you left me in peace?"

"Have I troubled you lately, Jon? I only called to compliment you for striking when you did."

"What d'you want? I'll help you if I can."

"You've already helped—more than you'll ever guess. Just don't go soft, now you're winning. I want your trucks kept off the street until further orders."

"You've no right to mix in this. The idea was mine."

"So it was, Jon. Therefore you'll bear the brunt if it fails. Not only from Mayor Newman—from *our* side as well. Remember, I can make you an orphan with a single cable—and end your own career as well."

"Why d'you want the strike to continue?"

"You don't ask *why*, Jon—remember? You do as you're told—like all good servants. Having your men off the street has suddenly become most important. Keep that in mind when the mayor tracks you down."

For a long time, Jon Marek sat alone in the dark, staring at the beam from a street light that fell through a broken blind. When a car ground to a stop at the curb, he darted to the broken slat to peer outside. Though he recognized the familiar silhouette of a squad car, there was no cause for alarm. These were traffic patrolmen, come to ticket weekend parkers.

Marek felt no sense of relief when they moved on. In a way, he could wish he was already face to face with Newman.

## 7.

Midnight at Manhattan Central was the hour Eve Bronson loved best.

Whenever she was off duty, it was her custom to ride up to the terrace outside the Bubble. Here, she could check the heartbeat of the hospital (a deep pulsation that never really stilled) and contrast

it with the heartbeat of New York. This midnight, when she returned
from the theater with Bob Trent, the muted pulse was constant: the
gossip of student nurses en route to supper, the rattle of a drug cart,
the moaning of a post-op in a recovery room . . . Beyond the terrace rail, Manhattan's pulse had all but ceased.

"Have the subways stopped already, Bob?"

The surgical chief nodded, with his eyes on the darkling plain below. Now she had identified the source, Eve found the silence had
a shattering impact. Buses had halted with the subways; most private cars had remained in their garages tonight. The taxi that had
brought them from the theater had raced like a homing banshee,
lest it be caught after zero hour.

"It only looks dead," said Eve firmly. "It's alive underneath."

"Of course it is. People will find ways to come to work tomorrow.
They always have."

"Doesn't the quiet frighten you?"

Bob Trent let his hand fall on hers. There was a kind of relaxed
camaraderie in the gesture. Even so she could feel the strength in
those surgeon's fingers.

"Right now," he said quietly, "I'm much too content to fear anything."

Eve smiled in the gloom. Bob had slept quite frankly through the
last act of *Affairs of Anatol,* but she knew he had enjoyed every second of their evening out. So had she. From their first date, over a
year ago, he had been an unending source of comfort—a wise inter-
preter of hospital intrigues, a friend and counselor in her progress
toward a medical degree. Nor could she deny that their evenings
out had had other stimulations . . . The terrace outside the Bubble,
by unspoken decree, was a trysting place after midnight. When his
hands moved to her shoulders, she turned willingly for his kiss.

"Shall we do this again tomorrow, Eve?"

"For shame, Doctor!"

"You needn't fence with me," he said good-humoredly. "I'm invit-
ing you for another evening on the town. I happen to know you'll be
off duty."

"You aren't, I'm sure."

"George Peters will cover for me."

"Sorry, Bob. I promised to drive out to Jones Beach with Eric. He's
taking me to dinner afterwards, at a place called the Beau Séjour."

The surgical chief's smile did not change by a flicker. "Enjoy yourself," he said. "I wish *I* had a white Ferrari roadster to turn the nurses' heads."

"I'm glad you approve," said Eve. She moved firmly down the terrace rail: somehow she had expected a quarrel at her announcement.

"Actually I don't approve at all," said Bob. "I can hardly object if you prefer public health to surgery."

"Is that a fair distinction?"

"You'll finish your O.R. service next month, Eve. Then, a final turn in the lab before you start your medical course. Naturally you'll want the best teacher."

"Have you thought I might enjoy Dr. Stowe's company for personal reasons?"

"The thought is with me constantly," said Bob. "Fortunately there are escape clauses. Two, in fact. My former Hopkins roommate won't be in our midst much longer. And I don't think he's the marrying kind, for all his charm."

"Aren't you looking rather far into the future?"

"By no means," said Bob. "Perhaps he *will* invite you to join his crusade to save humanity. If he does—and you accept—I'll never forgive either of you. Otherwise, I'm relying on chemistry to save the day."

"*Chemistry*, Doctor?"

"Yours and mine. It functioned well in the past—before this invasion from Utopia. It still functions, as we just proved." Bob turned to the sound of his name on the public address inside. The floor attendant had already moved toward the open door to summon him. "I'm on call after midnight. Perhaps it's just as well. I was on the point of speaking my mind. At this moment, it would never do."

Eve was still at the terrace rail (uncertain whether she was angered or amused) when she heard a step in the darkness. The white-coated figure, as she had expected, was Eric. They had met here before at midnight: it had become almost an unplanned rendezvous.

"I'd heard you were dining with the mayor," she said. "Don't tell me you've been working after hours?"

"Only a drug-room check. Manhattan Central has an impressive supply of pharmaceuticals. Enough antibiotics to protect us from almost any disease under heaven——"

"Are you *still* brooding over tomorrow, Eric?"

"It's part of my job," he said, with the same quiet good humor.

"After my talk with John Newman, I can't help wondering if my fears are justified. Would you like a fast rundown?"

Eve listened in numbed surprise while he repeated the gist of Pete Dalton's report and the mayor's plan to close in on Marek. When he had finished his low-voiced recital, she knew she was shivering, even in the breathless heat. It was good to feel that white-clad arm close about her shoulders.

"Tomorrow may prove you're mistaken," she said. "Perhaps the strikes will end. There may even be peace in the jungle."

"There can never be peace in a jungle, Eve. Not when it's man-made."

At that distance, they could not see the roof of the cold-water flat where Gladys Schreiber had long since risen from uneasy slumber to go to her cash register at the Millway cafeteria. They could not know that her germ-freighted breath (as she offered a practiced smile to each customer with his change) had created a score of fresh plague victims, long before her work day ended. . . .

The mission where Willoughby Fellowes had finally sought a bed during last morning's rain was also invisible in the maze of streets that faced the North River. Fellowes had snored there until midday. Later he had joined a stud-poker game with his fellow inmates —from which he had risen at dusk, ten dollars richer. By way of compensation, he had bestowed upon the other players a goodly share of the parasites he had supported since last midnight—enough to produce several fresh victims (by subsequent migration) in that crowded way station of the homeless.

*Pasteurella pestis* had scored brilliantly, via its first two hosts.

That same midnight, at the Blue Banjo bar (a cellar night club some fifteen blocks south of the hospital) another score was in the making. Its chief architect—the man on whom the amber-colored spotlights were now centered—was Brewster van Pelt, a poet of the new school, whose virile verses burned with so hot a flame that his devotees seldom noticed they made no sense whatever. Van Pelt was tall as a basketball forward, and scrawny as a whopping crane. But his tuft of red-brown beard was luxuriant, and the eyes he fixed on his audiences were twin thunderbolts.

Silence had fallen on the Blue Banjo, save for the throb of bongo drums in the background and the wail of a Chinese flute. It was played by the poet's legal wife, a hard-eyed girl dressed in an identical suit of rumpled corduroys. She watched van Pelt intently while he opened his sheaf of manuscript. All last night, he had paced the water front while he composed these verses. He had acted strangely since his return—even for a poet.

"The lines I am about to read," said van Pelt, "are called *Triumph of the Rat.*"

He lifted a hand—and the flute ceased its wailing. The drums sank to a murmur. Van Pelt's voice, muffled at first, rose line by line to a full-throated shout.

> Midnight is city's death-by-dying
> The hour of the rat
> The terror of the rat
> The triumph of the rat
> Ghoul eternal, soul-burglar, heart-destroyer
> Last tenant in the ruined temple when the gods depart
> Vile acolyte among the perished virgins
> Harbinger of tomorrow, foul Caesar, we salute you!
> *Ave atque vale,* companion of tortured midnights!
> We who were born without hope salute you!
> We who embrace death salute you!
> Hail and farewell. . . .

Van Pelt was howling now. His audience, eyes closed in ecstasy, swayed in the hot tornado of his words. Only the hard-eyed wife (whose ears were tuned to all the poet's nuances) caught the note of hysteria beneath the lines. She moved to catch van Pelt just before his knees buckled—and the scream she uttered came from the heart.

"Help me, someone—! Can't you see he's *dying?*"

The listeners, shocked out of their trance, made no answer beyond a confused babble. Then, at a ringside table, there was a second piercing scream. Van Pelt's wife glared at the screamer—the poet's current girl friend, a ceramist who had been lavish with her inspiration. Unlike the wife, she made no attempt to aid her fallen lover. Instead, she left the Blue Banjo with almost indecent haste . . . In another moment, the cellar was empty, save for a pair of sleeping drunks, and the frantic proprietor, who yielded at last to the wife's pleas and went to summon a doctor.

The exodus had been a sound one, obeying man's basic instinct for survival. Already, the twisted visage of Brewster van Pelt resembled a death mask, though the man himself still lived. This time the plague had struck with little warning. In that past hour—using the poet's hot breath as its vector—it had also claimed new victims in the smoke-filled room.

One was the ceramist. Though she had led the flight to fresh air, she had already made her appointment in Samarra—no less blindly than the sobbing wife who still rocked her husband in her arms.

Midnight, as van Pelt's swan song had stated, was the heyday of the rat. Between that hour and dawn, the original battalion from the *Sally Piersol,* ranging afield to fraternize with their kind, had spread their parasites by the thousands.

In a flat on Bleecker Street, an infant wakened screaming when an outsize specimen of *Rattus rattus,* bolder than his fellows, dared to invade her crib and nibble tentatively at her forearm. When the child's parents stirred, he whisked across their bed, bolting via the window and scattering still more fleas en route.

In the kitchen of the Village Bandbox (a cabaret that had raised squalor to an art on Sullivan Street) another nimble rodent, evading the chef's cleaver, dashed boldly among the tables, raising a tempest of terror among the female patrons and bestowing his parasites on a dozen new hosts.

North of Washington Square, in the delivery alley of an apartment building, a tenants' indignation committee was working in shifts to load a three-day backlog of refuse on a hired truck. The committee was attacked by a roving squad of sanitation workers, who clubbed them into retreat. A platoon of rats (waiting in the shadows to resume its interrupted repast) took the opportunity to explore the building. By morning, they had spread their freight of *Xenopsylla cheopis* through the lower floors.

In time—and this too was symptomatic—other plague carriers would develop their own approach. Some, like Gladys Schreiber, were unknowing menaces. Others, like van Pelt, might almost have been selected by a malign fate to serve its end. Still others were destined to prove that no corner of New York was now immune—including the town house of Jasper Merton. . . .

Tonight in that august mansion the fifth richest man in America slept deeply, wrapped in the cocoon of a recurrent dream. In this fantasy he was the world's richest surgeon, concluding an operation to roars of applause. In the spectators' gallery, a score of faces hung eagerly above the final knife stroke. All were replicas of Selden Grove. (The director of Manhattan Central was the man Jasper

Merton hated and feared above all others—much as a jungle chief might hate his head witch doctor.)

The philanthropist, who feared no man by daylight, was totally unaware of this trauma and the compulsion that drove him to use Grove as a whipping boy. His threat to withdraw funds from the Merton Project was part of that compulsion. Tonight, when he heard the whine of a police siren through his dream, he stirred resentfully—and reminded himself to repeat the threat next morning.

That Sunday midnight, the destiny of New York was truly in the balance—in sodden back streets, no less than in a billionaire's fretful brain. The pattern of destruction established by *Pasteurella pestis*, erratic as the finger-painting of a demented child, was now virtually complete.

# 3.  Monday

THE meeting with the Sportsmen, an all-Negro gang from East Harlem, had been scheduled at a half-hour after dawn. The chosen field was a vacant block at the northeast corner of the bulldozed Merton Project, a no man's land at the edge of the Royal Dukes' turf. The Sportsmen had been invited to appear at their peril. The fact that battle would be joined by daylight was a measure of the Dukes' new daring.

Nighttime rumbles, as war-lord Juan Lemayo had remarked when the meeting was endorsed by both gangs, were seldom conclusive tests. In the dark, weaker members could hang back with no real loss of face, if the odds were against them. The present meeting, scheduled for open ground, would permit no one to chicken out.

The Sportsmen had been guaranteed safe access to the field: the Dukes would await them at its center. Monitors along the way would check the invaders' numbers, which had been held to twenty-five. Juan Lemayo had promised his own force would be no more numerous. The group surrounding him this Monday morning was a hard-core cadre he could trust completely. He had trained them (singly and en masse) for a purpose he could divulge to no one—save to Ricardo Reyes, his second-in-command.

Juan surveyed the deployment of his forces and found it good. Each of the twenty-five youths had taken expert cover in the midst of this ruined plain, using such meager shelter as it afforded—remnants of walls the wreckers had spared or hollows that had once been basements. The war-lord's post was a cairn of bricks, masked by a clump of ailanthus trees, the leftovers of a backyard garden. The slender, weedlike branches, lifting against the promise of sunrise, gave the stark scene the air of a Japanese woodcut.

All of today's group were Puerto Ricans, swarthy of skin, deceptively slight of frame: the quick, hissing Spanish they used, larded with their special argot, would have been meaningless to other ears. Juan Lemayo, who stood a head taller than his companions, wore a cloak that all but concealed his well-muscled frame. Dyed blue-black and faced with red, the garment advertised his status. Beneath it were skin-tight black Levis, calf-high boots, and a dark shirt blazoned with the gang insignia, a knight's casque with a skull beneath the visor.

The other youths were dressed identically. Each face, framed in sideburns and crowned by glistening duck-tail haircuts, bore the same sneer. An adult interloper, stumbling upon this wolf pack, would have found the insolence comic, but the fangs that each cub bared were real. The brass-studded belts bore illegal switchblades (the knives were concealed at other times). The slight bulges at Juan's and Ricardo's left shoulders advertised the gun holsters beneath their shirts, a final proof the Dukes were out for blood.

It was full daylight now, though the sun had not yet shone above the white cliffs of the nearby hospital. The rumble should have long since been joined. Peering through his screen of leaves, Juan saw the group was beginning to grow restless at the delay. There was no doubting the bravery of their rivals. If the Sportsmen were late, it could mean the police had intervened—with an even chance the prowl cars would close in on this block as well. Prudence dictated dispersal, but the war-lord was not in a prudent mood. Anticipating Ricardo Reyes's errand, he shook his head when his second-in-command approached the cairn.

"They will not come, Juanito."

"Give them ten minutes. It could be a trick to spook us."

Ricardo nodded doubtfully and crept among the ambushed Dukes to repeat the order. Juan, watching closely lest he betray his presence to eyes outside the field, felt himself tremble with rage as five of the ten minutes dragged by. All night long, he had slept fitfully, but it had been eagerness, not fear, that kept his eyelids wide. War had been Juan Lemayo's only real satisfaction for as long as he could remember. His enemy's identity had ceased to interest him.

The *Jefe* had said that Negroes were an inferior breed, that it was part of the Dukes' mission to stamp them out. Juan had shrugged at the Leader's directive. All society was his enemy: his only security was the Dukes themselves, his only pride the supremacy he had won with fists and steel.

If the *Jefe* chose to give him foreign guns (and the expert training that made each rumble a victory), so much the better. The *Jefe* had said the Juan Lemayos would own the country someday, providing they obeyed his orders without question. Juan could accept the promise at face value—as easily as he kept the Leader's secrets.

Perhaps the promise was only a tempting lie. It did not matter greatly so long as his sense of power endured. In his eighteen years on earth, Juan had learned to live down most illusions, to trust no one but himself. Juan, and the man he served, were foes of the existing order. Both of them were dedicated to destruction. It was bond enough. . . .

The ten minutes were up. Juan clung to hope a moment more, his ears strained for the lookout's whistle that would announce the Sportsmen's arrival. When Ricardo Reyes crept toward him a second time, he held up a soothing palm.

"A moment more, Ric—"

"It is madness, *hombre.*" The second-in-command touched the bulge of his holster. "What if we are found with these?"

"We can take cover when we choose. If the *policía* come, we'll have warning."

"Why run the risk? There is no one to fight."

"Look again, Ric. An enemy approaches after all—and he comes alone."

Following the direction of the pointing finger, Ricardo joined the war-lord's chuckle. A figure had just wandered from street to vacant lot, as aimlessly as a lost dog who has abandoned all thought of shelter. Both youths had already recognized Willoughby Fellowes; he had visited the neighborhood often, wrapped in the same fog of alcohol that enveloped him now. Juan felt his heart thud happily as the old man approached the Dukes' ambush.

"The chance is too good to miss, Ric."

"*Matar?*"

"What else?" asked Juan. "Keep the others out—he is all mine."

The Leader had said the society of tomorrow would have no place for derelicts; the Leader had told the Dukes to strike down these human scarecrows at will, since they were better dead. It was poor sport at best, needing a touch of drama. Juan nodded to the group to break cover and unfurled the cape.

"*Toro!*" he called, in a heavy whisper.

Fellowes had entered a clear space among the rubble. Half-hearing the challenge, dimly aware of dark forms that had risen from the earth, he tossed back the hair that obscured his vision and made a solemn effort to wave the apparitions aside. The circle of Dukes, delighted by this show of defiance, drew closer. Willoughby Fel-

lowes bore little resemblance to a fighting bull, but that head-toss
was in character.

Lemayo flared his cape into an acceptable veronica and stamped
his foot, as though to provoke a charge.

"*Toro!*"

Fellowes's eyes were caught by the cape. He lunged toward it
drunkenly, to a chorus of approval from the circle. At a nod from
the impromptu matador, Ricardo bumped the old man sharply, tum-
bling him to hands and knees and dislodging the inevitable bottle
from his pocket.

"*Anda, toro, anda!*"

The bottle had skidded among the stones without breaking. Fellowes scrambled to retrieve it, only to find his head muffled in the
cloak. In the next few moments, the bottle was kicked repeatedly
out of reach; each time he rose, he was tripped and teased again by
the swirling cape. The wolf pack had played this game before when
they had flushed out other drunken flotsam at midnight. Somehow,
the sport was more thrilling on a flawless summer morning.

"*Olé, Juanito!*"

"*Mátale—ahora!*"

"*La estocada!*"

It was a call for the "moment of truth," the climax of the bullfight
—when the matador, fixing his target, drives the sword between the
shoulder blades to pierce the heart from above. Juan Lemayo, bow-
ing to the circle as gravely as though this were a true *plaza de
toros*, folded his cape and covered Willoughby Fellowes's eyes for
the last time. Then, while the derelict struggled to free himself, he
profiled gracefully, snapped open the six-inch blade at his belt, and
drove it deep.

Three strokes were needed before the victim crumpled.

Juan's shout of triumph rose above the old man's final scream. The
two voices reverberated from the blank-faced tenements in an eerie
echo. Almost at once it was topped by another sound. Lemayo's ears
(tuned to concert pitch, now he had renewed himself in this act of
violence) recognized the whine of car motors, moving in fast from
the east.

"It's the *policía*," he said calmly. "Clear out, everyone!"

The scurry of feet was almost noiseless as the Royal Dukes took
to their heels, following a dozen planned escape routes and utiliz-
ing each scrap of cover. Some fled down the nearest side street,
where a double row of parked cars stood between them and the po-

lice. Others bolted into an alley between two warehouses, just before the trio of prowl cars roared into view. Lemayo himself led the
second rush. It was only when they had gained shelter that he realized Ricardo had failed to follow.

The second-in-command had seen other killings of this nature. During the baiting of Fellowes, he had shouted as gaily as the rest: it
was his voice that had demanded the death stroke. Now, without
understanding why, he found himself rooted to the spot. He would
never know that the sight of that heap of bloodstained rags had re-
vived a memory of his own father—whom Ricardo had found years
ago on the family doorstep, stabbed through the heart.

The sob that choked him was brief. In a matter of seconds, he was
himself again—but the pause had been long enough to spell ruin.
The nearest police car had entered the lot in a storm of brick dust.
The two men who leaped from its doors had already spied the lone
figure standing above Fellowes's body.

Ricardo lost his head and fired first. The shot went wild. So did
the first policeman's return fire. The second, aiming with care, struck
the youth somewhere in the body, as he began his belated retreat.

There was no time to follow the escape route Juan had laid down.
Ricardo plunged for the first open door—a half-abandoned tenement
that stood at the very edge of the Merton Project, almost in the
shadow of Manhattan Central.

The dark space below the stairwell had served him before as a
haven from the law. It was only when he had barricaded himself
there, and drawn both gun and switchblade, that he realized how
badly he was wounded.

The bullet had entered the right flank and raked upward. Already,
he could feel the blood pump into his tight Levis. Sure that he was
dying, Ricardo Reyes felt his lips frame a soundless prayer. In another moment, with gun and knife still ready, he slipped into coma.

2.

The hospital was alerted by radiophone. In ten minutes, an ambulance brought Willoughby Fellowes to the emergency entrance,
where expert hands performed the usual ablutions and delousings.
In the accident ward, the patient was treated for shock, and given
antibiotic injections along with a blood transfusion. Treatment was
automatic, once the admitting doctor saw there was a chance the

wounds might not prove fatal. The blade had penetrated deeply—
but the mock *estocada,* unlike the thrust of a matador, had apparently injured no major vessel. The ambulance report stated that
the patient's pulse was fairly strong on arrival. Until the clinical
pattern was clearer (and a staff surgeon could be spared for a detailed examination) no further therapy was indicated.

A half-hour passed before the discovery of Ricardo Reyes. The police, hot on other trails, bypassed the hall where he lay groaning; it
was the tenement janitor who called Manhattan Central. A second
ambulance, with a brand-new intern at the strap, found Ricardo still
breathing, with weapons in each nerveless fist. Unaware that this
patient was ticketed for the prison ward, and unversed in procedure
for such cases, young Dr. Keller had pocketed gun and switchblade
in his haste to deliver a live body to the operating table.

Later, when questioned by the police, he remembered hanging his
ambulance coat in his locker. He could not explain how both gun
and knife had vanished.

Bob Trent was summoned to examine Ricardo. Dr. Peters had
made a preliminary evaluation just before the surgical chief entered the anesthetic room, yawning contentedly after the luxury of
five hours' unbroken sleep.

"What have we this morning? I'm ready for something serious."

"You've got your wish," said the resident. "It's a gunshot wound
of the right lumbar region."

Bob gave the patient a quick glance. He had seen such cases often. Usually they came to the table at midnight; it was odd to have
one so early.

"Any history?"

"They were knifing an old man when the police moved in. This is
the only one the prowl car cut down. We don't even have his
name."

Bob studied the bullet's point of entry. With no exit wound, he
could only guess at the track it had followed. A technician was ad-
justing the emergency X-ray unit to shoot a quick film that might
help locate the damage. It was easy to see the boy's condition was
desperate. Even with two transfusion needles in place, the rapid,
thready pulse showed the patient was losing blood more rapidly
than his veins could accept it.

"Let's get moving, George. We've no time to lose on this one."

When the surgeons entered the emergency operating room, the

patient had been placed on the table in the required position—an angle of elevation that would allow an incision to be extended to the kidney area. Pulling on a sterile gown while he moved into the midst of his hastily assembled team, Bob helped the resident apply the draping sheet.

"We'll use a transverse approach," he said. "There's no chance for second-guessing here. First we'll enter the peritoneal cavity. If there's no perforation there, we'll try the kidney."

He had set scalpel to flesh while he outlined fundamentals, to make an incision that extended from right flank to mid-abdomen. There was little preliminary bleeding, because of low blood pressure and the patient's state of shock. Towel clamps delimited the extensive operative field while the knife moved on, severing layers of fascia to expose the peritoneal lining of the abdominal cavity. The exploratory opening completed, Bob stood back while George and the assisting intern controlled the bleeders and cleared the wound with warm gauze pads soaked in saline.

Already it was evident that the bullet had ranged into the cavity. There were stains of bloody fluid beneath the transparent membrane.

So far the operation had moved as precisely as though a metronome had stood beside the table, beating an allegro tempo. Bob took a thumb-forcep and tented the peritoneal lining. George Peters did the same across the table. The surgeon's scalpel nicked the membrane between the forceps. Then, when he was sure there was no danger of damaging an organ beneath, he slit down the length of the incision. The rush of fluid into the wound was thickly laced with brown.

"*Bile!*" said Peters. The significance of that brownish tinge was unmistakable. Either the liver or bile passages (or both) had been touched by the bullet.

After the wound was cleared, the nature of the injury was shockingly apparent. When retractors beneath the rib cage opened the incision for a partial view, Bob saw that the copious flow originated at the dome of the liver. Sliding a gloved hand round the organ, he felt his finger slip into a mass of clot and damaged tissue. The blind approach made it impossible to determine the exact location of the tear, but it was obviously formidable.

Gauze pads came into his hand, enabling him to control the hemorrhage with pressure. During this procedure, the X-ray technician appeared with a still wet film. Placed on a ground-glass plate against the wall, it gave a precise silhouette of the patient's rib cage. As Bob had feared, the bullet had struck there, scattering chips over a space the size of a half-dollar.

"A bone explosion, George. The liver took it full force."

"Can we be sure it didn't reach the kidney too?"

"It seems a bit high for that. We'll have a look later, if he's in shape for it."

Both doctors knew the boy's chance for survival was remote. Soft in structure, porous, and profusely supplied with blood, the liver was the only human organ immune to repair. It did not possess the self-curing powers granted the rest of the body: with the presence of digestive bile as a complicating factor, a hemorrhage of this sort was virtually impossible to control. Outright removal was also ruled out; the liver was the single factor in the whole alimentary system that had no substitute.

"How's he holding up?" Bob asked the anesthetist.

"Still with us, Doctor. Maybe a bit better since you controlled the bleeding—but it's mighty close."

The surgical chief considered his next move. The injury could not be sutured; sewing would do as much damage to that porous tissue as the bullet. It could be packed with gelatin foam, which would absorb later, but the ooze would continue in the peritoneal cavity, an almost fatal complication after the initial blood loss. Another possibility, and a drastic one, was an approach by way of an exterior pouch. Surgeons of yesterday called this technique marsupialization, since the end product resembled the sac of the opossum or kangaroo.

Bob studied the X-ray, and spoke his mind aloud. "The track of the bullet is below the pleural cavity. We'll try to marsupialize. Make the window for me, George. I can't disturb pressure on this wound without losing him."

The resident nodded. The operative feat, bizarre though it might seem, was not too difficult, since it involved only the removal of a rib section and entrance to the peritoneal cavity by way of the liver dome. Once the window was opened, irritation from the wound itself would seal off the area. Thereafter, the hoped-for healing process, including the application of gelatin foam and pressure dressing, would come from without. The ruptured liver could then be handled like any external wound.

A four-inch incision gave George Peters the room he needed. Once the window was established, contact between the two surgeons would be possible, though difficult. Groping through the soft tissues that divided them, the resident made contact with Bob's hand, well inside the patient's body. Positive of his anatomy, he made his final incision boldly. A rib resector cleared the new operative field for a distance of several inches, removing a segment of bone.

The approach was still risky, since the pleural cavity was often extended to this area, to accommodate the expansion of oversized lungs. George cut carefully through the bed of the excised rib. The final scalpel strokes completed the shape of the artificial window. The resident could now see (as well as feel) the surgeon's fingers, on the pad controlling the basic wound.

"Ready to change, Doctor."

It was a simple matter for the surgical chief and the resident to switch places at the table. Bob slipped two more retractors into the opening George had fashioned, and motioned to the intern to hold them steady. The original pad, now anchored by the resident's fingers, still closed the liver wound.

When George released it at the surgeon's nod, there was a rush of blood, which Bob controlled with a second pad. Bits of lead had clung to the first square of gauze, to be discarded in the basin.

"Gelatin foam, please."

The white, spongy substance had been used originally to encourage blood clotting and to control hemorrhage in the brain. Today's problem was similar. Removing the new square of gauze, Bob risked a brief halt in the operation while he extracted other lead fragments from the wound. Then, sponging gently, he packed the gelatin foam into the new opening, as tightly as he dared. Over it, he placed several gauze pads. During this maneuver, George had finished the routine closure of the peritoneum.

Strapped snugly, the dressing would hold the gelatin pack against the damaged organ. In time, it might even stop the bleeding, since it afforded a practical framework where blood could clot. It was a last-ditch measure—and the only one that could save the patient.

Back in the anteroom, Bob noted an assistant resident in the doorframe. He paused in the act of shedding gown and gloves. Clearly the new day was developing on schedule.

"Better stay scrubbed, Doctor," said the newcomer. "We've brought another patient upstairs."

"What is it this time?"

"A repair job from outside: the old man who was knifed." The assistant glanced anxiously at the wall clock. "Multiple stab wounds on admission—with an outside chance to hang on. The kid was a prime emergency, so we let this one wait. In the last few minutes, he started downhill."

They moved to the hall together, while the assistant continued his outline of the case. Absorbed in the details, Bob was only vaguely aware of the two men waiting at the elevator. When the taller man spoke he realized it was Charles Tully.

"A busy day, Bob?"

"I've known busier ones—but it'll do."

"This is Sergeant Cates, Doctor. We heard you'd operated on one of the Dukes. As you know, I've been trying to make contact with that group for a long time——"

"So have I," said Cates. "When can he talk?"

"The answer's probably never," said Bob. "It was a bullet wound of the liver: he's pretty well exsanguinated."

The group entered the elevator together. "I'll ride up to the prison ward for a check," said the sergeant. "We were told he had a gun, but it isn't on the report."

"The ambulance intern will have to answer for that," said Bob. The man's voice seemed to reach him from a distance: already, he was deep in the problem that awaited him upstairs. "As you see, I'm on my way to another emergency."

"The old man those boys were working over?" asked Tully.

"So I'm told, Charles. Perhaps he can solve the sergeant's problem."

"I doubt if he'll remember much," said the social worker. "They never do. Still, it *would* be odd if he lived—and the boy died."

3.

The ward supervisor was waiting at the door of emergency. One look at her face was enough to hasten Bob Trent's steps.

"I'm afraid your patient's going fast, Doctor."

The sight of Willoughby Fellowes (inert as a waxwork figure on his cot) confirmed the judgment. An emergency oxygen mask showed only the slightest evidence of intake; the glass tube of the transfusion set gave the same ominous picture. Bob scanned the meager notations on the chart. Fellowes's age had been estimated in the mid-sixties. Routine emergency procedure was detailed, including the dressing of the three knife thrusts.

"Has there been much blood loss?"

"Not from the surface wounds, Dr. Trent. The bleeding is internal."

"Just how did it happen?"

"The police called it another fun killing," George Peters volunteered.

"There must have been witnesses."

"One or two. They didn't argue with switchblades. The gang was playing matador. This old fellow was *el toro.*"

Bob put down the chart. "Are the wounds in the back?"

"All three," said the resident. "How did you know?"

"In the bull ring, the sword drives into the bull's chest from above. The heart is punctured at the top."

"Could this be a tamponade?"

"That's my guess," said the surgical chief. "We may save him even now, if we can aspirate fast enough."

At Dr. Peters's nod, an intern had hurried up with a syringe and a size twenty needle. Bob had already lifted Fellowes's hospital gown to count the ribs in the skeleton-thin chest. Preparing to drive the needle beneath the fourth bony ridge, he did not pause to remind his assistant of yesterday's control of an extradural hemorrhage—a procedure which had also saved a life.

In both injuries, it was the site of the pressure that caused trouble, not its size. A six-inch knife, driven between the shoulder blades at a down-raking angle, could easily puncture the heart. When the weapon was withdrawn, blood would pour from the opening until the muscles of the chest wall had fallen into place, when it could no longer flow to the outside. In a lung puncture, a mixture of blood and air, compressing the spongy tissue of that organ, could stop the hemorrhage, providing the lungs were not squeezed beyond their capacity to breathe. With the heart (enclosed in a tough, fibrous sac called the pericardium) the situation was different. Here the blood rushed through the wound with every contraction of the organ, to accumulate within the sac. As pressure continued, the heart itself was increasingly constricted.

In Fellowes's case, the situation was classic: congested veins (because the blood could not empty into the heart chambers), a small pulse (because that powerful muscle no longer had working room).

Inevitably, the vicious circle would multiply itself until the beat was stilled.

The breathing bag on the oxygen mask was barely fluttering when Bob Trent thrust the needle home, at a spot just below the fourth rib and two inches to the left of the breastbone. There was a moment of resistance, then a sudden feel of release. Blood gushed into the syringe when the surgeon drew back the plunger.

"I've reached the pericardium," he said. "It's a definite tamponade. Tell the O.R. to set up for a thoractomy and closure of stab wound in the heart. We'll bring him up the moment he can stand the trip."

Bob continued to draw out blood while George Peters rushed to the phone. The pressure was violent: when he loosened the plunger, blood spurted through the syringe as though it were a faucet. Already, the change in Fellowes was startling. With the relief of the almost intolerable hemorrhage, the congestion at face and neck was clearing, and the thready pulse had taken on almost normal substance.

"Are you sure immediate surgery's indicated?" George asked. "Wouldn't it be better to observe him for awhile?"

The assistant's question was logical. The hospital files were filled with reports of similar injuries. Many of them, inflicted by narrow blades or icepicks, had closed without treatment. The viselike grip of the tamponade (as the accumulation of blood was called) often closed the wound long enough for its edges to adhere.

"This time we can't risk waiting," said Bob. "Not when there's damage on the posterior surface of the heart. We'll stay here just long enough to get that transfusion inside him, and finish with the aspiration needle. Then we must get him on the table."

Despite his general improvement, Willoughby Fellowes was only semiconscious when he was wheeled into an emergency operating room on the floor above.

Preparing for his task in the scrub room, Bob Trent studied the old man through the window. Obviously, the rescue of this bit of human flotsam (if it was feasible) would only postpone the inevitable. Fellowes had been marked for disaster from the cradle; the healing knife could only retard that process, not deflect it. At such moments, it was easy to wonder if the salvage process should continue.

"Don't scowl, Bob," said George Peters, busily scrubbing at his side. "You'll force me to read your mind."

"I wouldn't risk it."

"First the boy, now this," said Peters. "If the kid lives, he'll go into the street and kill again. If we save the old man, he'll destroy himself. Yet we'll do our damndest to pull both of them through. Do I qualify as a clairvoyant?"

"It's good surgery, George. It may be bad logic."

"Not if you're the sort of plumber who loves his work," said the resident. "Not if you remember a surgeon is lost if he starts asking why."

Bob Trent chuckled. "Thanks for putting me in my place. You're right, of course. We'll leave the aftermaths to our friend Dr. Stowe— and Charles Tully." He turned to the door, and the waiting senior nurse. "What's the situation, Miss Meadows?"

"Patient's ready, Doctor. We've injected atropine and morphine. Dr. Proctor feels he can take a general."

Bob nodded his approval. He had hoped that Hank Proctor would be free to act as his anesthetist. Through the scrub-room window, he saw that Hank was already at the table's head, holding the tracheal tube that would insure a fresh flow of oxygen while the chest was open. The device would also permit him to inflate and deflate the lungs in artificial respiration, if that drastic technique was required.

Masked and gowned, Eve Bronson waited at the instrument trays. Bob felt his heart swell with gratitude at her presence; he had guessed she would volunteer when she heard of his decision to operate. Behind her was the cardioscope, the instrument that gave a visible and audible record of the patient's heartbeat: it had been placed on a high stand to avoid the risk of sparks, in case Hank used an inflammable anesthetic like cyclopropane. Beneath it were two smaller cabinets. One held the defibrillator, an amazingly sensitive instrument designed to shock a runaway heart until it resumed its normal beat. Beside it was the "pacemaker," which delivered regular, rhythmic shocks to the organ itself—starting it in case of an abrupt standstill, and maintaining its pace artificially until it could regain its function.

The patient lay on his back, with sandbags under the left shoulder and hip, elevating the body sufficiently to permit the heart to be approached from either side. Proctor had just placed a catheter in the trachea. It would permit him to convert machine and lungs into a closed system, allowing rigid control at all stages of the operation.

At the surgeon's signal, the anesthetist switched on the cardio-scope. The electrocardiograph went into action at the same time, establishing its swift-moving, jagged pattern in the glass window of the cathode tube. The room was filled with the steady, thumping rhythm of the heart, modulated at a level that was audible but not intrusive.

"Ready when you are, Dr. Trent."

Gloved and gowned for the second time that day, Bob cast a glance toward the gallery, to find Eric Stowe's face among the others. While Peters rearranged the patient's drapes, he spoke into the hanging microphone.

"The diagnosis here is a stab wound of the heart, resulting in an accumulation of blood in the pericardium. The sac has already been aspirated. The case presents novel aspects as the wound is from the back. Since there may be difficulties, we will approach laterally."

The patient's chest had been shaved and painted. As Bob spoke, George Peters and the assisting intern spread a covering drape with its long rectangular window. Eve Bronson pushed the first instrument tray across the table below the spot chosen for the incision. Without need of words, she slapped the knife into Bob's palm. Her eyes were warm with encouragement above her mask.

"We will enter the chest at the interspace between the fourth and fifth ribs, on the left side."

His hand moved with the statement, dividing the skin down to the muscles for a distance of twelve to fourteen inches. This was surgery in its largest sense: the dimensions required (compared to most operations) were on the heroic side.

For the next five minutes, Bob and his assistants labored hard at the task of opening the chest with a minimum of damage. When the knife exposed the pleural lining, it was tinged with blood that had leaked into the cavity, mixed with a little air from wounds in the lungs themselves. Bob had expected the condition; he was relieved to find that the damage was not more extensive.

"We have some pneumothorax here," he told the gallery. "Fortunately it doesn't seem too important. Ready for me to open the chest, Hank?"

Proctor raised the volume of the cardioscope: they exchanged a look of satisfaction when the sound of the beating heart came through strong and clear, if somewhat hurried.

"Considering his years, and the Jersey lightning in his bloodstream," said the anesthetist, "your man's in amazing shape. Go right ahead."

The surgical chief slit the pleural lining for the full length of the incision. There was a hiss of escaping air while the left lung collapsed partially, due to the disappearance of the normal vacuum in the pleural sac. Its opposite number was functioning well. Already, the heart was revealed in its envelope. It was still beating regularly, and the vessels attached to it were emptying and filling in cycle. The pericardium seemed larger than usual and somewhat boggy. It was apparent the hemorrhage had resumed since Bob had relieved initial pressure in the accident ward.

Inserting his hand, he lifted up the heart. Inured though he was to the legerdemain of nature, it was still an odd sensation to hold this organ in his palm, to feel it slither against the glove as it contracted and relaxed. At such a moment, he could tell himself (in sober truth) that he was balancing life between his fingers.

George Peters had been busy with a suction tip, emptying the chest of remaining blood to allow better vision. There was no trace of damage at the front of the pericardium. When Bob rotated his burden toward the center of the chest and lifted it still higher, he saw blood gush from a small slit well back on the fibrous outer membrane.

"Tissue forcep, please."

When the delicate instrument came into his hand, Bob set its jaws on the edge of the gash. A second forcep, held by his assistant on the opposite side, enabled him to pull the small opening into a square. Holding it thus, he inserted the point of a pair of scissors and cut the sac for a distance of perhaps two inches. Peters was still holding the other forcep, while he manipulated the suction tip with his free hand. The technique permitted rapid removal of the blood pouring from the opened pericardium.

Bent above the window he had created, Bob could glimpse the matching wound in the heart muscle itself. The view was obscured by a fresh rush of red. It was enough to permit a well-trained finger to mark the spot exactly, to press against the muscle opening and prevent further flow.

"I think we have it, George. Clear the sac, and we'll see."

The suction tip proved that the surgeon's finger had found the opening. The location was unfortunate, much farther back than he would have liked. Bob knew it would take their combined skills to effect the closure.

"Put a guy suture in the apex, please. We'll pull it forward."

The resident (trained to take over the surgical burden at such a moment) accomplished the maneuver swiftly. The guy suture, attached to a curved needle, was anchored to the lower portion of the heart. When Peters lifted the anchor and drew it toward the sternum or breastbone, the whole organ was turned in its tented opening. The wound was now clearly visible, a roundish, puckered tear in the heart muscle, no larger than a button.

"We'll use silk to close," said Bob.

With Peters' anchor holding, and the surgeon's own finger hard on the wound itself, it was a relatively simple matter to place the strands of silk. Stitching neatly with his free hand until the wound was fully sutured, Bob nodded to the intern, who relieved Peters at the anchor. The resident tied off the sutures one by one. Breathing seemed to cease around the table as Bob released his pressure on the heart wall. There was not the slightest leak of blood.

"Surgically, I think that does it," said Bob. He glanced at Proctor —aware that the note of triumph might be premature. "How are we doing otherwise?"

"You got out just in time," said the anesthetist. "Pulse character is changing rapidly." He amplified the beat of the cardioscope, so the whole room could hear. Until then, the instrument had given off a steady, throbbing rhythm. Now the beat resembled a jungle tom-tom.

Prepared though he was for this setback, Bob found he was looking dazedly at the freshly sutured organ he had just restored to its normal position. When it had left his hands, the heart had contracted and relaxed normally. Within seconds the muscular flesh had changed its pattern. The present performance suggested the writhing of angry worms.

"It's ventricular fibrillation," he said. Across the table, a sudden intake of breath showed that Eve had taken in the threat.

"Open the electrodes, Miss Carroll," she said quietly.

The circulating nurse jumped to obey the order. The pause gave Bob a chance to down his panic. It was true that ventricular fibrillation (a sudden breakdown of the normal governing mechanism of the heart muscle) was the most dreaded of post-operative complications. Only a few years ago, a surgical team would have been forced to stand by and watch the heart, quite literally, thrash itself to death. Today, it was possible to restore its proper rhythm.

Eve placed the electrodes on the table. Bob felt his confidence return as their eyes met. The circulating nurse had already con-

nected the wires to the defibrillating machine. Once again George
Peters distended the squared-off opening in the pericardial sac.
Moving as swiftly as he dared, Bob placed the electrodes on the
madly writhing heart.

"We're ready, Hank."

The anesthetist flipped the impulse switch that delivered the jolts
of current. As the first was administered, Bob saw the heart leap
even more wildly, then sink back. The relaxation was brief. In another moment, the furious pattern of contraction was even more
evident.

"We are applying the defibrillator." He spoke into the microphone
automatically, without taking his eyes from the gaping window.
"Each time Dr. Proctor throws the switch, we deliver a pulse of one
hundred and fifty volts. As you observe, it enters the heart through
the electrodes. The machine is set so that the organ cannot be
shocked more than once a second."

The clinical picture was received in silence. There was no sound
in the operating room itself, save for the manic throb of the cardioscope, which the anesthetist had neglected to lower in volume. For
several seconds, each shock was followed by another disorderly
aftermath. Then, as Hank flipped the switch in the same rhythm, the
heart was strangely quiet. When the next shock came, the throb of
the cardioscope was constant, like the boom of distant cannon.

"I think the pattern's forming," said Proctor.

The deep boom was regular now. For the first time, Bob found
himself breathing freely.

"Tell me when you're sure, Hank."

"I'm ready to risk him now without stimulation."

"Let's hold off for a few seconds, then."

When the switch was disengaged, Fellowes's heart lay inert for
what seemed an endless moment. Bob was on the point of ordering
another shock, when the muscle contracted slowly, relaxed, and contracted once again. He felt his own heart swell, when the cardioscope missed but a single beat before resuming its normal tempo.

"That's it, Hank."

"So it seems." The anesthetist's hand was still on the switch, but
there was no missing his air of jubilation.

Bob addressed the gallery for the last time. "We'll leave the electrodes in place a moment more to be sure. Meanwhile, I think this
man will last—thanks to another man who discovered electricity."

Once the electrodes were withdrawn, the operation moved rapidly. When the chest wall was closed, a second injection of antibiotics was prescribed to combat infection. Less than a half-hour after the dramatic battle for his life, Willoughby Fellowes lay in a recovery room, where he would receive expert care around the clock until he was out of danger. Therapy would include a portable pacemaker. If need arose, it could administer a modified form of the same shock treatment without opening the chest.

Later—when it was learned that Fellowes's fight for life was only beginning—Bob Trent would recall those precautions with an ironic smile. At the moment, he was too elated to admit his weariness—until he stood before his locker in the dressing room, and felt himself stagger slightly.

George Peters thrust his head round the door of his own cubicle. "A thing like that *does* take your wind."

"All of us had it, George."

"Still asking questions about the caliber of our patients?"

Bob chuckled, as the spasm of exhaustion faded. "Not any more. I'm glad the old boy made it. If he does go to hell in a handbasket tomorrow, that's his privilege."

"Still plan to turn him over to Dr. Stowe?"

"Definitely—along with the kid in the prison ward. They're his problems now."

"What's he after?"

"I'm not sure, George. Some cosmic theory he shares with Inspector Dalton about crime and punishment."

"I doubt if we've helped him much," said the resident. "Fellowes was an innocent bystander today. The kid won't talk, even if he pulls through."

The surgical chief shrugged. It was true that most of these stony-faced youths classed doctors as their enemies, along with all organized authority.

"We could be wrong this time, George. Eric has helped the young to find themselves on more than one continent. Perhaps he can reach this one too."

"A Malay head-hunter would be easier to civilize."

"Aren't you being a trifle hard?"

"Not after two years on the accident ward—and a hundred stab wounds."

"I'll grant you pity's a dangerous emotion for a surgeon," said Bob. "I'll admit it softened me, seeing that heart come alive again. While it lasted, I could even wish our patient would find life worth living."

"Don't tell me you've still hope for the human species, Dr. Trent?"

"Hope is another emotion I'll yield to Eric," Bob said. "Right now I'll settle for a two-hour nap before my next case."

## 4.

Inspector Peter Dalton had spent the forenoon of the transit strike cruising in an unmarked police car, with a street map on his knees.

The tour had included a stop at Manhattan Central, where he had made pertinent inquiries at the prison ward. Otherwise he had seemed to drift with no visible goal. In Dalton's book, an impromptu exploration of this kind was an excellent stimulus for thought. This morning his musings were far more profound than his bland exterior suggested.

At noon he stopped in the plaza at Rockefeller Center to ring the mayor on his private phone. Others in the department were reporting to the commissioner today, and New York's finest were out in strength, alerted for possible violence during the one-day tieup. Pete was on direct liaison with City Hall, for reasons of his own.

John Newman came promptly to the phone. The detective grinned as he recognized the ice-cold voice. Like most born fighters, Newman seemed calmest when troubles thickened.

"The town's bearing up nicely," Pete said. "People are taking Ted Horgan's nuisance play in stride."

"Is that all you have to tell me?"

"Not quite. There's been another near-killing on Dr. Grove's doorstep."

"I heard that on the newscast, Pete."

"There are angles the commissioner hasn't released. First off, we know the kid's a Royal Duke. When he was shot, he was dressed for a rumble."

"Do you have his name?"

"Not yet. As usual, no one will talk. We do know he was carrying a gun. It was foreign made."

"You're sure of that?"

"Positive. He wasted a shot before he tried to get clear. The bullet lodged in a wall. It didn't come from an American model."

"What's your point, Pete?"

"The boy was brought in by a green intern. Instead of reporting the weapon at once, he left it in his ambulance coat. A half-hour later, it was gone."

"No leads on the thief?"

"Not yet. Sergeant Cates is combing the hospital. I asked Charles Tully to have a look: he knows the neighborhood backwards."

"What about the drunk who was stabbed?"

"He was just a target, John. Do you realize he's the fifth derelict to be attacked this month?" Pete hesitated, feeling the mayor's impatience vibrate down the line. "Last night, I told you *someone* was giving these hoods their orders. Today I was on the edge of proving it—if that damned gun hadn't vanished."

"You're still riding a hunch, Pete. Why not admit you've nothing solid to go on?"

"Call it what you like," said the detective resignedly. "At least I'm moving in on Marek. He's somewhere on Washington Heights, and we've pinned down the block. Even money says we collar him by dark."

John Newman chuckled. "I won't take the wager."

"Any blasts from old Merton? That near-murder was on his land."

"He hasn't called so far, thank God. I've headaches enough today."

"You seem to love your work," said Pete, and hung up the phone. Back in the police car, he could only shrug when his driver asked for directions. "Circle the plaza," he said. "Then we'll have a look at Madison and Broadway. You might go past the hospital again on the way to headquarters."

The silent expanse of Ad Alley did not depress Pete unduly. For the past two years, when the press of wheeled traffic in midtown had grown intolerable, all private cars had been detoured at Central Park South. Today the ban on personal transportation had been lifted: it was a throwback to the Fifties to find autos parked solid on each side street. The quiet, Pete reflected, was part of the emergency. Normally Madison Avenue would have been hideous with the war of jockeying taxis, the snarls of bus drivers. Today, it awaited the luncheon break in almost pastoral calm.

"East Side Highway, sir? Or shall we stay on Broadway?"

"Broadway will be faster today, Ed."

Even to Inspector Dalton's ear, there was something faintly sinister about that always dingy canyon. It was a strange sensation to drift through traffic lights without danger, to realize that these towering office warrens, though open for business, were operating with fractional staffs. Not that the situation was novel: New York had sweated out other transit tieups, and picked up its normal rhythm when they ended. Today, Pete felt there was a special quality in the silence, a threat that went deeper than idled subways and bus lines.

The fancy was absurd, and he had conquered it before the police car could reach Union Square. Ted Horgan had given the mayor his word that full service would resume tomorrow; the rank and file of Marek's union had virtually agreed to return to work. On that bright summer morning, the note of doom was still remote. Recalling the moment later, Pete Dalton knew that not even his radar-sharp ears could have caught that distant echo.

## 5.

Before returning to Manhattan Central, Eric and Eve had spent a sunburnt afternoon on a Long Island beach. They had dined early and regally at the Beau Séjour, a Lucullan roadhouse less than an hour's drive from the Triborough Bridge. Now as the last light faded in the west, the immunologist was driving faster than the law allowed to reach the bridge by dark—and hoping the MD on his license plate would explain his speed.

For several miles he had observed the heavy flow of outbound vehicles. Despite the hour, the last of tonight's car pools (fuming at traffic blocks on the bridge) were still following a gas-fogged homeward trail. By contrast the inbound lanes seemed virtually empty. The Manhattan skyline, lifting against the afterglow of sunset, seemed oddly hostile in this hour between day and night. Eric spoke lightly, reluctant to break the contented silence that had fallen between them.

"To my mind, dining by daylight's a barbarous custom. I wish we could have stayed longer."

"So do I," said Eve.

"Blame it on Bob. He asked me to get back by eight, to check on two cases in the accident ward. Didn't you assist while he was operating?"

"With the old man. Not the boy."

"Did he have any specific reasons?"

"We were busy finding a heart wound, Eric; there wasn't time to talk."

Eric kept his eyes on the looming cliffs of the city. "Apparently he thinks the next move is mine—since I'm unofficial head man of the hospital detective bureau." He was careful not to say more, now he had measured her unconcern; their day had been too precious to spoil. Swimming with Eve in the Atlantic surf, offering her *caneton aux oranges* and Montrachet at a famous roadhouse, he had found it easy to shed the depression that had plagued him—a sense of foreboding that had begun with his visit at Gracie Mansion.

Eve lay back in the deep bucket seat of the Ferrari as it spiraled down the ramp to the East River Drive. She, too, seemed entirely relaxed, but her voice echoed his thoughts when she spoke.

"I've enjoyed being outside, Eric. As you know, I don't escape often."

"If I suggested a permanent escape, would you consider it?"

"How can I, until I take my degree?"

"Surely you've post-graduate plans."

"Manhattan Central has given me so much. Perhaps I'll just stay there. We're beginning to sign on women residents, you know."

"The world's bigger than any hospital, my dear."

"Bob doesn't think so."

"Bob's a born surgeon. He's found his level in that service. Could you?" .

"I won't deny I've considered it."

"Don't you want to discover what's beyond an operating room wall?"

"Are you offering yourself as guide?"

Expecting the dare, he found he could answer steadily enough. "I'll be even more specific, Eve. Next year I'll be going to Afghanistan, to serve as W.H.O. consultant to their opposite numbers. It'll be an important job. If you're interested, I could use an extra supervisor."

"I'm not yet qualified."

"You will be—before this thing gets under way." He risked a quick glance; even in the dusk he could see her eyes were shining. "It's a firm offer—and you needn't decide right now. If the life didn't suit you, you could always come back to civilization."

"Back to Bob, you mean?"

"If that's the way things are."

"We aren't engaged," she said quickly. "It's the hospital that has the claim on me—not Bob Trent." She broke off abruptly. Once again, he was aware they had both said too much.

"Let's leave the escape hatch open then," he said carefully.

"Must you call it that?"

"I think it's my privilege, Eve. I'll mention it again, when my own tour of duty is over. Right now, I've two patients to visit, and I'm taking the short cut."

Eve let her hand rest briefly on his. "Please don't think I'm not grateful. But I *will* need time to decide."

They were approaching the next exit from the Drive, a utility road that cut through a maze of warehouses to approach the hospital via its back-door slum. Eric swung into the turnoff without conscious thought. They had used this timesaver often, when they hurried from beach to work; it was the first time he had risked it after dark.

"Sorry," he murmured. "I don't yield to automatic reflexes often. For all I know, there may be police blocks on this approach tonight."

The prophecy came true before they had gone a hundred yards. The gray-white sawhorse that stood across the alley ahead was warning enough that their usual short cut was closed to vehicular traffic after sundown. The narrow lane was crowded on both sides by the platforms of shuttered warehouses. A short block ahead (where his headlights bored into the dark) Eric could see the cleared vastness of the Merton Project. Beyond it, the glow of the hospital rotunda seemed unreal as a mirage.

"Apparently we must back up and start over——"

"*Cuidado, señor!*"

The hiss of warning came from a spot where shadows were thickest: the speaker had already drifted into view, a runty youth in dead-black jeans and T shirt. He was followed by an almost identical companion. Both of them had stepped boldly into the road, a scant foot from the rear bumper.

Sensing his danger, Eric gunned his motor. "I'm backing up, fellows. Watch it, or you'll be hurt——"

A third youth, ghosting from the alley's mouth, whipped a practiced hand into the open tonneau of the Ferrari and killed the ignition. Eric's own hand swooped to anchor the key in the lock. When he looked up, the alley was swarming with slender, black-clad figures. All of them talked a language of their own: their intent was clear, though he could only half-understand the rapid, pidgin Spanish.

The boy who had cut off the engine raised his voice a trifle, stilling the whispers around him.

"Somebody's gettin' hurt, mister. Only it won't be us."

There was a gleam in the darkness as a knife came alive in his hand. The others, responding to that wordless signal, drew their own knives—so quickly, that Eric missed the translation from pocket to palm. The threat had come with incredible smoothness, like an ensemble effect in a ballet. Had the gang moved to music, it could not have created that ring of steel more gracefully.

Expecting all-out attack, Eric braced to defend Eve, but the knives continued to hang motionless in the dark. The whispers had begun again, a surf of counterpoint to the dance of sneaker-clad feet about the car.

"*Sangre de Cristo! Qué carreta bonita!*"

"Know what that hot rod's worth, *amigo?*"

"The hubcaps are mine!"

"I'll take the spare tire——"

"*Caramba contigo!* Who stopped them—you or I?"

"I blocked the alley, *hijo de puta!*"

"Take the tires, *niño*. Just give me the *muchacha*."

"*Otro loco más!* She's mine, not yours——"

Eric cut across the hubbub in his best Spanish."

"Quiet, fellows! Tell me what you want!"

The lash of his tongue silenced the tumult briefly. The lieutenant recovered first, but there was a whine in his tone as he answered.

"Can't you guess, mister?"

"If it's *dinero*——"

"Don't worry, *señor*. We'll get your money too."

"After we take your *careta* apart——"

"The car first? Or his girl friend?"

Eric saw each threat was quite genuine. He raised his voice again, knowing in advance that anger would be as futile as yielding. The sport these young monsters had in mind would be as ritual as their ballet-like motion, their teasing dialogue.

"Let the lady go, you cowards! I'll fight the lot of you—fists or knives. Won't that be fun enough?"

"Don't move, Eric!"

Eve's whisper, catching him unawares, anchored him beneath the wheel. The circle moved nearer as she opened her purse, then paused when the gang realized the flash of metal was only a lighter. Making the gesture deliberate, she found a cigarette in her purse and lighted it, holding the flame at chin level while she took her first puff, so her face remained in clear relief.

"Where are you, Juan?" she asked coldly. "Isn't it time you stopped this nonsense?"

The knives still hung poised: the two hooligans who had surged toward the door with tire chains in their fists seemed frozen in mid-air. Each eye was fixed on the lieutenant, but the youth made no sign of combat. Eric saw why, as a tall figure stirred in the shadows on a loading platform, lifted a hand palm outward, then drew back into darkness. The knives vanished at the signal. The bearers of the tire chains, with a regretful shrug, drew back from the Ferrari's door.

"Forgive us, Miss Bronson," said the shrouded figure. "You should have spoken sooner."

"You hardly gave me a chance, Juan."

"Is this car yours?"

"It belongs to my escort," said Eve, in the same level tone. "He is a doctor—a close friend of Dr. Trent."

"Believe me, we did not set this trap for *you*."

"Move it at once, then. We've work to do at the hospital."

The figure on the platform (he had still refused to show his face) barked a command in Spanish. Two members of the gang shoved the stolen police barrier aside. Eve's hand pressed the ignition. The Ferrari streaked down the alley, burst into the dimly lit plain, and swung under the lights on the hospital drive.

On the ramp that led to the basement parking lot, Eric glanced at the dashboard clock. Their escape had been made in just under a minute.

"Tell me how it happened," he gasped. "I'm still not quite sure I'm alive."

"That, as you must have gathered, was Juan Lemayo," said Eve. To his chagrin, he realized her voice was still calm, now the ordeal was behind them.

"Weren't you even afraid?" he asked resentfully.

"Not when they didn't jap us at once," said Eve.

"Jap?"

"Beat us up, if you insist on English."

"It wouldn't have stopped with a beating."

"Perhaps it wouldn't," she said, with the same aplomb. "Did you see how they moved—like soldiers under a drillmaster's eye? That's part of Juan's training. I knew he was watching somewhere. He'd never let them hurt us."

"You speak like an authority, my dear."

"The Dukes are famous in this section of New York. All of us at the hospital know them."

"Don't tell me Lemayo was one of Bob's patients——"

"Last year, Bob operated on his mother. A case of massive gastric hemorrhage; the ambulance got her to the table just in time. I visited her after she was discharged from the ward; her tenement's only a two minute walk from this door. Living in their midst as we do, it seemed important to let her son know who'd saved her."

"I can see that. No wonder you were so confident."

The Ferrari was in its parking space now, but Eve made no move to step out. "Juan worships his mother," she said. "You might call it his one redeeming trait."

"Thank God for small miracles. I don't doubt it saved our lives tonight."

"Nor do I," said Eve. "She's a fine woman, Eric. One of those lost souls that can't escape its environment. She's done her best for Juan. It's hardly her fault that he's been an enemy of society from the start."

"A killer for the sake of killing?"

"I see you understand," said Eve. Her voice had trembled for the first time, but not from fear. "When society breeds that sort of misfit, would you blame me if I prefer to stay inside these walls?"

"After tonight, nothing you do would surprise me."

In the foyer, Eve gave him her brightest smile, and held out her hand. They were under the gaze of the night-admissions desk: it was no moment for tenderness. The urge to take this intrepid girl in his arms was still strong; he mastered it as best he could.

"Don't think I wasn't panic-stricken too," she said in a low voice that did not carry to the admissions desk. "I was just too stubborn to show it. And I hope you meant every word about Afghanistan. I'd like to consider that offer—carefully."

## 6.

The prison ward at Manhattan Central—like its counterpart at Bellevue—was a stern reminder that the patients it housed were dangerous, even during illness.

Opening from the emergency ward, it began with a heavily barred anteroom, where a police clerk and detectives kept constant guard. Here too was the check room, where the patients' effects were held against their departure; according to hospital rules, Ricardo Reyes' weapons should have been turned in at this counter on his admission. Eric gave the neatly labeled shelves a glance while the clerk was noting his visit on a regulation police blotter. He could understand Inspector Dalton's anger at the loss of these possibly vital clues.

"The boy's in 211, Dr. Stowe," said the clerk. "But I'm afraid he's turned in his checks."

Eric confirmed the news in the recovery room where Juan Lemayo's second-in-command had fought for life all through the day —only to succumb from blood loss. It was the complication Bob Trent had feared. The terminal notation on the chart indicated that the fear was justified:

*Massive hemorrhage from liver wound.*
*Uncontrollable by packing and continuous transfusion.*

The youth's body lay on the hospital cot beneath a sheet. Under the light, an orderly was solving a crossword puzzle while he awaited the morgue cart. Obeying an irrational impulse, Eric turned back the sheet to study Ricardo's face. In death the young hoodlum was oddly serene; there was no trace of the evil that had stunted him.

"Did he regain consciousness?"

"He tried hard, just before he copped out. He was too weak to get out a word."

"Does it happen often?"

"Oftener than you'd expect. Sometimes they remember their religion, and blab out everything. This wasn't the law's lucky night."

"Couldn't you even identify him?"

The orderly put down his puzzle. "We're sure he's one of the Dukes, and that's all. When he was brought in, he didn't have so much as a dog tag. Course, if they have records, we can pin 'em down with mug shots and fingerprints. This one was clean, it seems. All we can do is put him in cold storage, in case he has people to claim him—which I doubt."

"Why do you say that?"

"Two good reasons, Doctor. His kind don't like to mix with the law—and a funeral costs money. This lad is headed for Potter's Field, once he's worn out his welcome in our icebox. He had a ticket there from the start."

The immunologist replaced the sheet; there was no contesting that arid summary. It was logical that the boy should go to a nameless grave; it was the crowning irony that he would be mourned in secret, if at all. . . .

Back in the emergency ward, Eric was startled to hear his name on the public-address box. He was about to pick up a desk phone when an intern signaled at the corridor's end.

"I put through that call, Dr. Stowe. There's something here you must see to believe."

"I'll join you in a moment—after I examine a patient called Fellowes."

"*He's* the one I'm talking about, sir."

The blinds in this recovery room were drawn, blurring the glow of the street lamp outside. In the pale light, the derelict resembled a crusader unhappy with his bier. Eric saw that he was barely conscious, and plucking irritably at the bedclothes. The chart mentioned a mild delirium, and a slowly rising temperature. Otherwise the post-operative picture was excellent.

"When did this fever begin?"

"In the late afternoon, Dr. Stowe. There's a complication we didn't foresee when he was admitted."

"Why isn't it mentioned here?"

The intern's eyes dropped. Eric would have sworn the man had blushed. "I hesitated to enter it, sir—without consultation. But the cause is obviously gonorrhea."

"At *his* age?"

"You can't ever tell what'll turn up in emergency. Will you have a look?"

There was no mistaking the swollen masses in the patient's groin. These were the lymph nodes known as buboes. Their enlargement was a standard warning of the venereal disease the intern had mentioned.

"What do you make of this body rash?"

"Vermin of some sort, Dr. Stowe. Looks like he scratched himself raw while he was floating in alcohol."

"Was he deloused on admission?"

"Thoroughly, sir."

Eric moved out of the cone of light while he fought for calm. "I'd like a needle biopsy from that swelling."

"I'll bring a tray," said the intern.

"Fair enough. It's best not to move him."

The immunologist stood at the window blind while he awaited the man's return. His pulse had steadied now—enough, at least, to cover his thoughts. Routine was a salvation after the tray had been placed on the night table. His hands were firm with purpose as he set out syringe and needle, opened a jar of antiseptic and a pack of sterile gloves. If the thing he sought was present in Fellowes's body, this was a technique that admitted no bungling.

An orderly and a nurse had returned with the intern. They stood ready now to anchor the patient for the biopsy.

"Shall I light the alcohol lamp, sir?"

"If you please," said Eric.

Avoiding three pairs of curious eyes, he moved to the sink in the corner to scrub his hands. The discipline of years was in control when he approached the feebly moaning patient. Donning the sterile gloves, he painted the distended skin of the groin, and tented a small windowed sheet above the largest swelling.

"Bear down, Bert," said the intern. "He's bound to squirm a bit."

Eric tested the painted skin surface, confirming the shiny, reddish hue of a fulminating inflammation. Then, attaching syringe to needle, he thrust the point deep into the swollen lymph gland. The plunger drew back, bringing only a drop of blood into the syringe before the glass receptacle filled with straw-colored fluid.

"That'll do nicely," he said. "As of now, I'll want this man in complete isolation."

The intern was obviously startled, but his discipline was adequate. "Very good, Dr. Stowe. I'll give the orders. He already has a special nurse."

"I'll check his progress in the morning. Call me if there's any significant change."

"May I ask what to look for, sir?"

"I won't know myself, until I've made my smears."

During the exchange, Eric had kept busy above the alcohol burner, where he had flamed the mouths of two culture tubes before letting two precise drops fall into them from the syringe. It was a technique he had followed a thousand times. Tonight his hands performed it with no help from his brain, which still insisted what he was witnessing could not be real.

When he had made his smears he placed the slides on the instrument tray, racked the two culture tubes on the same receptacle, and carried the lot from the recovery room. It was only a short walk to the laboratory—and he was thankful that he had encountered no one en route. Once he had settled at the work table in his own quarters, he was breathing more easily.

Here the techniques he followed were just as mechanical. The culture tubes were consigned to an incubator. The slides were flamed lightly over a burner to fix the material upon the glass, then defined further with the familiar Gram's stain—a standard application to differentiate classes of bacteria. When the first slide was ready, Eric placed it on the movable stage of his binocular microscope and put a drop of oil on the smear. The highest power-objective of the microscope was then lowered almost to the glass, until lens and oil were in contact. The procedure gave the best possible visibility—an absolute need if he hoped to pin down his quarry.

Working with the concentration of the researcher whose objective is almost in view, the immunologist lowered his head to the eyepiece of the microscope. Expert as he was at fixing his sights, he needed only a few touches at the controls to bring the material into brilliant focus.

A glance at the myriads of rod-shaped organisms confirmed the assumption he had made in the recovery room. Only the final culture reports would make the diagnosis certain—but he had seen enough to start his mind functioning like an electronic computer. With no need for conscious thought, he found himself turning the leaves of his address book to search out Selden Grove's home telephone. He was in the act of dialing when he heard his name called across the shadowed laboratory outside his cubicle.

Eric looked up in annoyance at the interruption. It was Dr. Peyton King, a soft-spoken Texan who was one of the many assistants in the pathology department. Deliberate in all his actions, he seemed to be breathing fire tonight.

"I'm afraid I'm rather busy, Dr. King."

"Sorry, sir—but this might be important. I saw you come in just now, and reckoned it couldn't wait."

"What's on your mind?"

"I've been studying some lung-tissue specimens Dr. Maynard took from a cadaver yesterday. One of 'em looks right funny."

A bell rang faintly in Eric's mind. It was a tocsin he had long since learned to heed.

"Lung tissue, you say?"

"The diagnosis at autopsy was broncho-pneumonia. Well sir, it's the strangest kind of pneumonia I ever saw. The regular sections hadn't come through yet—so I cut another block and made a temporary preparation. The organism's rod-shaped, and the tissue's solid with 'em."

"You're sure?" The query was automatic; the tocsin was clanging in earnest now.

"I thought of Friedlander's pneumonia," said King, "but this baby's the wrong size. So I looked up the possibilities. There aren't many, Dr. Stowe—besides the pneumonic form of plague. And that's out, of course. There hasn't been any *Pasteurella* in these parts for close to a century."

Eric left the microscope he had been using. "Take a look."

The younger doctor glanced at the slide, studied it with great care for a moment, then looked up with bewildered eyes. "It's the same bug I found in the lung tissue. Where did you——"

"That's a smear of material aspirated from a massive buboe down in surgery."

"Buboes—*and* pneumonic. The two forms of plague, in *New York?*"

"I'll want to see cultures from that lung case. I suppose Dr. Maynard took them."

"He did, sir," Dr. King said dazedly. "There's a note on the chart to that effect." He indicated the record he had placed on the table when he sat down at the microscope.

"Bring them, and we'll make some smears," said Eric. "Meanwhile I'll check the record. Naturally, you'll say nothing of this to anyone."

The young pathologist's face was ashen, but he managed a vigorous nod. "Naturally, Dr. Stowe."

7.

Dr. King returned promptly from his work table, bearing a rack of test tubes still warm from the incubator. The brief absence had given Eric time to scan the police report, and the laconic notes of Dr. Gilbert Maynard had dictated during his autopsy. They completed a story he could have recited from memory, now he knew precisely what to look for.

"As you'll observe, there's a heavy growth," said the pathologist. "It must be a pretty virulent organism."

"It has that reputation, Dr. King."

Eric took up one of the platinum loops used for transferring bacterial cultures. Flaming the loop in a burner, and repeating the process with the test tube King handed him, he lifted a section of the culture and made his smear.

"You can leave these cultures with me," he said. "I'll keep them in my own incubator for the present."

The slide was flamed in turn to kill the bacteria now spread on its surface, then stained and fixed in the field of the microscope. The picture revealed sent a chill to Eric's heart. He had observed that almost solid mass of rods too often to mistake its significance.

"We must warn Dr. Maynard at once," he said. "Unless he was masked, he was almost certainly exposed during the autopsy."

"There's no chance it could be anything else, Dr. Stowe?"

The immunologist studied the culture record and glanced again at the rack of tubes. The pattern of media in which the germs were increasing most profusely fitted the growth characteristics of *Pasteurella pestis* exactly.

"We'll double-check, of course," he said, "with special culture media. As of now, we must presume there is plague in New York."

"How did it enter?"

"The dead man who supplied this lung tissue was captain of a freighter that called at a West African port. My guess is he took on infected rats there. Or possibly some crew members who started the disease-cycle at sea."

The pathologist was staring at the record lying on the desk, his eyes filled with sudden terror. Eric looked at him anxiously, and put out a hand to steady him.

"Dr. King! Did *you*——?"

"I've handled no fresh tissues or cultures, except in the tubes. It's Dr. Maynard."

"What about Maynard?"

"He was admitted to the respiratory ward at noon. He and Al Novak, the technician who helps him with p.ms. The diagnosis was URI."

Eric grasped King's meaning instantly. URI—or upper respiratory infection—was an inclusive label, extending from the common cold to illnesses resulting from more than a hundred viruses pathogenic to man. Sometimes the layman diagnosed his troubles as grippe, dosed himself with aspirin, and sweated out the misery: in the end, the disease ran its course—and if there were no major complications, the patient recovered. Sometimes even with the best of medical care the patient died. URI could strike for no apparent reason. Or it could spread epidemics whose explosive effect could be traced as easily as the spatter of a shotgun. . . .

Eric had no real worries about himself; as a public-health officer, he had long since been immunized. The vaccine might not protect him from the pneumonic form of plague, which invaded the lungs directly, carried by what epidemiologists called "droplet infection." Still, with a first rank of antibiotics already in his blood, he could face *Pasteurella pestis* without fear; the worst he could expect would be a minor infection.

What concerned him now were the dozens, perhaps hundreds of people who had already come in contact with Maynard and Novak. Such victims of these two walking incubators, unless they had traveled recently in the Orient, would have had no protection whatever.

Before hastening to the respiratory ward, Eric had put in a call for the chief resident of the hospital's medical service. Dr. Norris Weaver, he recalled, was a no-nonsense type who would take the news he bore in stride. Weaver's acceptance of his report was a confirmation of that estimate, when they met in the anteroom of the ward.

"I visited Maynard an hour ago," he said. "He isn't doing at all well. In fact, I'd already half-decided this was no simple URI."

"I would advise rigid isolation technique, beginning now." Eric said. "Gowns, gloves—the whole routine."

"I'll order the supplies at once." Weaver took up the house phone, and barked his commands. His expression had not changed when he faced the two visitors. "Naturally I'm hoping you're dead wrong, Dr. Stowe."

"Have you seen Novak too?"

"His course is about the same as Maynard's."

The floor nurse appeared with the equipment Weaver had ordered. Gowned, gloved, and masked to the eyes, the three doctors filed into the room where Gilbert Maynard lay. The assistant pathologist was staring wide awake. When he noticed his visitors' garb, the fever gleam in his eyes was heightened by a rising light of fear.

"This looks like full isolation, Norris."

"We'll call it that for now, Gil," said the medical chief.

"So I've picked up more than bargain-basement flu. I know I should feel honored. I don't." Maynard went into a spasm of coughing, as Dr. Weaver put a soothing hand on his shoulder.

"So far, there's no need to be alarmed."

"Then why's Dr. Stowe with you? *What's wrong?*"

Eric joined Weaver at the bedside. "We think you've picked up a rare bug, Doctor. So rare we'd like to isolate it, as a matter of precaution." He was looking at the chart while he spoke. The steady rise of the patient's temperature, the up-and-down spikes of marked toxicity, told him volumes. "Will you answer a few questions briefly?"

"I'll try, Dr. Stowe."

"Did you notice any symptoms before noon today?"

"Headache this morning. Felt worse fast. A chill-and-fever pattern."

"Where's your discomfort now?"

Maynard touched the head end of his chest and spoke hoarsely, after another fit of coughing. "It's pneumonia of some kind, I take it."

Eric nodded. Technically this was true, since pneumonia meant only an inflammation of the lungs, in which bacterial secretions solidified all or part of those normally spongy organs. Tonight, at least, it would be a needless cruelty to give Maynard the real name of the invader.

Al Novak was in the same two-bed ward. The proximity of the patients, Eric reflected, was one good break in the tragic sequence of events he had just uncovered. The picture in the assistant's case was almost identical. The three doctors did not speak again, until they had filed into the hall and shed their coverings.

"I'll call the night supervisor and order specials," said Weaver. "Any other suggestions, Dr. Stowe?"

"Have you tried antibiotics?"

"Not yet. We usually bypass them in URI cases—to avoid staphylococcus pneumonia. With an impending if not actual pneumonia, they seem indicated here. What's your idea of medication?"

"The broadest scale of injections you can use—preferably with the tetracycline group. I'd give the sulfanamides as well. Sulfamerazine should produce the best results."

Weaver gave the immunologist a hard-eyed look. "Will you note the probable infecting agent on the chart?"

"Not yet, Doctor. But I'll stake my reputation it's plague."

"The pneumonic form, in this case. If you're right, we couldn't have worse news."

"There's a case of the bubonic form here too—in the surgical recovery section. He's already been isolated."

"Is that the extent of our troubles?"

"So far as the record shows."

"Meaning that we should run a check on everyone who has been in contact with Maynard and Novak—as well as your man downstairs."

"We can't settle for less, Doctor. All of them should receive an initial dose of plague vaccine at once—including yourself and Dr. King."

"I'll handle the details," said Weaver. "The night pharmacist will know how much we have on hand. We can get more in the morning."

*Before this thing is ended,* thought Eric, *we'll need more vaccine than this whole country can supply—to say nothing of more sulfamerazine.* New York was no oriental city, immunized, in some degree, by centuries of exposure to plague. Now it had found lodgment, the tiny, rod-shaped enemy would have the most fertile soil imaginable for its growth, and almost no natural resistance to deflect its spread.

He did not voice the thought—but it was a leaden weight on his shoulders when he shut himself in the first phone booth, and dialed the home number of Dr. Selden Grove.

Grove answered on the first ring. His voice was jubilant.

"I was about to ring you, Eric."

"Does that prove extrasensory perception's more than a theory?"

"How's that again?"

"Forget it, Selden. My jokes aren't too brilliant tonight."

"I've just talked to John Newman," said the hospital director. "They've collared Marek. Sanitation trucks will be on the street by morning."

"That's good news."

"It's the best news we could have, Eric—short of a real start on the project. With our labor troubles settled, we can really get to work on Jasper Merton."

"We've other problems tonight, Selden. Worse than an army of Mertons——"

There was no way to break his news gently. Pulling no punches, Eric described the events of the past hour.

Grove heard him through without interruption. "Is there an outside chance you're mistaken?" he said hoarsely. "I still can't grasp what you've told me."

"I'm afraid there's no chance whatever."

"In that case, I can only thank God you're here to take charge. What do we do first?"

"We're taking every possible control measure in the hospital. Starting tomorrow, we're going to present the health commissioner of

New York with a king-sized headache. To say nothing of the Public Health Service."

"Can't we immunize everyone who's been in contact with these cases?"

"If we could find them, yes. But where do we start? Dollard's dead. How do we pinpoint his whereabouts since Saturday? Or Maynard's? Or Novak's? Or a homeless drunk like Fellowes? Besides, no one knows just how protective vaccine will be in an epidemic."

"We aren't facing an epidemic, so far."

"We will be day after tomorrow. Take my word for that much now."

"Give it to me straight, Eric. Is this bacillus completely beyond control?"

"I didn't say that. But we must remember that people *have* died after vaccination—before the antibodies could build up resistance in their blood."

"Then we'll need more than serum?"

"Put it this way, Selden. With our head start, we've a better than even chance to cover the hospital and its personnel. Even if we have to supplement the vaccine with some form of chemical prophylaxis. The technique has worked elsewhere. Outside Manhattan Central, we'll have to rely on straight medication."

"Surely not for a whole city."

"Our best hope is to destroy the germ in the body *before* the disease pattern starts. We've about two million people on Manhattan Island alone. With those numbers, we can't rely on vaccine, even if it were practical. What we'll be wanting are drugs in quantity. Streptomycin, sulfamerazine——"

"That's a job for Public Health. We'll put the problem in their laps tomorrow."

"Meanwhile, will you call up key personnel, and set up a morning meeting? I'll do the same at the W.H.O. Obviously, we'll have to look for help overseas before we're done."

"I'll start at once. Do you want me at the hospital?"

"We won't need you at this moment. As I said, Dr. Weaver's taking every precaution."

"I'll issue an order tomorrow, putting you in emergency charge. You've my verbal authorization tonight."

"Thanks, Selden. So far, I've had full co-operation."

"You'll keep on getting it. Be assured of that."

8.

Jon Marek had been pacing the detectives' squad room for the past hour, while he cursed the luck that had brought him here.

The clock on the mustard-yellow wall hung close to midnight. It ticked loudly in the stillness; there was almost no other sound to disturb the stagnant repose of the Police Department's Eighty-first Precinct. The occasional raucous lament of a drunk in the cooler downstairs did nothing to destroy the illusion that Jon Marek had been left here alone, to meditate on his crimes and their probable punishment.

It was a point in his favor, the Sanitation Union leader reflected, that he had not been locked up as well. The fact that he had not yet been formally booked was of small comfort—and he had found no real target for his rage so far. When the law had banged on the apartment door at last, he had been wise enough to go quietly. When the desk sergeant had told him (with deceptive politeness) that Inspector Peter Dalton would soon be arriving to ask a few questions, he had not protested too strongly at the highhanded summons.

He had been ushered into the empty squad room; though he knew the door was guarded, there had been no threat of restraint. Should he storm back to the sergeant's desk, demand that this game cease at once? The impulse was futile, of course—there was no further point in flight, no haven where he could close his ears to the whisper of the Voice. His hand closed on the phone he had been allowed to use freely, but the gesture was as pointless as the urge to escape. There was no reason to call his lawyer again, or the union's vice-president. Both numbers had failed to answer: he knew the reason well enough.

*Rats and a sinking ship,* he thought, even as his mind rejected the well-worn metaphor. This time, the rat might become king of Manhattan, thanks to his holdout; he could hardly tag his underlings with so convenient a label. Nor could he blame them too much if they sought the easiest escape from the city's retribution.

Was this soiled room his journey's end? Jon Marek had spent too much time on the threshold of jail to mistake his present plight. Yet even now, though his spirit cringed within him, the ghost of an old defiance took over. He raised a fist to heaven, damning Inspector Dalton and all his works. The malediction comforted him a little.

The bluster died when he heard the cough of a motor in the street. Hoping it was the inspector's car, he hurried to the window—and stopped dead, shaken by what he saw. One of his own department trucks had just rolled into view, loaded to the brim with refuse. It was followed by a second and a third. A driver sat at each wheel, with two helpers riding the running boards. Wise in the details of his trade, Marek realized they were headed for an uptown incinerator.

He opened his mouth to shout, then struck the window sill a bruising blow—obviously, his voice would not carry beyond these panes of leaded glass. The strike had been broken against his orders—and he could name the breakers, as accurately as though Saul Gordon and his craven vice-president stood before him.

A little later, when the door opened and Dalton appeared on the threshold, Marek was almost sobbing. He turned aside, unwilling to show his tears.

"Sorry I couldn't get uptown sooner," said the detective.

Marek kept his eyes on the window. Trucks were now passing in a solid file. (His vice-president, he decided, had opened the reserve garage to speed collections.)

"How did you end the strike?"

"Simply enough. We had you declared a missing person, which put your next-in-command in charge. When your lawyer convinced him he was facing jail, he didn't waste time. I'm afraid neither of those gentlemen has your stamina."

"We'll omit the sarcasm," said Marek. "You've won this round, inspector. What comes next?"

"There won't be a next time."

"We'll see about that, when I've talked to my lawyer."

"At the moment, you have no lawyer. Saul Gordon was always quick on his feet; he's joined the opposition."

"Nothing's cheaper than a mouthpiece. You can't scare me that easy."

"A good mouthpiece is expensive, Jon. Can you afford one now?"

"I've bought bigger men than you. Why can't I afford a lawyer?"

"This time you overplayed your possum act," said Pete. "Your union not only endorsed a new president today. They gave *you* the boot as well."

"They *couldn't*. It isn't legal."

"In your place," said Pete, "I wouldn't quibble about legality. It was also voted to put your funds in escrow, including the war chest you're so proud of. They're asking for an accounting. Are you ready to give one?"

"What business is this of yours? If I'm under arrest, say so. If not, let me crack a few skulls——"

"It's true you were brought here on my orders," said the detective. Throughout, his voice had not lost its strange note of pity. "I had to move fast, Jon—before you did yourself real harm."

"Tell me why I'm here, Dalton! I've a right to know."

"Couldn't you use a little protection, after tonight?"

"From my friends, perhaps?"

"I'm referring to the man who rules your life. You can hardly deny you've let him down."

Staggered though he was, Marek held his ground. "Try again, Mr. Policeman. You've lost me completely."

"We both know *he* wanted the sanitation tie-up to continue. Surely he'll take his revenge, now you've failed him."

"This strike was my idea, and mine alone."

"Perhaps it was, at first. Isn't it true you were told to prolong it?"

Aware that the detective was bluffing—or at least guessing wildly —Marek turned to meet his eye. "Can you prove a word of this?"

"I think it's the reason you stayed in hiding," said Pete. "I'm sure your life will be worthless if you walk out that door alone."

"Because I failed?"

"Because you couldn't do as you were told," said Pete. "There's no worse crime in the country you serve."

"Are you out of your mind? I'm an American citizen."

"You've never served America, Jon. When you aren't lining your pockets, you're helping one of our enemies. Shall I mention his name? Or shall I name the city where your parents are held prisoners?"

"I'm alone in the world."

"It's too bad we couldn't spare your people," said Pete. "Given the present situation, we had to think first of New York's health. There's still time to save *you*—if you'll play ball."

"You're talking wild, Mr. Policeman." Marek's eyes were stony now, and he had never felt more at ease. Already the airless room and the tired man who faced him seemed hopelessly remote. "I won't say you're talking nonsense—that wouldn't be polite."

"Tell me who gives your orders, Jon. It's all I ask."

"I've yet to take an order."

"There's no way to persuade you?"

Marek's chin lifted. Fear was an emotion that had lost its tyranny. "If that's a threat, forget it," he said. "I don't know what persuasion means. May I go?"

With a shrug, Pete Dalton opened the squad-room door. Marek felt a brief surge of pique at the ease of his escape. It was true that he had renounced the world. He would have still enjoyed proving (to a final antagonist) that he was master of his fate.

The night was deliciously cool. He stood for a moment under the green lights of the precinct house, then walked into the darkness—smiling a little, when two plainclothesmen fell into step behind him. Aimless though he seemed, he knew where he was bound and why. It was a bourne not even a detective could enter.

Midnight was chiming from a distant steeple before he could reach the corner. As though answering the final chime, the subway grating beneath his feet rumbled faintly. He recognized the sound. It was a pilot car, sent out to test the tracks before Ted Horgan ordered the first train to leave the barns.

Bemused by the sound, he paused at the curb and lifted his face to the stars. The cross street was at the top of one of New York's many hills. He was in clear relief against the sky when the explosion came—a rending blast that shook surrounding buildings and etched the whole city against a backdrop of flame.

Stunned by the sound, Marek needed a moment to identify the threat, before he rushed toward a parapet at the street's end. Behind him, his two watchdogs began to run in turn. With his lead, he reached the dead end long before they could overtake him, and paused at the parapet, against the spout of flames, to show this was no attempt at flight.

Less than a quarter-mile away, the power station that served the West Side nexus of subways had been all but demolished. Evidently the bombing had taken place within. The building was already a mass of flames, and only fragments of the walls remained. While Marek watched, he heard a second booming crash from Manhattan's eastern plain. The matching power station, he saw, had been wiped out with the same precision, in the first five minutes after midnight.

The saboteurs' intention was evident. Because of giant strides in automation (and the fact that the island's rigid geography made one pattern inevitable) the power grids that fed the subways had recently been concentrated in those two stations. City planners had warned the Transit Authority that a double breakdown could paralyze the whole system of tracks.

The Authority had answered that no other system was financially possible, without doubling the existing twenty-five-cent fare.

Now, in two blinding flashes, the prophecy had come true.

The Voice, Marek thought, had been in deadly earnest when it demanded that the sanitation strike continue. A near-paralysis of business life would now be inevitable: office toilers who had accepted a one-day shutdown could not be asked to beat their way to work indefinitely. Nor could they be expected to go on festering in their own refuse. The union chief felt his heart contract as the full import of his failure sank home.

He turned toward the detectives, while he fought down the urge to summon them. He might still have called himself a hero, had he given the Voice a name; he might still have saved New York from a fate he had just begun to vision clearly. Yet even now he knew he would never turn informer. Once he was shorn of power, Dalton's offer of protection had lost its value.

Jon Marek stepped up to the parapet quite calmly. Long before the precinct watchdogs could reach him, he had plunged head foremost into space.

# 4.  Tuesday

THE emergency meeting of department heads had been called for Tuesday noon. It was the earliest feasible time for such a gathering, after a night that had demanded the utmost of every service in the hospital.

To mark his new importance, Selden Grove had insisted that Eric occupy the director's chair. A place at his right was reserved for Dr. Ernest Thurlow, New York's health commissioner. Still involved at City Hall with the aftermaths of last night's sabotage, he had sent word he would be late.

Grove sat at Eric's left. Department heads were scattered about the oval table in the board room with no emphasis on protocol. Sorting his notes, the immunologist studied the gathering. Some, like Bob Trent, were old friends. Others, like Dr. Greer of the Outpatient Department, and Dr. Poore, the custodian of the hospital files, were summer-long intimates. Still others (the men from Orthopedics, Laviosek from Neurology, and the chief psychiatrist Bela Kempert) were only names on the call list.

After that covert appraisal, Eric kept his eyes on his notes. No attempt had been made to call the meeting to order until the health commissioner arrived; conversation was still both lively and general. Had the situation been less dire, he would have taken ironic amusement from the comments tossed about the table.

Manhattan Central's alert had been called a few minutes after midnight, to accept its share of accident cases from the blasted power stations. The state of emergency had just been lifted; these doctors, to whom an overflowing accident ward was no novelty, had accepted last night's pressures as routine. There had been ample resources to meet the challenge. Most of them, after all, had faced other disaster alerts, in peace and war. Eric could only wander at their reaction to the testing they would face tomorrow.

Like any staff member, he had given the alert what time he could —though the long-distance phone had claimed most of his attention until dawn. As always, the main pressure had fallen on the surgical service. Most cases had gone direct to the operating theatres, where Bob Trent and his staff labored steadily—débriding burns, closing chest punctures, putting fractures together, and finding room somehow for the normal flow of emergencies that every metropolitan hospital handles. Not all of last night's injuries had come from the power plants. There had been broken bones on more than one sanitation truck—and broken heads on Fifth Avenue, where department-store watchmen had been assaulted by thieves as they made their rounds.

Looting, Eric realized, was an expected by-product of any major disaster. Last night's pillage had special aspects—as though the looters had concentrated at chosen spots. Lofts had been sacked in the garment district, and bookstores had been gutted on college campuses. There had been food raids—at such widely separated spots as Harry's Delicatessen (an all-night rendezvous for café society in the East Sixties) and a downtown lunchroom next door to the New York *Record*. All over town, newspaper delivery trucks had been stripped of their late city editions; Eric suspected that the looters preferred to spread their exploits by rumor rather than cold reportage. Precisely timed assaults had wrecked a score of buses in garage and parking lot; as a result, few drivers had ventured out that morning. . . .

Working to save lives, with no chance to look beyond the tasks of the moment, Manhattan Central had picked up such facts in snatches. Eric had seen from the first that Pete Dalton's surmises were justified. So far his mind had refused to move beyond that sober certainty. The tracking of these human jackals was a job for the police. The problems in his own sphere were more immediate —and even more sinister.

Somewhere between midnight and dawn, a second, expected weight had tipped the scales downward: among the lines of injured pouring through admissions had been three unmistakable cases of plague. There had been no more sleep for Eric that night, even when his volunteer work in the wards had ended. . . .

The details, he reminded himself, were in notes. The hospital would be immunized by nightfall. He could trust that chore to Dr. Norris Weaver: his own tasks, like Selden Grove's, lay in other fields. All through the night, the hospital director had lived with the telephone, alerting city and state officials to the crisis in New York and asking their immediate help. Eric himself had worked through contacts in Washington and the special services at the UN.

Now while he waited for Dr. Ernest Thurlow in the hospital board room, he was sure he had done everything possible. If the city could be saved, the techniques of survival were launched.

The doors of the board room opened to admit Dr. Thurlow—rotund, glowing with the tan of a recent holiday, and apparently unshaken by his meeting with the mayor (to say nothing of the fearful knowledge he shared with Eric). His presence was a tonic for the keyed-up room. Eyes around the table invited confidences—but the health commissioner had come to listen, not to talk.

"Sorry to delay you, gentlemen," he said. "The situation's in hand —at our end: we've called in the best help available. You'll understand my meaning if you'll give undivided attention to Dr. Stowe. I warn you he's about to blast you from your chairs."

Eric got to his feet, as quiet clamped down on the room. "I'll begin by telling you that Dr. Grove has just placed me in complete control in this hospital—for good reason. Manhattan Central must meet the worst challenge in its history, along with New York. The emergency may be the greatest any city in the Western world has ever faced."

He had their attention, he saw—if not their belief. *Emergency* was a standard word in these men's lives. They were accustomed to hearing it without a soupçon of panic. And yet, some degree of panic was a *sine qua non,* if he meant to attain his objective.

"Last evening," he said, "I was able to diagnose three cases of plague in our wards. Others were admitted during our alert. I have compelling reasons for believing that many more are developing in the city. We are here this morning to devise a strategy for what I am forced to call Operation Epidemic."

The words fell like stones in an immense silence. Glancing round the table, Eric saw the dawn of fear, the inward, questing look all men give when faced with a threat beyond their ken. Complacency had been swept away, the assumption of the medical expert that he was equipped to cope with any situation. Here was a danger foreign to the experience of nearly every man in the room—a direct menace to themselves, as well as to the composite individual they served under the generic name of patient.

"Thanks to Dr. Thurlow," said Eric, "we have learned just how the disease entered New York——"

They were hanging on his words now. He made the most of the pause before he went on to describe the docking of the *Sally Piersol*, the lax discipline aboard, the grilling of the first officer that had revealed the whole hideous picture.

Dr. Laviosek was the first to interrupt. Eric recalled that the chief of Neurology was famous for his bluntness.

"That ship captain should be electrocuted."

"He died almost that quickly, Doctor."

"From *bubonic* plague?"

"From the pneumonic form of the disease—which is far more serious."

"How could such a thing happen?"

"Don't blame the people at quarantine. The master listed no illness; he conveniently forgot the men who died at sea. At the time, New York had had no word of an epidemic in Africa. There was no reason to suspect the presence of diseased rodents aboard."

"Aren't there guards on the hawsers? And watchmen at the gangway?"

"Of course—on a well-run ship. I've told you the master was mortally ill, and the first officer a drunkard. That, plus the dockers' strike, was enough to give *Rattus rattus* shore leave——"

Selden Grove spoke for the first time. "It may clear the air if Dr. Stowe explains how this disease spreads. I doubt if many of us have the clinical picture."

The blank stares Eric encountered endorsed the director's estimate. It was reasonable to assume that none of these men of science (who stood at the very top of their specialties) had investigated the activities of *Pasteurella pestis* since its routine textbook demonstration at medical school.

"Bear with me while I spell out the basic facts," he said. "The bacillus that causes plague may follow one of two courses in the body. Usually it is carried by two vectors, the rat and the flea. Rats serve as reservoirs of the disease; the insect is the actual agent. A person bitten by an infected flea can become ill within forty-eight hours. Symptoms are fever and general malaise——"

Dr. Greer, head of the Outpatient Department, spoke up grimly. "Meaning the first signs are identical with flu or grippe."

"In isolated circumstances, yes. Next comes a characteristic swelling of the inguinal lymph nodes, or buboes. By this time, there is marked prostration and toxicity——"

"What's the usual death rate?"

"Around twenty-five per cent in bubonic plague. Mortality figures run much higher in actual epidemics."

"And the pneumonic form?"

"Pneumonic plague is spread in an entirely different way. This form involves the lungs and resembles pneumonia. It can be transmitted directly, like any respiratory infection. Mortality is almost always eighty per cent. I've known it to approach a hundred."

Dr. Greer's voice was loud in the silence. "How soon do symptoms develop?"

"From thirty-six to forty-eight hours after exposure to an acute case. In severe epidemics, when the germ has built up its virulence, symptoms have been noted in twelve to eighteen hours. Pneumonic plague has killed in thirty-six."

"We've both forms on hand, I take it?"

"Both have been diagnosed beyond question."

Dr. Poore spoke from the table's end. His dry tone was precise as the hospital files he handled so flawlessly. "Surely this threat can be contained on the water front—the neighborhood of the ship."

"It might be, so far as the rat-borne form is concerned," said Eric. "Bubonic plague has a tendency to work in pockets. The fact remains that one of the three cases admitted last night was the janitor of an apartment building a good ten blocks from the pier. The others were pneumonic. As I've told you, that form can be picked up as easily as a cold."

"Do they tie in with the ship?"

"One case ties in directly. The patient involved is named Gladys Schreiber. She's a friend of Captain Dollard's—he was in her apartment when he died. I'm sorry to add that she was employed as cashier in a Times Square cafeteria."

Bela Kempert, the chief of Psychiatry, struck the table with his fist: the cheeks beneath his luxuriant whiskers were drained of color.

"*Vot* cafeteria, Dr. Stowe?"

"It's called the Millway."

"I took coffee there yesterday. Haff I infected myself—*und* my family?"

"You'll receive prophylactic treatment this morning, Dr. Kempert. So will your family, and any contacts we can reach. There will be other preventive methods——"

Dr. Greer cut in, as heavily as before. "Let's stick to what we know for sure. You say two pneumonic cases were admitted last night, Dr. Stowe. Who was the second?"

"A poet named Brewster van Pelt. The kind of poet who sings for his supper in *avant-garde* bars. On Sunday, he collapsed in one of them. A place called the Blue Banjo."

"I gather those two cases alone could have scatter-gunned half of Manhattan."

"Your estimate is all too accurate, Dr. Greer."

"Will you define the preventive measures you mentioned?"

"*Rattus rattus,* naturally, is our immediate target. Dr. Thurlow will brief you there."

The health commissioner spoke without rising. "We began that war last midnight—concentrating on the dock area. The job will be done thoroughly: it's my concern, not yours. I've said the situation was in the hands of specialists. We're marshaling an army of them. Not just from my own ranks—from the United States Public Health Service and matching services in the United Nations. *Your* concern is to put Manhattan Central into this fight, on the human side. Dr. Stowe is waiting to tell you how."

This time Eric felt the silence was more ominous. He broke it quietly, aware that he was nearing dangerous ground.

"Because of its location and its importance, most plague victims will come to this hospital for treatment. With Dr. Grove's consent, I'm preparing to receive the maximum number."

"So we're to become a pesthouse!" boomed Laviosek. "Isn't this rather highhanded, Dr. Stowe?"

"Perhaps the occasion demands highhandedness," said Eric. "If we concentrate the victims here, I'm convinced we can handle the expansion of the disease."

"What of our staff—and patients already admitted?"

"Staff members known to have had contact with present cases have received the first injection of vaccine."

"How long will it hold out?"

"Thanks to the overnight help of a wholesaler in Brooklyn, we're heavily stocked at the moment. We've already cabled to every known supplier in the world. I'm glad to say a Canadian freighter is docking on Thursday with a large drug cargo. It includes vaccine—and sulfamerazine, which is a first-rate preventive agent. The cargo belongs to the World Health Organization, on consignment to India. Our radiogram diverted it to New York."

"Can vaccine alone prevent infection?" asked Dr. Greer.

"Frankly, we aren't sure. Oddly enough, we've had help on that angle recently. From a rather improbable source—the Soviet Union."

"Not my former countrymen?" said Laviosek.

"It's part of the W.H.O. literature," said Eric. "A report from the Expert Committee on Plague. Russian epidemiologists have been fighting both forms of plague for a long time, in both Europe and Asia. Their preventive agent is streptomycin. They've proved that one-gram doses, spread over a proper interval, will prevent the disease developing in most contacts."

"Can we follow that procedure here?"

"We already have, at hospital level," said Eric. "We're organizing our campaign around vaccine *and* streptomycin, as long as the former holds out. Afterwards we'll rely on streptomycin alone. The sulfamerazine aboard the freighter will be used for mass immunization, if that becomes necessary——"

"Vill all hospital contacts receive treatment?" asked Kempert.

"Not only contacts, Dr. Kempert: the entire personnel, both staff and patients. In cases like yours, protection will be extended to family members. Dr. Thurlow will give the same protection to his own department, as well as to police and firemen."

"The public will scream like minks when *that* gets abroad," Dr. Greer warned. "They'll say we're favoring people in the driver's seat."

"So they will. We've no option, when these same people will be working to save the whole city." Eric met Greer's black-browed frown head-on. "You'll like the next item even less, Doctor. Beginning this afternoon, all city stations will start broadcasting warnings. Anyone who feels ill from respiratory infection or lymphatic swelling will be urged to go to his doctor or clinic for treatment. Our entire medical resources must be devoted to meeting this need."

"Who'll take responsibility for such procedure?"

The health commissioner bounced from his chair before Eric could frame an answer. "After hearing what's been done is so short a time," he said, "I think you all know who will head Operation Epidemic. This morning, the mayor handed me a commission placing Dr. Eric Stowe in full authority. As of now, he's in charge of us all, including John Newman."

There was a brief silence at the announcement, then a burst of applause; even such holdouts as Greer and Laviosek joined in heartily. Eric had not anticipated this reaction, and found himself at a loss for a proper acknowledgment. The commissioner's well-trained orator's voice, booming above the hand clapping, covered his embarrassment.

"The mayor will join us before we adjourn, to receive the city's orders. Meanwhile Dr. Stowe can assign your own battle stations."

The hiatus had given Eric time to collect his thoughts. "The program I'm outlining may seem on the drastic side," he said. "Believe me, gentlemen, our first concern is to catch incipient cases, *before* they develop. We must make each patient his own diagnostician—there's no other way."

"Including a description of symptoms on television?" asked Greer.

"That most of all."

"You're telling New Yorkers there's plague in their midst?"

"A few cases, all of them isolated. Eighteen years ago, the same procedure was followed during a threat of smallpox. On the same broadcast, we'll say that preventive medicine will be available for all, in good time. We must work in the open from the start. One thing we can't afford are rumors that turn into facts later."

"Dr. Stowe, you know as well as I such publicity will swamp us."

Eric suppressed a smile. "We're aware of that, Dr. Greer. As head of OPD, you're facing a heavy task."

"I haven't the personnel to give even cursory examinations on this scale."

"No one expects you to. Fortunately a check on body temperature will identify plague victims early. Most laymen can read an oral thermometer—and stay at home if the reading's normal."

"Any trained hypochondriac can run a temperature. So can a man with a summer cold."

"Genuine fevers must still be hospitalized, Dr. Greer. Long enough, at least, to establish a secondary diagnosis."

"The wards will overflow."

"When they do, New York will use its major-disaster plan, at Civil Defense level. We'll set up emergency wards in every municipal development. We'll set up churches, schools, theaters—any place where we can spread blankets."

"You'll never vaccinate that sort of multitude."

"We won't try," said Eric. "We'll use antibiotics in the tetracycline group. Plague bacillus responds rapidly to these drugs; a few doses should clear up any case that isn't too far advanced. Those, of course, will be isolated for definitive treatment."

"You'll get hundreds of bad reactions. Some patients have an idiosyncrasy to any drug, including aspirin."

"I know that too, doctor," said Eric. "It's one of several calculated risks we can't avoid taking." Actually, he welcomed Greer's hard-headed objections: they drove home the magnitude of this task for every man in the room.

The OPD head sighed, and leaned back in his chair. "I'm with you, Dr. Stowe," he said. "If I sound stubborn, it's only to define my job and yours. I guess you know I wouldn't occupy your shoes for a million dollars."

Eric permitted a grin to break through. "May I endorse that sentiment completely?"

"He's right, Dr. Stowe," said Laviosek. "You'll be New York's hero —when the mayor introduces you on television. Wait till some cheese-parer on the Board of Estimate asks what your program will cost. Wait till the papers claim the job could have been done cheaper, if we'd waited for bids from the big drug companies——"

"That too is a calculated risk, Dr. Laviosek."

"Suppose this wholesale salvation doesn't get results? You'll be ridden out of town, on the biggest rail ever split."

"I'll accept that punishment."

The neurologist leaned back in turn. "If you mean that, I'm with you—same as Andy Greer." He glared round the table. "Any nays in the room? If there are, I'll ask 'em to step outside and take off their glasses."

Eric held up his hand to stem the laughter. Even more than the spontaneous applause, it proved he commanded a team of realists.

"All of you are familiar with the Civil Defense disaster plan," he said. "We needn't rehearse its details. The big thing is to stock up on drugs and keep them moving. Here again, the OPD will be our first line of defense. Another thing we can't afford is the psychological kickback in people who think they're ill, come to their doctor or clinic, and are turned away."

"Meaning they'll worry themselves sick if they don't have something to swallow?" Greer asked.

"For such would-be patients, we'll prescribe one of the sulfonamide drugs. You'll recall how valuable they were in wartime, whenever there was an outbreak of respiratory cases in camp."

A youngish doctor, who had not spoken before, held up his hand. "There's another point worth making. How will organized medicine react to this program?"

"Will you identify yourself?" Eric asked.

"Dr. Philip Sherwin. I'm on the President's Council of the Medical Society. Don't misunderstand me, Dr. Stowe; I'm with you all the way. I can't say the same for every Society member. Some of them will spit snakes when you tell them how to treat their patients——"

"Refer such men to me, Dr. Sherwin." The new voice came from the hall doorway; it was John Newman, who had entered unannounced. "Not that there'll be much need, I assure you. Copies of Dr. Stowe's commission have already gone to every M.D. address in New York." He approached the table's head, ignoring the wave of applause that greeted him, to shake hands with Eric, Grove and Thurlow. His springy step, and his firm-jawed confidence, lifted every heart in the room, long before he turned to address the gathering.

"This isn't a speech," he said. "There isn't time for speeches. It's a vote of absolute confidence. I heard enough from the door to know you all mean business. With men like you to guide us, we can fight this thing to a standstill. New York City is backing you, to the full power of my office. The proclamation Dr. Stowe requested has been prepared. It will have its first broadcast this afternoon. What more can I say but God bless you?"

The meeting broke up on that high note of confidence. Besides the mayor, only Eric, Thurlow and Selden Grove remained at the oval table. John Newman's eyes had clouded while the last of the grave-faced department heads left the room.

"I can only stay a moment," he said quietly. "Any special instructions, Eric?"

"You've done enough for now, John."

"Do any of these doctors suspect there's a connection between last night's damage and those cases in your isolation ward?"

Eric shook his head. "Since last midnight, most of us have been too busy to speculate. Naturally there's been gossip—but that's all."

"I'm buying Pete's theory—a bit late." The mayor's face had aged abruptly, now there was no further need to exude confidence. "After last night, it makes sense. We *do* have an enemy in our midst, and he'll stop at nothing. Is it possible he brought in the plague?"

"Does Pete think that?"

"No, Eric. He claims it's fortuitous, and so do I. We're hoping you'll agree."

"The tragedy of the *Sally Piersol* was sheer happenstance," said Eric. "Call it the chink in our armor, if you like. The germ found it, not the enemy. Captain Dollard's logbook proves as much."

"Were our inspectors at fault?"

"The inspection of the freighter was up to standard. The mere presence of rats can't stop a clearance if there's no reason to believe they're infected. If we'd known there was plague in Africa, the ship would have been refused entry. Unfortunately there was another revolution in the Cameroons: the story was late in reaching us."

The mayor gave a bleak nod of comprehension and turned toward the door, a man whose first concern was the giant task awaiting him. Watching his hesitation, Eric could pity him with all his heart. Busy though he'd be hereafter, Newman would be infinitely busier—and the command decisions awaiting him would have broken most spirits.

"Don't let us detain you, John," he said. "And above all, don't blame yourself for anything. Not even if our program fails—as it well may."

"That I'll never buy," said Newman. "Can you picture this city, if plague gets the upper hand?"

"All too well," said Eric. "So can you."

"So it was just bad luck," said the mayor. "The worst kind of luck that could strike us. Don't think the enemy—whatever he calls himself—won't use it to his advantage."

"I gather he already has," said Eric.

"By urging Marek to prolong the sanitation strike?"

"That was one attempt. Naturally it was meant to backstop last night's sabotage. From here to the finish line, Operation Saboteur and Operation Epidemic will run neck and neck."

"I'm betting on the second horse," said John Newman. "Good-by for now, gentlemen."

They moved to the door together. "How soon can the subways be repaired?" asked Selden Grove.

"Not for five days, at least. Even then, they'll be on auxiliary power. Whoever planned that demolition knew his business."

"Never underestimate the enemy, John," said Dr. Thurlow. "Especially when he's working inside the city gates."

The mayor squared his shoulders, now that they were standing on the edge of the rotunda, with curious eyes upon them.

"You can say that twice, Dr. Thurlow. So far, there's just one detail in this business I approve. When those plants are rebuilt, they'll do it my way. With *double* sources of power. I'm giving the city that, if I have to run for governor."

### 2.

When he emerged from the board room, Bob Trent was not too startled to find Eve Bronson awaiting him. He saw at once that Eric's fearful tidings had not yet reached her.

"I hope you're off duty," she said. "Inspector Dalton wants to see us both. What do you suppose he's after now?"

"I don't have a notion, Eve—and I wish he'd stop playing 'Dragnet' here. We've problems of our own to chew on."

They found Pete Dalton sprawled on the sofa in Grove's sanctum; the director himself, said his secretary, was on his way to a conference at Bellevue. Bob was glad that Eric was not present. The immunologist would need every precious minute to lay the groundwork for his program. This afternoon it was only turnabout that his friends should intercept the probings of the police.

Pete did not rise from the couch.

"Forgive my bad manners, Miss Bronson," he said. "In my trade, one rests where one can. I've just talked to Dr. Keller. Can either of you add anything to his story?"

Bob and Eve exchanged glances. Dr. Keller was the intern who had brought Ricardo Reyes to Emergency without pausing to turn in the boy's weapons.

"I gather you can't describe the gun?" said Dalton.

"The patient was on the point of death," said Bob drily. "It wasn't *my* job to frisk him."

"And you, Miss Bronson?"

"I wasn't even there," said Eve.

"They told me you were Dr. Trent's surgical special."

Bob smiled at Eve. "So she is, usually. She wasn't present when I tried to save the boy."

"He was on the brink of a confession when he died," said Pete. "Even knowing his name would help." His hand dropped into the brief case and came up with a photograph. "We took this shot in the morgue. Maybe it'll ring a bell."

Bob studied the photograph and shook his head. It was no time to explain that he had scarcely noticed the boy's face as he lay on the table. Or that his whole being had been concentrated on tracing the course of a lethal bullet. Even had Ricardo Reyes been a neighborhood fixture, he would scarcely have remembered him now.

"Do you know him, Eve?"

Eve Bronson was staring hard at the floodlighted picture. "I've seen him at the Lemayos. I'm sure he lived there for awhile."

"We've shown that picture on the street," said the detective. "No one will give it a tumble, including Mrs. Lemayo. They never do, of course. When did you notice him last?"

"A few months ago, when I made a nursing call. Mrs. Lemayo had just been released from the hospital. The boy was eating in the kitchen with Juan. I didn't follow their Spanish, but I *think* they called him Ric."

"Ricardo, probably," said Pete. "Will you go to the Lemayos now, and try to learn more?"

Bob cut in quickly; without knowing why, he resented the request. "How could Miss Bronson help? You just said these people are clams."

"Mrs. Lemayo might talk, Doctor—if you went along. Didn't you save her life?"

"You're asking a great deal, Inspector. I've a jammed-up schedule today."

"This needn't take twenty minutes. After all, you must be one of the few gringos the woman trusts."

Bob shrugged, as he intercepted a pleading nod from Eve. "I'm game, if Miss Bronson's willing," he said. "Just what would you like to know?"

"The origin of that gun. Who trains the Dukes—and why."

"Aren't you relying pretty heavily on two amateur sleuths?"

"Sending you to the tenement is a gamble, Dr. Trent. I won't say it'll pay off. It may even backfire."

"Why not bring Juan in and make him talk?"

"You've seen these kids in your wards. I don't need to remind you how hard they can be. It isn't an accident that Lemayo is a warlord—" The detective looked up as someone tapped the office door. "That would be Charles Tully. Don't go yet. He may give you a lead."

The social worker entered the room with his usual poise. Evidently he had come direct from the basketball court of Merton House; he was still wearing gym clothes, and carried an early edition of an evening paper. After this half-hostile encounter with Dalton, Bob found himself taking comfort in Tully's mere presence. *Here is a man who speaks our language,* he thought. *A man who knows the score in Juan Lemayo's blacked-out domain.*

Charles Tully listened attentively while the detective repeated a gist of his remarks. He shook his head after a careful scrutiny of Ricardo's photograph.

"I looked at the boy in the recovery room. Didn't Sergeant Cates tell you?"

"I thought I'd try again," said Dalton. "Still no sound of bells?"

"Unfortunately, no. He isn't one of mine."

"Doesn't your work bring you in contact with the Dukes?"

"The Dukes shun my company," said Tully, with a smile. "In their vocabulary, I'm a *lengua larga*—a possible informer."

"You've never met with them—or offered them help?"

"I've tried incessantly, Inspector—to no purpose. The worst of our youth gangs are beyond redemption. The Dukes are a completely evil brotherhood; dedicated to fighting all that's decent. They accept no member under eighteen. By that time, the mold has hardened. Only death can break it."

"Surely that's a drastic statement, Mr. Tully," said Eve.

"Boys like Lemayo are natural enemies of society, Miss Bronson. Storm troopers in miniature—the Hitlers of tomorrow." The social director held up a pleading hand. "Don't call me a cynic, please; I know whereof I speak. Thank Heaven such throwbacks are a minority, even in the worst neighborhoods. They'll vanish from our midst, I'm sure, once the Merton Project opens its doors."

"Will Jasper Merton build it now?" Bob asked.

"I've every hope of persuading him to keep his promise," said Tully. "Granted, the outlook is bad today, with saboteurs at large, and six cases of plague in this hospital——"

"Who mentioned *plague* to you?"

Tully unfolded his newspaper. "It's the lead in Ronald Sharp's column, Bob. Don't tell me it's just another rumor. His information's always accurate."

The surgical chief frowned at the smear of type. Ronald Sharp was a diligent—and unscrupulous—journalist, famous for his undercover sources. It was like him to break the story, with no regard for consequences. Bob glanced at Eve, and noted proudly that she had taken the news with her poise unshaken. Already he was a little ashamed of his reluctance to visit Mrs. Lemayo. The inspector, like every hard-pressed public servant, needed friends badly today.

Dalton barely glanced at the newspaper. "We were told Sharp would run the story," he said. "News of this sort always leaks. Not that it matters too much; as Dr. Trent knows, we're about to broadcast our own warnings." He gave the social worker a level look. "As for you, Mr. Tully, I hoped you'd have a theory on last night's troubles."

"I'm afraid I'm as bewildered as anyone," said Tully. "Do you think the explosions and the disease are connected? Was the virus spread *deliberately?*"

"The answer is no."

"On my way here, I heard street-corner arguments over Sharp's column. The words 'germ warfare' were used frequently."

"We'll kill such talk fast enough."

"Are you sure you can, Inspector? All major powers have training programs in biological attack. It *could* have happened."

"It could, Mr. Tully. But it didn't."

"May I ask why?"

"I've two good reasons," said Dalton. "The boys overseas would never take such a risk—any more than they'd launch the first rocket. Not when they know we're ready to hit back in both fields. Second, we've proved this bug arrived by accident, from a freighter that called in Africa. Anyone who says different is a lying propagandist. Pin back his ears, all of you."

"We'll do our best, of course," said the social worker. "Stories of that kind can do great harm."

"Stories like that can be fatal, Mr. Tully."

"The fact remains, Inspector: The city *is* faced with twin threats to its survival."

The detective sat up at last. "In your opinion, which is the worse enemy?"

"I wouldn't dare say, at the moment. Obviously, we must conquer both, if New York's to have a sane future. We can hardly afford to fail. Our prestige abroad would suffer a body blow."

"That's why I need help all down the line," said Dalton. "Are you ready to visit the Lemayos, Miss Bronson?"

"Of course. We'll phone your office, if we have any news."

Pete got to his feet and extended his hand. "I know it's asking a great deal today, when you're starting a disaster program here."

"Disaster's our job, Inspector."

"And this is positively our last chance to play detective," said Bob. Somewhat to his surprise, he found himself shaking hands in turn. "Thanks to Eric Stowe, we're ready for Operation Epidemic. Let's hope you do as well with Operation Saboteur."

3.

Reporters were waiting for Dalton outside the office. They swarmed about Eve and Bob, forcing them to escape via a service elevator to the hospital garage, which offered a short cut to the street.

Stepping into the wide, dimly lighted haven, they exchanged unhappy smiles.

"Tell me frankly, Eve," said the surgical chief. "Aren't we behaving like damned fools?"

"Not if we can really help."

"*I'm* here for just one reason," said Bob, "to get Dalton off Eric's back. There isn't much a surgical department can contribute."

"Don't be too sure of that, Bob. They expect another bumper crop of accidents tonight. At least you'll be taking weight away from other wards."

"Will you assist?"

"Of course."

"It's your privilege to work elsewhere, if you prefer."

"I'd rather stay with you."

They had paused on the street ramp, to scout the exit for lurking journalists. Noting the presence of Eric's Ferrari in its usual parking space, Bob struck the mudguard with his fist. The cream-white sports car was a threat he could define all too accurately. *Regardless of the outcome of this program,* he thought, *Eric Stowe will remain a knight in armor for Eve.*

"Was I too short with our friend the detective?"

"A little," said Eve. "Don't you like Pete Dalton?"

"Maybe I'm tired of prophets of doom. Dalton overdoes it. Why can't he take a balanced view, like Tully?"

Eve had advanced halfway up the ramp, with Bob a dogged pace behind her. She turned now, with a detaining hand on his arm.

"If you like, I'll see Mrs. Lemayo alone."

"I wouldn't hear of it," he said. "Just don't be disappointed if we fail to uncover a nest of foreign agents. It's my guess we'll learn nothing."

"Eric agrees with the inspector," said Eve.

"Do you honestly think some evil genius abroad is planning to destroy New York? That our street hoodlums are part of the plot?"

"Is it too hard to believe?"

"Maybe I've the wrong sort of brains, Eve. I'm a surgeon, not a cloak-and-dagger boy. Saving people's lives is hard enough: don't ask me what makes 'em tick. That goes double for Juan's mother."

Outside the hospital, rain was falling with a hint of late afternoon sun behind it. The misty light softened the ugliness of the nearby tenements as they entered the vestibule of the Lemayos' building. Eve pressed Bob's hand warmly and rang the bell.

"You saved her life too, Bob—don't forget that."

"Does that mean she'll confide her heart's secrets?"

"Perhaps not. But I need you with me now."

Rita Lemayo had long been a neighborhood fixture. While he lived, her husband had eked out a living as janitor for their tenement; as his widow, she kept a precarious toe hold there. For years, it had been her custom to sit at her second-floor window, gossiping volubly with friends and deploring the wickedness of her only child —whose training ground, even then, had been the street.

After her illness, her personality had seemed to change abruptly. The window-sill gossip had ceased; her shades were drawn now, and she sat behind them night and day. Occasionally she descended to the sidewalk for meager purchases at the grocer's; her only diversion was her weekly visit to the Spanish-speaking movie in the next block. Bob knew that Eve had called often to check on Mrs. Lemayo's health; in her opinion, Juan's mother was a good woman according to her lights, with an inevitable blind spot where her son was concerned. To Bob's own mind, this was a poor time to seek the truth about Juan, even if the woman could supply it. Yet he felt his heartbeat rise when he rapped on the Lemayo door and turned the knob after a whispered permission to enter.

Rita Lemayo sat in her usual armchair; despite the heat, there was a heavy quilt about her shoulders. The shades, as always, were tightly drawn; the candles on a *prei-dieu* in one corner gave the only light. The room seemed incredibly cluttered—jammed with bed and clothespress, stacked ceiling-high with old newspapers. More den than dwelling, it exhaled an odor of its own—an acrid reek that spelled poverty in any language.

The woman in the chair summed up this dry rot perfectly. In the bluish light from the candles, she seemed an aged tigress. Yet the voice that issued from that sagging body was almost cringing.

"Enter, *señorita*. And you too, *Señor médico*. I feared you would come like this."

Bob moved forward quickly. There had been an undertone of terror in that whisper.

"Are you ill, Mrs. Lemayo?"

"*Sí. En el alma. No en el cuerpo.*" The woman smiled wanly. "Forgive. When I am troubled, I think in my own tongue. My body is well enough. But I weep in my soul."

Eve settled on a footstool beside the armchair to take Rita Lemayo's hand in hers. Bereft of his healer's role, Bob kept his distance. Already he realized Eric could have come in his stead; his friend's Spanish was flawless.

"Can you tell us what's wrong?" Eve asked.

"We must not speak aloud, *señorita*. My son lies behind that door asleep." The worried eyes darted toward the bedroom entrance. "I would have come to hospital had I dared. It seemed better to send a *carta*——"

"You sent me a note, Mrs. Lemayo?"

"*Sí*, Nurse Bronson. An hour ago—by a hand I could trust. Is it not why you are here?"

Eve and Bob exchanged a wide-eyed glance. "It must still be in my hospital mailbox. Can you tell me what it said?"

"*Cino palabras, señorita.* I could say a few words only. More we cannot risk." The woman beckoned her visitors closer; the whisper, sinking in volume, was still hoarse with dread. "Pretend you came to examine me for illness. This is the time Juan wakens. We must not seem to conspire."

Bob lifted the stethoscope from the pocket of his coat; at his nod, Eve began to record Rita Lemayo's pulse. Standing over her thus, they could talk freely, merely by moving their lips. In another setting, the surgical chief would have found the subterfuge grotesque, but he could sense the threat behind that bedroom door.

"Juan is your son," he said. "Why do you fear him?"

"Juan has turned devil."

"We all know your boy is a war-lord," said Eve. "Is it news to you?"

"The Dukes are his life. How can I ask him to desert them, when they give him back his pride?"

"They are a gang, *señora*," said Bob. "Troublemakers, hunted by the police——"

"*Es verdad*," said the woman. "I admit the fights, the broken heads. But I could not believe Juan took orders from above. I called those stories lies."

"What kind of orders?"

"To destroy. To kill——"

"Who gave such orders to Juan?" asked Bob.

The woman's eyes were closed, as the pretended examination continued: her mouth was a hard white line that shaped words in agony. "I do not know. There is a *Jefe*—a Leader. Juan does not say his name aloud. Nor did Ricardo Reyes."

"Ricardo Reyes? The boy in the prison ward?"

"Ricardo died in your hospital. I have just been told."

"Who was he, Mrs. Lemayo?" Eve demanded softly.

"A *perro perdido*. A lost dog that slept here awhile. Until Juan fed him, he had no one. Juan gave him hope again—and a gun."

"The gun he carried yesterday?"

"*Si, señorita*. They always take these guns to *batallas*—what you call rumbles."

"Why say these things to us?" Bob demanded. "You could call the police."

Mrs. Lemayo shook her head. "*You* must get word to them—you or the *señorita*."

"Won't you tell us more?" Eve pleaded.

"Read my note, Nurse Bronson—" The woman broke off, and lay back in her chair. All of them had heard the sound of the turning doorknob.

When Juan emerged from the bedroom, he was still knuckling drowsiness from his eyes. The pause gave the visitors the chance they needed. Eve spoke first, at Bob's nod.

"There's still a little scar tissue, Doctor——"

"It will make the wound stronger."

Eve smiled at the boy in the doorframe. "We've good news for you, Juan. Your mother's really cured. I brought Dr. Trent to make sure."

Juan was wide-awake in a flash, as his eyes took in the tableau.

"What does this mean, mama?"

"Can you not see?" Mrs. Lemayo's face was placid, her voice a blend of love and scolding. "Busy though he is, the *señor médico* comes to our poor abode to assure me I am well again. Thank him for me properly. I do not have the English words."

Juan came into the room; Bob noticed he was careful to close and lock his bedroom door. "Why *here*, Dr. Trent? Don't clinic patients come to the hospital for their checkups?"

"Miss Bronson wished to spare your mother a journey."

"Suppose I won't swallow that? Suppose I figure you're snooping?"

"For shame, Juanito!" cried the mother. "These are your friends——"

"Maybe things have changed across the way," said the boy. "I wouldn't know—and I'm not calling Miss Bronson names. But I don't take this visit kindly, Dr. Trent. And I'll thank you both to leave us be."

Eve rose from the footstool. "As you like, Juan. We came here only in kindness. I wish you'd believe me."

"I saved your life last night," said the boy. "That pays back what you did for mama. From now on, stay on your side of the street."

"What have we done to upset you, Juan?"

"Ain't there a detective-inspector at the hospital askin' questions —because Ric died without talking? Didn't he tell you to come here?" Aware he had said too much, the boy backed hard against the wall. Bob could see his fingers were itching for the hidden knife, the swift, bright answer to every threat.

"We came to help your mother," said Bob. "If you'll let us, we'll help you too."

"I thanked you once for saving mama. Now leave us in peace."

"Do you want to live like this forever?" Eve asked.

"Course I don't, Miss Bronson. But I'm changin' things *my* way——"

"Don't you want us to build the Merton Project here?"

"Are you sayin' that old moneybags would give me a plugged nickel? He wants this land to make himself richer. That's why we're fightin' back—" Once more, Juan swallowed hard as the unwise avowal escaped him.

"We know you've felt cheated all your life," said Eve. "Take my word, this is an attempt to right the balance."

"Is that somethin' you read in a book?"

"Won't you even try to listen?"

"Miss Bronson, rich men's promises are moonshine. Why do you swallow them? I know better—'cause I've been told better——"

"By whom, Juan?" asked Bob.

"By people who've been around. Believe me, when *we* change things, we'll really change 'em."

Bob shrugged, and his eye sought Mrs. Lemayo's. She gave him the barest of nods. Caught up in the heat of his anger, Juan had forgotten his original suspicions. It was time to go.

"Have it your way, Juan," Bob said. "I hope you learn better, before it's too late."

"The same goes for you, Doctor."

"Can't you even recognize enemy propaganda when you hear it?"

"Don't give me more highbrow labels—they're for the birds." Again, Juan was almost screaming. "I don't want old Merton's money as a gift. When the time comes, I'm taking it——"

"Have you gone *loco*, Juan?" wailed Mrs. Lemayo.

"Leave this to me, mama. You won't be here much longer."

"Where will you send me, my son? To jail—or to a madhouse?"

The question gave Bob the lead he needed. He moved boldly toward Juan, and spun him by a shoulder, ignoring the knife that sprang into view like an adder's tongue.

"You might try answering your mother," he said. "We saved her from dying. We can't save her from *you*—if you won't mend your ways."

The knife hung between them, and the boy did not speak again. Instead he nodded at the outer door. Bob shrugged and walked into the hall. Eve pressed Mrs. Lemayo's hand and followed.

Neither of them spoke while they moved from tenement to street. It was only when they were on the sidewalk that Bob risked a low-voiced comment.

"His mother's right," he said. "The boy's refused to think so long he's lost the power."

"Are you sorry you came along?"

"What did we really accomplish?"

"I'll answer that, after I've seen Mrs. Lemayo's note," said Eve.

They were on the hospital driveway now. Taking her hand, Bob hurried toward the Nurses' Home—and the row of mailboxes just inside the portal.

4.

Six o'clock was striking when Bob and Eve entered Manhattan Central—and New York, facing its second full day of dead subways, was strangled in the bottleneck of the evening rush hour.

With bus service reduced to a trickle, taxis were at a premium all over town and prudent drivers were choosing their own routes. The northwestern corner of the island, a grid of some eighty blocks served by the West Side power station, was blacked out completely. Here, TV sets were silenced and iceboxes stricken. Apartment dwellers had already snapped on their burglar chains and locked their windows. The sound of patrol cars, crisscrossing the area to warn off vandals, was the only sign of life from Inwood to Washington Heights.

At the railroad terminals, bomb scares had kept homeward bound passengers in an uproar. Railroad police had reduced such threats to a single minor explosion in Grand Central. It had halted the Twentieth Century in the tunnel and made a shambles of commuter schedules until midnight.

Theaters and movie houses had seen their audiences reduced to a trickle. Citizens in good health who reached their homes safely, it appeared, had made up their minds to stay there. Sharp's column had two million readers. It had spread a chill across the metropolis. The fear was not yet panic, but it was next of kin.

John Newman's personal proclamation, printed on the front page of each afternoon paper, and repeated in half-hour broadcasts, had helped to calm jangled nerves. The mayor had spoken confidently of the control measures that had isolated each case of plague, of the Health Department's all-out war on rats, of the drugs available to any citizen who believed himself exposed to the disease. As Eric had foreseen, doctors and clinics were promptly swamped with patients. Each would-be victim was certain he harbored a bacillus that only yesterday was virtually unknown to New Yorkers.

At Manhattan Central, applicants with authentic bronchial ailments and fevers of unknown origin were admitted to special isolation wards, until Eric and his hard-pressed staff could make a positive diagnosis. The procedure was repeated in every borough hospital.

The doctors in charge were aware that some of this bumper crop of patients were malingerers. Others were suffering from honest (but relatively harmless) ailments and were simply frightened out of their wits. Still others—no less honest, in their own minds—had always made a career of producing symptoms at the first rumor of mass illness.

There were also authentic plague cases in that first near-stampede; before Tuesday ended, nearly a score had been identified beyond question. Such identifications in themselves had made the warning broadcasts worth while: if the first foci of the disease were to be pocketed, there had been no other course. Had Tuesday's therapies been less sweeping, the Black Death could have stalked the city at will, as it had once stalked through King Charles's London.

That evening, five inmates of the mission home where Willoughby Fellowes had played his Sunday game of poker found themselves racked with chills and fever. The settlement doctor had viewed them with rising concern. Before midnight, he had heeded the mayor's advice and conveyed them to Manhattan Central, where they had been sent promptly to the isolation ward.

Fellowes, oddly enough, had already passed his crisis. Initial doses of broad-spectrum antibiotics (given to combat infection from the stabbing), though they could not completely control the pace of the disease, had permitted body processes to fight back. As a result, this plague case had followed a conventional course. Unlike the first patients struck down by the pneumonic form, Fellowes had turned the corner with the monstrous swelling of the buboes, which had now been relieved by lancing. By midnight, his temperature was falling and his chances of recovery seemed excellent. Eventually he would go down in the records as a shining proof of man's will to endure, regardless of his habits.

In that same contagious ward, time had run out for lab assistant Al Novak and Dr. Gilbert Maynard. The tide in their lungs had risen beyond control. By early evening, each had developed the dark, splotchy areas that gave *Pasteurella pestis* the name of Black Death. As the last pulmonary lobe had filled, the fatal complication of oxygen lack had taken over. Fighting wildly for breath, their lips blue from cyanosis, they had gone under in the same hour.

The two deaths had occurred well after the passing of Gladys Schreiber, whose story of Captain Dollard had given Eric invaluable clues in his campaign of prevention. No more than three cases were discovered in her apartment building. It was another story at the Millway cafeteria. Since Gladys had a night shift, Eric had hoped that a stern warning to all after-dark workers who had supped there on Sunday would alert potential victims in good time. He had forgotten that the cafeteria was in the theater district, that most of its patrons belonged to a footloose city group with no settled abode.

When the list of Gladys's contacts was complete, it included over fifty names, most of them already clear-cut cases. Theaters within a five-block radius had contributed their backstage quotas. The fraternity of beggars that haunted the marquees at curtain time had given two victims. So had the ragged youths (both white and Negro) who scrambled for coins at taxi doors.

A patient whose death would make headlines was a vendor of entr'acte cigarettes, a Times Square legend for a quarter-century. So was the hunchback who stood outside stage doors, to collect tips from actors who touched his shoulder for luck. It was a final irony that no actual playgoers were stricken. Most drama lovers scorned the fare at the Millway and repaired to night clubs across town, which were still immune.

The Blue Banjo bar and the Village Bandbox had not been so fortunate. At the former, Brewster van Pelt had done yeoman's service in assisting the rod-shaped bacillus, partly through direct physical contact with friends of both sexes, partly through the sheer violence of his poetic rantings.

The Bandbox, in time, had sent its share of patients to Manhattan Central. So had the apartment house whose tenants had fought with striking sanitation workers. All these were of the bubonic type. Consequently, the case-load was not quite so heavy.

The spread of bubonic plague (as Eric's records had shown in the past) tended to saturate certain pockets, contrary to the scatter-gunning of the pneumonic form. At times, however, it could seem just as wildly capricious in its impact—as a vector named Adolph Bruin was to prove.

Bruin was a repairman, a slovenly, overalled giant whose specialty was air conditioners and the generators that powered them when electric circuits failed. He occupied a ground-floor apartment in the building that had defied the garbage collectors; as a good tenant, he had taken a notable part in that battle—and his apartment had been one of the first to be explored by *Rattus rattus*. On Monday he went out to his first job with a swollen lip and a bad humor, aggravated by a headache and a mysterious rash that resembled prickly heat.

At nine-thirty, he rang the service bell at the donjon-like residence of Jasper Merton, to make a yearly check of its generator. Minor parts needed replacing, and a clogged feed-line eluded his probings. The mansion's cooling system did not extend to its service areas. The electrician's clothes were dripping, and the rash had become a torment when he ascended from the basement to report his work complete.

It was Bruin's custom to visit with the butler while he drank the bottle of ice-cold Bavarian beer he considered his due. This noon, it was a letdown to find that the Merton servants were on their summer holidays. The kitchen was empty, save for the magnate's frost-faced secretary, who was in the act of removing a French cheese and a plate of cold cuts from the icebox.

The repairman had hoped to find the owner absent. On previous service calls, he had been allowed to roam upstairs at will. In the paneled-library, he had gaped at erotic Gobelin tapestries and towering shelves of first editions; in the master bedroom, he had dared to bounce on Jasper Merton's mattress beneath a valance of fleur-de-lis from the Emperor Napoleon's couch. The secretary (whose name was Boles) informed him coldly that Mr. Merton had been nursing a migraine in that same imperial bed and had complained of noise in the cellar. Because of the servants' absence, he planned to lunch in the kitchen. Boles suggested the electrician depart at once to avoid his employer's wrath. With that advice, he had rushed out in response to an explosion from above.

The encounter, topping Bruin's private miseries, left him hot with rage. He lingered awhile, striving to nerve himself to a search for beer. In the end, he had cut a generous slice of Brie, wrapped it in prosciutto, and swaggered out. As a final defiance, he neglected to close the cellar door.

If Boles had greeted him properly, Bruin would have reported that one of the gratings had rusted through. As a result, the basement now had rodent tenants; several had scurried underfoot while he finished his repair job. Five minutes later, when Jasper Merton entered his kitchen, two of these monsters were on the serving table, gorging on imported cheese.

The magnate (who secretly rejoiced in his servantless fortnights) had looked forward to this pick-up lunch: he had looked forward even more to an afternoon of slave-driving, when Boles would dust each book in the library, under his personal supervision. His first reaction to the invaders in his kitchen had been shocked incredulity. His second was a bellow for the secretary.

Boles found his employer armed with a poker. The two rats, cornered in the pantry, dodged in vain. Merton killed one with a single blow. The secretary (who had a pistol permit, since he doubled as his master's bodyguard) shot the second on order.

Both rats had had sufficient contact with the repairman to take on numerous specimens of the parasite he harbored. While the two hunters pursued their quarry in the kitchen, *Xenopsylla cheopis* had changed hosts one more time. Merton celebrated the twin killing with champagne. Afterwards he had napped too deeply to realize that unwanted visitors were nipping his wasted (but always immaculate) body. The damage was done when he went to his bath in the dusk. Boles, soothing his own bites, had already phoned the exterminators. He had not ventured to ask his employer if he harbored fleas of his own. It was the sort of question no one would put to Jasper Merton.

The philanthropist rose late on Tuesday, mistaking a faint malaise for hangover. He had fumed when Boles failed to answer his ring. Descending to the kitchen to brew his own coffee, he heard the exterminators at work below. He was still unaware that he was dangerously ill, or that the white-jumpered men in his cellar were also in peril of their lives. Jasper Merton had left grade school in Texas to help bring in his first gusher. His donations to science were the tribute of ignorance to marvels beyond his grasp.

In the early afternoon, his secretary arrived with office mail and the newspapers. Merton was on the phone, listening with thin-lipped scorn; Selden Grove had just called to report the conclusions reached at the doctors' meeting. As chief contributor to the hospital, Merton insisted on receiving all such bulletins. He was exhaling brimstone when he banged up the receiver and turned to Boles.

"Where have you been since noon, you damned shirker?"

"You told me to go downtown for the mail, sir." Boles stood with bowed head, until his employer finished his tirade. Submitting to tongue lashings was one of his duties.

"D'you know what Grove just said?"

"It's in the afternoon paper, sir."

"I won't believe a word. Bubonic plague in *New York?* The very idea's asinine."

Boles held his tongue. Had he wished, he could have told Jasper Merton a great deal about *Pasteurella pestis*. His early youth had been spent at a mission in the Burmese jungle. He had seen what plague could do, once it gained a foothold. Most of his missionary-father's flock had fallen in one such epidemic; his parents had been among the victims. Boles had escaped with a token illness, and consequent immunity.

"Speak up, blockhead! Do you believe this nonsense?"

"It could be true, sir."

"Then Grove's an even greater fool. He should have killed off this bug long ago. I'm damned if I'll give another cent to a Dr. Quacken-bush. Bring me a double scotch—and one of those tranquilizer pills. My head's splitting."

"You aren't looking at all well, Mr. Merton. Shall I call your doctor?"

"Of course not. Just because I support a stable of doctors doesn't mean I trust 'em. *Whisky*, dammit!"

Boles slipped from his employer's presence. In the serving pantry, he knew an icy moment of fear. The news in Sharp's column had begun to sink home. His hands were shaking when he took out Merton's pills and his Highland Nectar. While the chill lasted, he considered abasing himself further. (There was no escaping the fact that Merton was in deadly peril.) Then, as he poured the whisky, his hand steadied.

When he returned with the drink and the tranquilizer tablet, Boles was only the self-effacing servant. The impulse to flee had vanished. He, after all, was safe. It would be a pleasure to discover how a billion dollars faced extinction.

## 5.

Rita Lemayo's note was waiting in the mailbox when Eve rushed through the nurses' lounge to claim it. Bob Trent had left her with a quick handclasp. The public-address was clamoring for his presence.

"Tell me what it says later," he ordered from the doorway. "I'd wait if I could."

"I'll do that, Doctor," she replied, primly correct once more under the eyes of the receptionist. Staring at the single sheet of notepaper, she kept her face blank. The note, a scrawl of Spanish, told her nothing whatever.

Should she phone Inspector Dalton at once, or seek out Eric? The dilemma solved itself when she saw the bold-typed notice on the bulletin board, reminding all hospital personnel to report promptly to Dr. Norris Weaver for vaccination. Eric might be there. Busy though he was, he could spare a moment to advise her.

So far Eve had not let her mind dwell on the threat of plague. There had been no chance to test the hospital grapevine, but she could sense the excitement as she hurried from the nurses' wing and took the stairway leading to Personnel Dispensary.

Here she discovered the immunization program was proceeding at a steady pace, with lines in every hallway. She took her place behind a student nurse and an intern from the Outpatient Department.

"You're lucky to be in surgery, Miss Bronson," the intern said. "OPD's been jumping all afternoon."

"I can believe that, Dr. Cary. Are many really sick?"

"Most of 'em are trying hard. Still, it shows how this thing is spreading. I heard that two thousand cases have been identified in the past six hours."

"Not that many, surely."

"The governor of New Jersey is closing the state border tomorrow," said the nurse. "There goes my date from Newark."

"You wouldn't be off duty anyhow," said Eve. "The order was on the board—no more leave."

"It'll be a long time before any of us see the outside again," the intern confirmed. "Already, people are in a bad mood. They're demanding vaccine and sulking when they have to take sulfa. They're saying it's an outrage for police and firemen to get theirs first."

The babble of voices was constant while the line inched forward; for the most part, the war of words seemed good-humored, but there was no escaping the note of anxiety beneath. On the stair above her, a striking redhead in the uniform of a hospital volunteer was airing another grievance, in a honeysuckle accent.

"I declare, Dr. Parelli, this reminds me of a mumps scare at Sweetbriar. They put up quarantine signs everywhere and ruined the spring formal."

"That must have been rugged, sister," said the Italian intern beside her.

"It was a false alarm, too. Not more than a dozen caught it."

The line behind Eve was filling rapidly; she had moved from hall to stairwell now.

"Did you see Ron Sharp's column?" asked the student nurse.

"I've been too busy to read it."

"He claims this is germ warfare. Says you-know-who sent a freighter here loaded with plague rats. All the Iron Curtain people at the UN were warned weeks ago. They've been getting vaccine ever since."

Eve was conscious of the note in her pocket. Again, she wondered if she should give up her place (and the chance to protect herself) in order to seek Eric at once. The scene at the Lemayo flat had troubled her badly. Here in the hospital, it was hard to believe that the scrawled message had any connection with the epidemic. She could see the dispensing table now. Three staff doctors were making the injections, using a battery of syringes from nearby sterilizers. Beyond the injection stations was a second bank of tables, where pharmacists were handing out packages containing the required four doses of streptomycin, in addition to the first capsule, which was taken on the spot.

There was a brief flurry when the Sweetbriar alumna fainted under the needle, and two interns sprang forward for the privilege of assisting her.

"Easy does it," warned a voice from the line. "Two buttons will give her enough air."

The girl coughed over an ammonia inhaler, and sat up. "Did I pass out *again?* I'd do that at college, every time they gave me a shot." She smiled at the faces around her—then, somewhat tardily, refastened her blouse.

It was Eve's turn now. She felt the jab of the needle, the brief congestion as the vaccine was injected. At the second table, she swallowed her tablet, and dropped the drugpack in her uniform pocket.

"One dose a day for five days," the pharmacist chanted, and she was shoved on gently by the next in line.

Even now she hesitated to ask Eric's whereabouts. Knowing the task he must face tonight (and the nights to come), she felt she had no right to break in on the strength of a detective's whim. *Pete Dalton should do his own police work,* she thought resentfully. *Today, of all times, he has no right to use us as his decoys.*

The resentment faded when she heard her name called. Eric was beckoning from an adjoining office.

He was seated at a card-index file—the hospital roster, arranged by services. The smile he gave her was an instant reassurance.

"I see you've had your medicine, Miss Bronson."

"How's the program going?" Eve was glad to find her voice was just as tranquil. It could hardly be otherwise, with that file of personnel outside.

"In another hour, we'll be down to maintenance. We'll also be down to our last cartons of vaccine. We'll have more by air in the morning."

"Enough for New York?"

"We can protect our police and firemen. Let's make a two-part wish—and hope it comes true. One, that we're short of true epidemic status this time tomorrow. Two, that our Canadian freighter docks on schedule."

"Don't leave out Inspector Dalton," said Eve, dropping her voice to a whisper. "*He* could use a little help from Aladdin's djinn."

The immunologist listened with the same false air of relaxation while she described her visit at the Lemayos. His face was unchanged after his hand had closed on hers beneath the table to take the note.

"Wait for me in the lab, Miss Bronson," he said. "I'll consider your problem there."

"Are you sure you'll have time, Doctor?"

"At the moment, I'm only pretending to supervise." He stood up as he spoke, opening the office door wide.

Eve slipped through the line and took the fire stair to pathology. Save for a few busy technicians in a far corner, the main laboratory and Eric's workroom were empty at this hour. Charles Tully's cubicle was dark: Tully himself, she remembered, was in the upstairs corridor, chatting with friends in the line.

She settled at his desk, feigning immersion in a medical journal, lest the technicians wonder at her presence. She was still staring blankly at the page when Eric sat down beside her.

"Pete's hunch paid off, it seems," he said.

"Can you understand her note?"

"It wasn't too hard—if you overlook the señora's lack of grammar." He spread the crumpled sheet on Tully's blotter, and translated slowly, as though he still half-refused to accept its meaning:

Dear Miss B:

There are few peoples woman like me can trust. You, I hope, are one.

My boy Juanito (whose word I took only yesterday) has show himself to be an enemy of man. So far, he does not know I know.

*He must be stopped, while there is yet time.*

I have always realize he is war lord of Dukes. That I forgive. I did not know these Dukes are train to loot and to kill, on a leader's orders. A man who is never mention by name.

Juanito tell me he work nights—at a farmacia in Harlem. Now I find he work only for this man, who pay him well and arm him.

I say no more: to write this much, I risk my life. These things I learn only by chance. Juanito think me a fool, because I am old. *Why else does he keep guns in room next to mine?*

Night after night, he take these guns to Dukes, when he think me asleep. Night after night, I lie in dark and listen. Now I must speak.

Tonight at nine, I go to cinema. Come when apartment is empty. Look in armoire—in Juanito's room. You will see I speak true.

I leave two keys—on ledge above street door. One open my apartment. The other, the lock on armoire.

Call the police, if you must. I do not wish to know your decision.

                                        R. Lemayo.

Eve did not stir while Eric tore the note across, tossed the pieces at Tully's wastebasket—then repented the gesture, and burned it in the ashtray.

"Shouldn't you keep that for Pete Dalton?"

"I think we'll remember the contents." He got up from Tully's swivel chair, and extended his hand. "We're in this together, aren't we?"

"If *you* want to be, Eric."

"Pete's my friend. I haven't much choice." Her hand was still in his: she could feel the eagerness of the pressure as his eyes went to the wall clock. "It's almost nine: I'm afraid you'll have to come with me. There's no time to find another witness."

"Aren't you going to call the police first?"

"Not until I've something definite to report. Let's go."

Eve had no clear memory of reaching the Lemayo apartment. On her visit with Bob, she had been calm enough. Tonight, she was a breathless conspirator, following a trail she could not sense clearly.

Eric had picked up a doctor's bag as a passport, and tossed a raincoat about her shoulders. At the corner, they paused in a doorway to let a familiar, stoop-shouldered figure pass by. Despite her slipshod walk, the woman had her own dignity. Positive that she had marked their presence, Eve put down the impulse to call her name. Now that Rita Lemayo had made her peace with God and man, they could never speak again.

Rain had begun to fall heavily when they mounted the tenement stoop; the sidewalk was deserted. Letting the street lamp fall on the black bag in his hand, Eric went through the routine of consulting an address book. Playing the game to the end, Eve rang the Lemayo bell, while her escort returned with the keys. He had found them in their promised place above the lintel.

"Move fast," he whispered. "If we're stopped, we'll say this is an emergency call."

The stairwell was black as a coalbin, save for a feeble bulb on the landing. The first key admitted them to the Lemayo apartment, where a candle still burned before the *prie-dieu*. The door to Juan's room stood open. A splinter of light from the street, catching a wall mirror, showed there was no furniture but a cot and a chair without a back.

*So far,* thought Eve, *our timing has been perfect.* And yet, when she drew the bedroom shade and touched the light switch, she could almost wish they had stayed away.

Eric bent on one knee to study the wardrobe lock. There was a rasping protest as the tumblers fell; the key was evidently not an original, but it fitted. The door swung on oiled hinges, opening the shallow closet to the glare of the ceiling bulb. The entire space was a makeshift gun rack, where a dozen thick-handled automatics rested. The floor below was stacked with ammunition boxes.

They had found precisely what they sought. The discovery shocked them both to silence.

"Why did she tell us?" Eve demanded. "I still don't understand."

"Call it a forlorn hope. Being his mother, she couldn't turn Juan in herself. She hoped we'd handle that detail." Eric had lifted one of the guns from its rack. To Eve's eye, there was nothing to distinguish it from a hundred others. She was unprepared for Eric's reaction, after he had read the letters on the butt.

"Do you recognize the make?" she asked.

"Ever hear of the Skoda works?"

"The munitions factory in Czechoslovakia?"

"Hitler risked war to annex it. For almost twenty years, it's been part of the Soviet orbit."

"Don't tell me this street gang is taking orders from the Kremlin."

"We can't go on blaming Moscow forever," said Eric. "I've seen this same gun all over satellite Europe—even in parts of Asia."

"And now New York?"

"At least it proves we've an enemy on our doorstep," said Eric. He replaced the weapon on the rack. "Obviously, one of these was stolen from Dr. Keller's locker yesterday. I'd give a great deal to return the compliment."

"What's our next move?"

"A fast report to Pete. This is his baby now."

"Shouldn't we search the whole room?"

"If you insist. I'm afraid we'll find nothing more."

Eric's prediction was accurate. Though they ransacked each corner, and turned both carpet and mattress, they found no further clues. The *Jefe* to whom Mrs. Lemayo had referred so vaguely remained an enigma when the interlopers put out the light, raised the window shade to its former position, and prepared to depart.

The glow of the *prie-dieu* was enough to guide them through the crowded living-room; even so, Eric just missed colliding with a lamp in his progress to the hall door. Eve's hand was on the knob: she moved to steady the lamp before it crashed to the floor. At that moment, she heard the sound of footsteps outside, the sibilant murmur of Spanish. She recognized Juan's voice instantly, riding above the others.

Eric, flattened against the door, listened with complete detachment while the war-lord of the Dukes was fumbling for his key.

"They've come for their arsenal," he whispered. "Hide in the clothespress. Remember, they think the place is empty."

The key was in the lock before Eve could seek refuge among Rita Lemayo's scanty wardrobe. Eric, she saw, had chosen the ambush of a clothes hamper, seconds before the hall door opened. The visitors entered single file, with Juan bringing up the rear. Tonight they wore nondescript garb; though they continued to chatter like magpies, there was tension in their movements, an unconcealed haste.

Small as the room was, they seemed to fill it with their presence. Eve choked down a gasp when a hand fell on the light switch, then dropped in response to a command from the war-lord. He was already in the bedroom, starring the armoire with a flashlight. This time, the lock turned silently. In another moment, the guns were passing from hand to hand.

The arming was accomplished smoothly. Now that her first dread had subsided, Eve found herself watching the group in mingled fascination and dismay. Though their language was strange, she could grasp their intent: beyond a doubt, this was a unit of what Bob had called Operation Saboteur. Each of them was prepared to kill and destroy on order.

The Dukes did not leave in a group. Instead, they slipped into the hallway one by one, to appear briefly on the sidewalk before drifting into the dark. Eve saw the reason when the lights of a squad car, roving the district in a routine check, probed at the Lemayo stoop.

Juan had been the last to depart. He waited a few seconds after the last dark-clad figure had vanished. Then he locked the empty wardrobe and ran from the apartment.

Eric was on his feet at once. "Are you all right, Eve?"

"Reasonably. Could you understand what they said?"

"Enough. Not that I'm much the wiser." He had already moved to the *prie-dieu*, to make busy notes on a pocket memo. Once again, Eve marveled at his ability to put first things first. "These are for Pete Dalton. Call him on the number I've jotted down——"

"Why should *I* call the inspector?"

"This is your assignment now," he said. "I won't have time, I'm afraid." He was handing the memo to her, sheet by sheet. "Will you read these back?"

The notes were an almost verbatim transcript of Juan's orders. For a man in haste, Eve thought, they were surprisingly complete. As Eric had said, they revealed no new factors. Juan had ordered a rendezvous in the tenement basement, to await his mother's departure. Every youth who had followed him to his bedroom was a lieutenant —a privileged aide, allowed to carry a pistol. This was the cadre on which the Dukes were based. Tonight they were assigned to a mission requiring full use of the arsenal.

The group was bound uptown (the war-lord would reveal the site when they reassembled). The purpose of the raid was unstated (the

*Jefe* himself would be present to give the final orders). The Leader's identity, it seemed, had been revealed to no one besides Juan and Ricardo Reyes; tonight, the same precaution would be followed. Tomorrow, a new second-in-command would be chosen. The choice would be based on the group's impending performance.

"Shouldn't we follow them, Eric?"

"We've taken enough risks tonight. Besides, we'd never pick up their trail."

Eve tucked the notes into her uniform pocket. "How will these help Pete Dalton?"

"At least they'll backstop his hunch."

In the downstairs vestibule, they pressed close together lest their white uniforms betray their presence. A dozen youths (run-of-the-mill members of the Dukes) were loitering near the stoop; it was a poor time to leave the tenement.

"I hope you'll forgive me for bringing you here," he whispered. "When we left the hospital, I'm afraid I wasn't thinking too clearly."

"I *had* to come, Eric. You know that."

The Dukes had moved on, but Eric made no move to step outside. Instead, he drew Eve still closer and kissed her. The risks of the past hour, the unknown perils that waited at Manhattan Central, were lost in that unexpected embrace. Eric's kiss, she reflected, was well worth having. It was good to know she had earned it.

"That was a reminder," he said, "of our date in Afghanistan. I hope you'll keep it."

"I'll let you know when Operation Epidemic's over."

"That'll do nicely for now." He opened the door and emerged on the stoop. For the first time he seemed really anxious. The distant whine of an ambulance siren explained his haste.

"Do you suppose that one's for you, Eric?"

"It's for *all* of us, my dear," he said. "They've been arriving steadily while we were upstairs. So far I've counted seven."

"Is that why you gave me these notes?"

"Yes, Eve. I can't spare a minute more. Not even for a phone."

It was still important to walk slowly until they had left the asphalt jungle; if hostile eyes were upon them, a false move might wreck the work they had done for Pete Dalton. Only when they moved under the arc lights of the hospital drive and saw the file of ambulances awaiting their turn at the emergency platform did they break into a run.

A small group had gathered at the gates. It parted with a murmur to let the two white-clad figures pass, then fell into silence as the woman in the first ambulance rolled into view on the wheeled stretcher. Eve saw that the group on the unloading platform wore masks, gowns, and gloves. It was part of the technique of isolation Eric had ordered for each admission, from the moment the case entered the hospital portals.

At the Lemayos, she had had no chance to lose her nerve. There was something in this floodlit scene that caused her to shiver uncontrollably. Eric sensed her revulsion, and paused with an arm about her shoulders.

"Thank God for the vaccine," she said. "At least we're prepared for whatever happens."

"Let's *hope* it's effective, Eve."

She gave him a startled look. "Hasn't it proved itself in Asia?"

"Of course—in long-range immunization. I've never been forced to use this precise technique before. In Asia there's native resistance, built up over the centuries. The disease could never spread there so rapidly."

"Then no one's absolutely safe at the moment?"

"I'm afraid not, Eve. That's why I ordered gowns and gloves, all down the line. What I'm relying on most heavily is the streptomycin. And we're taking the word of Russian scientists for that."

On the platform, the woman on the stretcher gave a piercing shriek. Both her arms lifted, as though in supplication to some dark deity. Her face, in clear view at last, was livid with cyanosis; in the garish light, she was like a witch daubed with blue clay. While the tableau lasted, she seemed to hang in midair, suspended by the sheer will to live. Then, with another shriek, she fell back on the stretcher. The arms she had raised to heaven hung limp. This was a case for which no hospital bed would be needed.

At the hospital gate, the knot of onlookers gave an answering moan. Then they began to move, slowly at first, until the contagion of fear had struck at every heart. Almost before Eve could turn to look, the street was deserted.

She lifted her eyes to Eric's, grateful for the strong hand on her shoulder. Without his touch, she too would have joined that mindless flight.

"I'm needed in there," he said. "Will you take my notes to a phone, and give them to Dalton?"

He left her without another word. She was grateful for the brusque order, since it gave her flight toward the nurses' wing a purpose. While that row of ambulances waited, nothing on earth could have forced her through the emergency-room door.

# 5. Wednesday

THE six men gathered in the committee room adjoining the office of Selden Grove were gaunt from lack of sleep. That Wednesday noon, all of them had good cause for near-exhaustion, though each of the six was doing his best to cover his weariness. Surveying the gathering from the hall door, Dr. Eric Stowe took a deep breath before he joined them. He could sense the controlled despair in the room, the burning need for guidance.

John Newman was in the presiding chair this time. Selden Grove sat on the mayor's right hand, Health Commissioner Thurlow on his left. Beside Thurlow was Dr. Manuel Fernandez, who headed the United States Public Health Service in the area. Next to Grove was Norris Weaver, the capable head of medical service at the hospital, now in complete charge of personnel. Clive Decker, the police commissioner, faced Newman at the table's end.

The spacious committee room, with city maps on each wall and towering statistical charts, made the circular table seem absurdly small. The group around it suggested a council of war. Eric knew the metaphor was accurate.

"Thank you for coming here, gentlemen," he said quietly. "It was the only way we could gather as a body, since I can't leave the hospital at this time. From what the mayor has told me, such a meeting is essential."

"We won't move until you've briefed us," said Newman.

The immunologist glanced at the clip-board in his hand. Shocking though its tidings might seem to a layman's eyes, he had learned to accept them during his long hours on the wards.

"I gather you want the bad news now," he said.

The mayor forced a wan grin. "Can we take it?"

"I think so. In the past twenty-four hours, we've admitted ninety-eight cases of plague to our isolation wards. That figure includes this hospital only. Elsewhere in the city, hospitals have accepted forty more cases for treatment. Out of this number, about two thirds are of the pneumonic variety——"

"What's the mortality rate?" asked Dr. Fernandez.

"In spite of intensive treatment, there have been thirty-six deaths. Over thirty more are listed as critical."

Police Commissioner Decker looked up from his notes. "How about hospital and government personnel? Right now, they're more heavily exposed than anyone."

"The story there is more hopeful. So far we've had only five cases —two here and three on city staffs. There have been no deaths reported."

"New Yorkers won't like that average," said Decker. "Our switchboards are flooded with calls, complaining the police were protected ahead of the people."

"So is mine, Mr. Commissioner," said the mayor.

"People are also saying protection must be bought."

Eric settled into a chair beside the commissioner. He had expected this report, word for word.

"Has there been much medical bootlegging so far?"

"Enough to keep my detective bureau hopping," said Decker. "The usual shysters have bought up all the plague vaccine they could get. They're using practical nurses to give injections at a hundred dollars a head. That was the last reported price." He glanced pointedly at Eric's clip-board. "If those figures get out, the cost will jump."

"Perhaps not, Mr. Decker—if we can convince people they've been hoodwinked."

"How so?"

"Vaccine alone may not be effective in this epidemic."

"Are you using that word now?"

"I am—in this room. The figures I've given you prove one thing beyond question. *Pasteurella pestis* is moving quickly. A patient's body may not have time to develop immunity from that source alone."

"Is there a better remedy?" asked Thurlow.

"I think so, Doctor," said Eric. "Providing all new contacts report promptly. My plan, from now on, is to rely mainly on antibiotic and sulfonamide prophylaxis. Naturally, where we have vaccine available, we'll immunize our personnel; if the epidemic continues, they'll build up an anti-plague level. It's just possible we'll need that kind of work force later——"

"If things get really out of hand?" asked Thurlow.

"At this moment, I refuse to anticipate the worst. I'm merely saying we'll be prepared. Meanwhile, may I have Mr. Decker's report on Operation Saboteur?"

The commissioner's eyes were dagger points. "What's the connection, Dr. Stowe?"

"None, perhaps. It does seem the two patterns overlap." Eric was careful not to press the query. Selden Grove's committee room was no place to mention the discovery he and Eve had made at the Lemayos: Pete Dalton's follow-up on that information was—by its very nature—a departmental secret.

"Last night was no worse than Monday," said Decker. "Not if we forget the power plants. We expected wholesale looting and cracked down. The mayor knows the whole force is on emergency alert."

"I'm sure of it," said Eric. "What's the estimate for tonight?"

"That depends on the decisions you reach today," said Decker.

"Meaning that Operation Saboteur will step up its tempo if epidemic figures go on rising?"

"Doesn't it stand to reason, Dr. Stowe?"

"Naturally," said Eric. He let his eyes duel with the commissioner's —if only to establish his point in that quarter.

Dr. Fernandez spoke up before the impasse could deepen. "May I ask my most important question? Is it possible to contain this thing to Manhattan Island? My own figures say disease rates in the other boroughs are still negligible. I've no reports whatever in the suburbs——"

"No cases have been diagnosed there, so far," said Eric.

"I'm aware that isolation of this borough could spark a first-rate panic," said Dr. Fernandez. "Isn't it still the best solution?"

The mayor cut in. "Albany's been pressuring me since yesterday," he said. "The governor wants to block off the rest of the state."

"So do New Jersey and Connecticut," said Fernandez. He turned to the health commissioner. "What *is* the over-all picture in Manhattan? Will things improve by tomorrow?"

"The rat-war is swinging our way," said Thurlow. "So far as medication's concerned, we're getting delivery by the ton—and I'm being quite literal." He turned to the mayor with a shrug of apology. "Naturally, I've had to sign vouchers for tons of money. So has Dr. Stowe."

"You'll both be covered," said Newman. "I promised that much yesterday. Dr. Fernandez is still waiting for an answer."

Thurlow and Eric exchanged glances. Eric spoke first, at the other's gesture.

"If you're wondering about the case-load—I'm afraid it will be climbing fast. My last report lists two hundred probables among our admissions after midnight. At best, we must expect at least sixty more pneumonic patients here—which means twice as many elsewhere in the borough."

"I've a return call waiting now in Washington," said Fernandez. "May I have a decision?"

Eric glanced at Selden Grove. The director had abdicated in his favor, but he could not make the next commitment without Grove's nod.

"Quarantine's the word, I suppose," he said. "Plus a full-scale immunization, once Manhattan Island is sealed off."

John Newman leaned forward. "How can we take such a risk?"

"*Pasteurella pestis* had established its beachhead," said Eric. "We can defeat it within these boundaries. If we hesitate, we'll have two thousand cases tomorrow in Greater New York. The day after, there could be ten thousand in the metropolitan area alone. Don't think I'm romancing. I've seen this bug in action."

"What do you propose?" asked Newman.

"Quarantine tonight. Borough-wide prophylaxis tomorrow. We'll cover the island—and no more. It's our only chance, while geography is in our favor."

The mayor took the challenge calmly. "How soon must I close the exits?"

"Not before tonight's work force leaves." Eric had moved to the nearest wall map. "Traffic in this borough can easily be managed at such key spots as the terminals and the toll gates. My plan is to let the commuter rush depart as usual. Thanks to the tie-ups, it's far below normal. Once that tide has ebbed, I'm asking the mayor to go on TV and proclaim a state of siege here—until our enemies are defeated."

"*Enemies*, Dr. Stowe?" asked the police commissioner.

"I've named mine, Mr. Decker," said Eric. "Perhaps you can track down yours in time. Until then, let's fight our war inside those boundaries."

"We've had commuters here for three days," said Thurlow. "What if they take our epidemic into the suburbs?"

"Such contacts can be controlled at exit points."

"How, Dr. Stowe?"

"By medication, when each commuter departs—whether he has a railroad ticket or a car pool."

"You'll create the worst jam in history."

"Not if departures are staggered. I'll grant you it would be impossible, if we had to police bus lines and subways. As things stand, you and Mr. Decker can handle the load between you."

"What drug are you distributing?" asked Dr. Fernandez.

"Sulfamerazine," said Eric. "We've enough on hand now to give each commuter a standard package. That's our curtain raiser. If it works, we'll shoot for our real miracle tomorrow."

"Which is prophylactic treatment for all Manhattan?"

"Precisely, Doctor."

"Today's miracle is tall enough for me," growled Decker. "If I can clear our commuters without bloodshed, I'll take tomorrow's miracle in stride."

Eric glanced round the table. He could read approval of his strategy in every face, now the pattern was clear. Even Decker's complaint had been automatic.

"Let's keep this fact in mind," he said. "Once those commuters are home, they'll *stay* home. The mayor's broadcast will take care of that angle. Of course we'll order a temporary shutdown of business, and permit only essential traffic between island and mainland."

"How will you define the word?" Decker demanded.

"By your usual disaster standards. When the mayor announces the quarantine, he will also promise mass distribution of drugs."

"Through local depots?" asked Thurlow.

"It shouldn't be difficult to spot booths all over Manhattan and arrange a schedule. Not with the streets free of traffic, and the country's best police force to keep applicants in line."

Dr. Norris Weaver entered the discussion for the first time. "What if those applicants don't apply? Even here in the hospital, I've had volunteer workers refuse the needle."

The mayor rose from his chair. "These are my people, Dr. Weaver," he said. "They'll take their medicine, after I've told them why it's needed. Any more instructions, Dr. Stowe?"

It was a call to action; Eric accepted it in that spirit. "Once our medication's on hand, we're prepared to administer it. This is the final stage of Operation Epidemic. I trust it'll prove decisive."

The mayor glanced round the table in search of dissenters. When he found none, he banged the surface with his fist. "In that event, gentlemen, I'd suggest we hit the road. There's a backbreaking task ahead, and damned little time to complete it." He turned again to Eric. "I gather we'll forego all announcements until tonight?"

Eric addressed the gathering for the last time. He could still read doubt there—but he knew there would be no faltering when the real test came. "Those leaving Manhattan Island will be given drug packets, and instruction for self-medication. If that exodus is handled quietly, there should be no real trouble, above rumor level. I'd suggest eight o'clock as the best time for the mayor's proclamation. It can hardly be delayed longer."

John Newman met each pair of eyes in turn. "You've heard Dr. Stowe's idea of timing and the need of secrecy until I go on the air. If there's a premature leak, in Sharp's column or elsewhere, I'll know someone in this room gave out the information. Be assured I'll personally make that man wish he'd never been born. You all know your jobs. Conference dismissed."

2.

Once the meeting had broken up, the mayor, Eric, and Selden Grove entered the director's own office in a solemn file. Grove had taken little part in the discussion: there had been no need, with the immunologist in charge. Now, he turned to Newman.

"I'm sure you realize the burden we've put on you, Mr. Mayor."

Newman shrugged. "I'll do my best," he said. "Before I start composing my broadcast, I'm asking just one favor—a first-hand view of our enemy in action."

The three men exchanged a glance. Both doctors knew just what the mayor intended. *Pasteurella pestis* was the immediate antagonist. Pete Dalton would pursue their other, all too human Nemesis.

"Why risk exposure?" asked Grove.

"I must know exactly what you've done here before I show my face on television."

"You won't like what you see, John."

"I'm braced for shocks. Will you lead the way, Eric?"

"Since you insist," said the immunologist, "we'll check the women's ward. You'll find it revealing enough."

Four wards at Manhattan Central had already been set aside for plague patients, with reserve units available in city developments nearby. In the common anteroom that connected them, both Eric and the mayor donned gloves and gowns from a sterile press, and

caps and masks from another. Cocking an ear toward the surf of
moaning inside, the guide gave the visitor a last searching glance.

"Do you remember your Dante, John, and the inscription over the
portals of hell?"

"*All hope abandon, ye who enter here?*"

"Things aren't quite that desperate—but it will prepare you."

The volume of sound rose sharply when they pushed through the
ground-glass doors—the senseless mutter of patients in delirium,
the shuddering gasps of lungs in the viselike grip of the pneumonic
virus. There were twenty beds in the section Eric had chosen; with
a sinking heart, he saw the three empty cots had been filled since his
last visit. One of the three newcomers was in the early stage of the
disease. The others had already been touched by the fatal bluish
tinge of cyanosis at lips and ear lobes.

Moving from bed to bed, Eric gave the mayor a run-down on
each chart. It included a concise estimate by the admitting physician, the probable place of infection, and all subsequent contacts.
Several of these patients had visited the Millway cafeteria on Sunday: others had heard van Pelt's communion with the muse at the
Blue Banjo. In a few cases, it had proved impossible to trace the
route of the infection.

"How can you start immunizing all down the line?" asked Newman. "The numbers must be astronomical."

"Not always. You'd be surprised what loners some of these people
are. Families are harder, of course—but not impossible, for epidemiologists who know their business. Each name and address goes
straight to Dr. Thurlow. Antibiotic teams from the Department
take over promptly: the police make spot checks later."

When the last bed was covered, the mayor paused on the threshold with haggard eyes. "How many will die, in spite of everything?"

"With twenty in the ward, at least ten would go—on a straight statistical basis. Unfortunately many of these cases were diagnosed
late. I'm afraid we'll lose at least fifteen."

"Is this room typical of all your wards?"

"No, John. I'm showing you the worst, so you can visualize our
problems. Bubonic cases are segregated on another floor. In them,
the disease is slower-paced, so we can hit it harder. With pneumonic cases, the determining factor isn't treatment; it's how soon
after contact we get them."

They paused a moment more in the doorframe, while Eric described the techniques he had installed to make these victims' lot

endurable. Each life was being fought for, even where the battle
seemed hopeless. At more than half the beds, intravenous sets were
in use, pouring massive doses of the tetracycline drugs into the
patients' circulations. Others were battling for survival in oxygen
tents. Here and there, particularly high fevers were treated with
the cooling packs ordinarily used for refrigeration anesthesia in
heart surgery—a last-ditch attempt to lower skyrocketing thermometer readings.

"Those jolts from the tetracycline group are the only positive
medication," Eric explained. "All we can do after that is supportive.
It's a matter of whether the patient holds up until the *Pasteurella* in
his body can be finished off. Sometimes even that development
can prove fatal. When the bacillus itself is destroyed, it releases its
toxic products in the blood stream. It acts like a dose of strychnine."

They moved to shed their masks and gowns in the anteroom; before leaving the isolation area, they were careful to wash hands and
forearms at antiseptic basins, drying their hands on paper towels
consigned for burning. The mayor performed these macabre rituals
without speaking. Something about his set jaw told Eric that the
experience, unnerving though it had been, was precisely what the
moment demanded. John Newman would face the television cameras tonight well aware of the game he was playing and the stakes
involved.

"Would you care to see the stock of pharmaceuticals we've built
up since yesterday?"

"That won't be necessary," said the mayor. "I've got the picture
I needed. Just tell me one thing more and I'll get on my own
treadmill. If you had an option, would you change careers at
this moment?"

Tired though he was, Eric found he could laugh aloud.

"Of course not. I'm doing what I was meant to do: it's something few men can say nowadays. Even if I fail, I'll be grateful for
the chance."

The operating lights were on in the Bubble, Eric saw, when he
passed through the surgical wing. Yielding to a familiar impulse,
he turned into the empty spectators' gallery. As he had hoped, Bob
Trent and Eve were the center of the busy team below. The task
at hand was an intestinal resection. It seemed formidable enough
to the visitor's eye—though he could tell from the surgical chief's
easy tempo that the procedure was routine.

Leaving the closing to George Peters, Bob lifted a hand in greeting. "Believe it or not this is our last accident case," he said via the microphone. "I'll join you in another moment."

Eric picked up the spectators' microphone. "Bring Miss Bronson with you, please. I'd like a word with you both."

Over coffee in the empty lounge, he told his two friends of the mayor's visit to the wards and the troubling statistics they had found there. He made no effort to minimize the pace of the epidemic, though he did not dare reveal the plans he had made for tomorrow.

"Selden told me you volunteered to cover all emergencies," he said. "It's been a great help in freeing personnel for isolation work. I'm sorry we had to restrict you to that type of admissions."

"If last night's a sample of things to come," said Bob, "we'll do well to handle those. Incidentally, when did you have any sleep?"

"I can't remember. Can you—or Eve?"

"I'm sending *her* to the sack right now," said Bob. "Did you hear that order, Miss Bronson?"

"Let me stay a moment more." Eve turned to Eric as she spoke. "Has there been word from the inspector?"

"Only a note of thanks for what happened at the Lemayos. Did you brief Bob on that?"

"Of course; *he* played detective too."

The surgical chief frowned at his cup. "I understand the Dukes have gone to earth. God knows how much work they made for us last night." He got up with a cavernous yawn. "Speaking only for myself, I'm still glad I chose surgery at Hopkins. Remember to sleep while you have the chance, Eve." He dropped a hand on Eric's shoulder. "As for you, *Herr Direktor*, let me know if I can do anything more."

"You're handling three men's work already."

"Three men who can help you fight *Pasteurella*," said Bob. "It's a fair deal."

Watching his friend cross the lounge, Eric felt a familiar sense of guilt at this respite, however brief it had been. He pushed his own cup aside and turned to Eve.

"Thanks for the vote of confidence," he said. "You've both done more than I'd the right to ask. Now I insist you follow orders and build up that backlog of sleep."

"What's your next tour of duty?"

"I'm headed for Merton House. We've just made it an immunization station for contacts." He did not add that similar distributions were taking place at other key points in the city. It was a substantial attempt to reduce the crowds that would be pouring into the prophylaxis stations tomorrow.

"Let me walk over with you," Eve begged. "I need a breath of outside air."

"Only if you'll promise to go to your room afterwards."

In the playground that adjoined the youth center, a long line waited for admission. Skirting the queue to enter the building by its side entrance, Eric studied each face swiftly for latent hysteria. As he expected, he found nothing on the surface. Most of these tenement dwellers had lived with trouble since their first breath: like all their resentments, today's fear was a wound they nursed in secret.

"They're scared," Eve whispered. "The fear is buried—but you can sense it."

"Fear is nothing to be ashamed of," he said. "Not if it's controlled."

"Let's hope they'll be this quiet tomorrow."

"Want to come inside and see how things are going?"

"No, Eric. This breather was all I needed. *I'll* stay controlled, no matter what happens."

"I'm sure of that, my dear."

She pressed his hand quickly before she crossed the sun-baked asphalt to the nurses' wing. He studied her confident carriage for a moment before turning into Merton House, without daring to ask himself how much she knew of his plan for tomorrow. Despite John Newman's order, the secret could not be kept. By evening, it would be praised or damned in every service at the hospital.

Inside the youth center, the basketball court had been utilized as a distribution point. The line was moving toward the tables where nurses were handing out the neatly packaged drug, with printed instructions in both Spanish and English. Dr. Weaver, who was supervising the team, joined Eric at once, to lead him into a corner of the vast, airy gymnasium.

"Our vaccine is going fast, Dr. Stowe. So's the streptomycin."

"Will it last?"

"Just—if they don't pile up on us."

"Where's Tully?"

"Observing you from on high, Eric." The social worker's voice

had boomed down from the shallow balcony that circled the basketball court. It was a natural vantage point; Eric wondered how he
had missed that imposing figure.

"How do things look to you?"

Tully lowered his voice. "I've covered the area round the project,"
he said. "People are on edge, of course. So far, I'd say they were
bearing up."

"How long will they bear up? Through tomorrow?"

"I wouldn't risk a guess, Eric. Meanwhile, I'll spread what cheer
I can. Right now I'm about to have lunch with Irene in my apartment. Why not join us?"

"I'm afraid I haven't time."

"Not even for a drink? My guess is you could stand one."

"Sorry, Charles."

Returning to the hospital (and the endless, grinding pursuit
of sulfa drugs) Eric asked himself if he had been too brusque. At
the moment, he needed a change of scene badly—and he could
have used one of the continental lunches for which Irene Lusk was
famous. Oddly enough, he was still glad he had refused. Today
he could not have borne Tully's brand of optimism.


                                    3.


New York had come to work that Wednesday in greatly dimin-
ished numbers, because of the continued transit tie-up. The pre-
vailing mood was mixed—running the gamut from bad humor to
near-terror.

Actual emotion, for the most part, continued to be well masked.
New Yorkers, like most city breeds, took pride in their *savoir-faire*.
As an outward proof of urbanity, Manhattan Island accepted its
subway breakdown (and the report of pestilence on its doorstep)
with a cynic's shrug, with a stubborn inner hope that both evils
would vanish with the morrow.

Deep uneasiness remained; its symptoms were constant, regardless of the worker's station, as the familiar army streamed into its
warrens. That Wednesday morning, copywriters on Madison Avenue and cloth cutters in the Thirties, earthshakers in Radio City
and brokers' runners downtown, Park Avenue doormen and air-
conditioned demimondaines gave identical proofs that man under

stress is a creature of impulse. Wherever New Yorkers gathered, there was the same urge to glance over one's shoulder for an invisible enemy, to bark at underlings, to hate one's rulers more bitterly than before. . . .

The mayor's Tuesday address on television (which, only yesterday, had done its part to steady nerves) was repeated at regular intervals on the airways. Early broadcasts from the Health Department assured the five boroughs that the situation was well in hand, and listeners were told again that the Canadian freighter *Admiral Beattie* had been diverted to New York with enough drugs aboard to protect all Manhattan Island. Today these soothing voices did little to dissipate the fog of rumor that had thickened with each passing hour.

It was said that hundreds of plague cases had died in every contagious ward, that the bodies had been incinerated to keep the infection from spreading down the hospitals' own corridors.

When an uptown warehouse was padlocked to safeguard stand-by cartons of sulfamerazine, the neighborhood buzzed with reports that a nearby clinic had resorted to the Dark Age practice of sealing the dead in airtight coffins, because it was now unsafe to transport them for burial.

A hearse, crossing town to a funeral home, was sideswiped by a careless motorist—so violently that the basket containing the body spilled to the sidewalk. After the accident even the mortuary attendants fled the scene. The police were forced to summon a Manhattan Central ambulance to complete the delivery of a cadaver whose only ailment was old age.

Drunks who had once slept unmolested in tenement doorways were driven out by furious landlords, lest they prove to be victims of the new disease.

An epileptic, writhing at a busy intersection, caused a lunchtime stampede and a riot call to the nearest precinct before the victim could be cared for.

Authentic collapses, of course, were still the exception. In Union Square, a crank spread poisoned grain for the pigeons. When dying birds fell on window sills, stories of yet another form of plague swept through midtown offices and garment lofts. The story created a climate of hysteria. It subsided reluctantly after the next city broadcast had given the facts.

At street corners, hawkers braved arrest to sell patent cures. Churches were jammed; itinerant preachers led prayer sessions,

shouting that God had smitten Babylon while their assistants
passed the hat.

After the luncheon break (as a hundred office managers noted
wrathfully) efficiency tapered off sharply; it was as though each
desk-man, wrapped in private musings, ignored the ledger or the
typewriter before him. Transistor radios in filing cabinets continued to whisper the latest bulletins. And yet, though each worker
listened avidly, the soothing words continued to lose impact.

In bars, viewers banked six deep before each TV set. That
Wednesday afternoon, beer and prayer were sovereign specifics
against disease.

Actual mortality figures were still moderate, though the number
of genuine cases admitted to the wards was now rising astronom-
ically. The figures reported at the morning meeting in Manhattan
Central had nearly tripled, and Eric's experience warned him that
the present case-load might double again by nightfall. Working
desperately to isolate and track down each new source of infection, he had left the handling of New York's commuting public to
Dr. Thurlow and the police. The plan was now ready to go into
effect, with dispensing stations at every exit point, and doctors
available to diagnose all suspected cases.

At noon, the health commissioner had appeared on the city station to announce that all out-of town offices would close on a staggered schedule. Dr. Thurlow's matter-of-fact instructions had given
no hint that Manhattan Island would be sealed off after tonight's
hegira to the suburbs. Nor did commuters and car pools realize, as
they began their carefully staged journeys, that they would receive
a medical check and prophylaxis.

The exodus was managed smoothly. There was still no open fear
when the last office door was locked and the last wearied executive (damning the dead subway and the lack of taxis) began to
beat his way homeward. New York was a colossus held line by
habit-patterns. Today, it had done its job in nervous snatches, held
its terrors to a murmur, and avoided each coughing desk mate.

The urge to flee an unknown peril burst through on occasion.
At the time, such sporadic breaks in the city's orderly rhythm went
unnoticed. They too would be magnified beyond all reason when
Manhattan became a truly beleaguered island.

Russell Harrington was one of the few New Yorkers who missed
the health commissioner's broadcast.

All that hot forenoon, the stockbroker had fought a racking head-ache in his pine-paneled Wall Street eyrie, while he drove through the paper work of an oil merger. He had already planned on a long weekend at his estate at Cold Spring Harbor. The plane was waiting now in the heliport. His personal secretary had taken his bags and brief case there. Gloria shared her employer's relaxations when his wife was traveling abroad.

At three-fifteen Harrington had snarled a good-by to his lawyers, donned the straw boater that had been his hallmark for a half-century, and strode into Wall Street for the short walk to the heliport. This afternoon, prey to a sudden fit of vertigo, he had waited in the shadow of the Sub-Treasury until his head cleared, then en-tered a taxi that had providentially drifted to the curb.

Ten minutes later, seated at the controls of his 'copter, with Glo-ria nestled at his side, he had regained both his vision and his cour-age. Enough, at any rate, to roar with anger when two policemen (unaccountably on duty on the heliport deck) attempted to halt the plane's skyward lift. At the same moment, a white-jacketed doc-tor had appeared to demand a medical check of both pilot and passenger.

It was the first physical coercion Russ Harrington had suffered since the age of nineteen, when his father had thrashed him in the family garage for borrowing the second-best limousine without per-mission. On that occasion, he had done his best to throw in the clutch before his father's fist connected with his jaw. Today, obey-ing the same impulse, he gunned the 'copter's motor in a deter-mined effort to foil the hands outside.

The attempt was almost successful: for an instant, it seemed that the whirlybird would shake off police and doctor like unwanted fruit. When three attendants added their weight to the others, the plane faltered in its takeoff, then crashed to a halt against a gas pump.

There was no need to admonish the pilot, once the door was open. A moment before, he had been turkey-red with fury. Now he lay stone dead across the controls. The plump young woman be-side him had slipped into a fainting fit from which she never really roused.

When he made his examination, the doctor had taken the stand-ard precautions. Twenty-four hours earlier, he would have assumed the financier had suffered an apoplectic stroke, that his secretary, fearing the plane would topple into the East River, had gone into simple shock. Now, thanks to his briefing at Manhattan Central, he knew the import of those mottled-brown spots on Russ Harrington's wattles, the trickle of dark blood on his lips.

Once Gloria's pancake make-up was removed, it was found that she was similarly discolored. Autopsies proved her case of plague was even more advanced than Harrington's. Later investigation revealed that she had gone to the now famous poetry reading at the Blue Banjo, where Brewster van Pelt had greeted her with a hirsute kiss. She had finished the evening, as usual, in Harrington's New York apartment.

The broker and his secretary had been unaware of the true nature of their illness. It was a different story with the three wasp-waisted young men in the borrowed Ford, racing at that moment toward the Queens Midtown Tunnel. The trio were also intimates of van Pelt; all of them had been in the Blue Banjo. Now, reeling through fevered torments, they were sure they were dying. Scornful of society to the end (and its refusal to accept their all-too-common deviation) they had planned to expire together on Fire Island, chanting their own wild poetry, even as van Pelt, with their final breath.

At the toll gate, their reckless speed had alerted the police. Run down by patrol cars, they were brought to the psycho ward at Bellevue. Here it was discovered they were suffering from nothing worse than narcotics poisoning caused by excessive fixes of heroin while they awaited their last hour.

Save for two wrecks in the tunnel, at an hour when traffic was light, the capture of the addicts had caused no real stir. Like the attempted flight of Russ Harrington, the story had added its weight to tip the scales of rumor. So did three other victims of the rod-shaped bacillus, who also strove to flee Manhattan Island—each of whom had been exposed to Adolph Bruin, the repairman who had already served as a male Typhoid Mary in the town house of Jasper Merton.

One of the three was a maiden lady named Felicia Bingham, who lived in her own brownstone a few doors from the Merton mansion. A true recluse, she had no friends but the cats that shared her bedroom. Since she had installed air conditioning, she had seldom opened door or window. That Monday, after she had grudgingly admitted Bruin for his annual tune-up of the generator, she

had refused to believe his preposterous story that her basement had
been invaded by rats; forgetting that Fifi, Gisela, and Moppett
were nearly as infirm as herself, she had insisted they would have
frightened off such interlopers. Later, she had gone with a flashlight to disprove the repairman's story, only to run shrieking upstairs when *Rattus rattus* converged on her in force.

Brief though it was, the encounter had been sufficient for direct
infection. Two mornings later, when she rose to unlock the grocery
container in her kitchen door, Felicia Bingham was almost too
dizzy to find the keyhole. About to call her doctor, she realized she
no longer had one; the family physician who served her had not
been needed for years, and she had read his obituary months ago.

The problem of summoning a stranger was too onerous at the
moment. Instead she had gone upstairs with her morning tea and
a saucer of milk, to discuss the matter with Fifi, Gisela, and Moppett. A little later, she had fallen into an uneasy doze on her chaise
longue, to dream of the house in Philadelphia where she had
passed her girlhood before her father had moved his business to
New York.

When fever wakened her at dusk, she had yielded to a sudden,
irrational desire to see that Philadelphia house again, only to collapse at the phone before she could summon a taxi.

Her cleaning woman had found her there next morning, and run
wild-eyed from what she saw. She had left the service door wide
open, permitting the cellar invaders to scamper upstairs at will. Fifi,
Gisela, and Moppet had had little chance to mourn their mistress.
They had been overrun by sheer weight of numbers, long before
the ambulance arrived from Manhattan Central to transport yet another body to the auxiliary morgue.

The next victim of Bruin's lethal visitations was named Nick
Azandian. He was a blind newsdealer, with a kiosk outside a subway stair on Lexington Avenue, a half-block from the Bingham
brownstone. Business had been poor that morning because of the
tie-up, but Nick had gone to his stand from habit. He had welcomed Bruin when the latter ducked inside to escape a shower.
For ten minutes, the two friends had sat in the tiny enclosure, trad-
ing gossip and amiable insults until the rain slackened. It had been
time enough for another migration of body parasites.

On Tuesday Nick had harnessed his lead dog and come to work
with a light fever. On Wednesday he had made the same journey

—now but half-aware of the figures that flowed past his counter. Most of his customers, intent on their own affairs, had not noticed his illness. The few who spoke were dismissed with a jest—for the newsdealer, despite his lot, had an iron will to survive. His endurance had not snapped until midafternoon, when delirium usurped the place of reason, bringing an image of the wife who had loved him, after her fashion, before his blindness.

In those days (before Louella had deserted him), he had owned a candy store in the Bronx, with living quarters behind it. When he harnessed his dog and set out for Valentine Avenue again, he was sure he would find Louella waiting, with shaslik in the oven and a jug of California chianti to erase the day's tediums. A moment later, when he ignored his dog's warning and stepped into the path of a truck, he could see his wife as clearly as though his optic nerve, by some special alchemy, had resumed contact with his brain.

Here too, the ambulance doctor, wary of any sudden death in the streets, had diagnosed bubonic plague. Once more the chilling ritual of decontamination was enacted for hundreds of awed witnesses, until the body vanished in the metal container all ambulances now carried. The story was on every tongue by nightfall, though the papers played it down, backing the mayor's attitude of disaster in control.

Bruin's third target (other than Jasper Merton himself) was Patrolman James Morison, one of the officers assigned to the apartment building where tenants and sanitation workers had joined combat. After the battle Morison had assisted the precinct detectives in their check of the premises, including the repairman's ground-floor apartment, which they had found in a shocking state of untidiness. Patrolman Morison had lingered long enough to handle the bathrobe Bruin had worn to the garbage men's war, and to suggest it be consigned to the incinerator. The repairman, wise in the ways of policemen, had offered Morison a drink to ease the rigors of the dawn patrol. Exposed to infection a good two days before the immunization of the force, Morison had been a marked victim when he departed.

A direct descendant of King Brian Boru, Jim Morison gloried in his service record no less than in his dark good looks. For three full days, he had fought off his illness. His splendid physique had given him reserves of strength to combat the enemy in his blood stream.

Once his defenses were breached, he had gone down with a rush; but even then, the collapse had been mental.

It had occurred in the police lane of the Triborough Bridge. Morison was driving a district captain on a check of the toll booths. Seated in the car while his superior conferred with an attendant, he had felt his mind turn a long cartwheel into the country of his youth. With that painless backflip he was a boy again, en route to a cove on the Liffey where he had once taken a dare and plunged from the top of the highest tree.

The memory picture was compelling. He had driven on to the nearest cable tower, halted traffic with a white-gloved hand, and ascended the ladder to the catwalk. It was a fair substitute for the tree: the tide-roiled waters of Hell Gate had the same gleam as Dublin's river. While traffic snarled below, Jim Morison had thrown off his uniform, hung poised above the flood like a marble Apollo, then plunged cleanly. He was laughing like a boy when his neck snapped on contact.

The urge to flee the present, to relive some treasured experience, are symptoms of most fevers. Historically (as Dr. Eric Stowe's notes would remark later) it is more characteristic of bubonic plague than any other disease. Another symptom is the urge to shed all clothing and run naked through the streets, almost as though the victim anticipated the nakedness of death, in itself a throwback to man's entrance into the world. Patrolman Morrison was not the only New Yorker to succumb to that urge, as fear and fever mounted in parallel patterns.

An hour after the patrolman's dive, in her apartment on Sutton Place, Mrs. Patricia Maltby was sipping her third gin and tonic since lunch, while she awaited a call from her dentist.

An authentic queen in her cosmopolitan heaven, a three-time winner of the Best-dressed Woman award, Pat Maltby was a perfectionist in all things, including her smile. On Monday, she had parted with four of her molars; Dr. Pollard had promised matching bridgework before noon today, and the dentures were late. She had meant to drive to Beachampton early, if only to escape the ridiculous gossip about an epidemic; the journey was unthinkable with a mouth in disrepair.

Despite perfect air conditioning, her apartment seemed stifling this afternoon. With no enemy eyes to judge her, Pat had let herself go completely. Yielding to the cleanliness fetish her analyst had explained to her years ago, she had lunched in her nightgown, showered twice since noon, and wondered why she was still furnace-hot, without a trace of sweat. (Oxen sweat, men perspire and ladies glow, she told herself, and continued pacing the pearl-white rug in her living room.)

The gin had begun to give her a feeling of lightheadedness that was a pleasant contrast to her burning body. Obeying an impulse she would not have admitted to consciousness at another time, she ripped the nightgown from her shoulders. It was a delicious feeling of release to pace the apartment naked, to scold the absent dentist with a gutter eloquence that would have startled the husband awaiting her in Beachampton.

The maid, who spoke only French, came in a moment later to say that Dr. Pollard had phoned at last, to announce the tardy arrival of the dentures. He was awaiting Madame's arrival now in his office.

"*Bien, Denise. Je viendrai, sur-le-champ.*"

"*Comme ça, madame?*"

"*Comme çi, idiote! Pourquoi pas?*"

Mrs. Pat Maltby snatched her purse from the mantel and left her apartment. The maid, frozen in disbelief, made no move to detain her when she entered the automatic elevator. In the lobby, the doorman could only gape in turn. He had often undressed this ice-cold goddess with his eyes. For a split second, he could believe that romance and reality had coincided.

Magnificent in her nudity, America's Best-dressed Woman stalked from the lobby to a nearly empty street. A taxi driver almost wrecked his cab when she waved from the curb. By this time, the doorman (recovering his lost poise) was struggling to wrap her in his coat. The maid was on his heels, adding a babble of French to Mrs. Maltby's fishwife profanity.

It was the taxi driver who first realized what was wrong. "She's got the plague!" he shouted. "Just like that cop who jumped from the Triborough!"

He left the curb in haste, ignoring the red light at the intersection. The apartment manager had already emerged from his maisonette-office. Estimating the situation at a glance, he ordered his secretary to phone for an ambulance. He was careful to stand well apart from the struggle at the curb. It was hardly his fault that doorman and maid, in the performance of their duty, had been touched by the hand of death.

## 4.

Dr. Norris Weaver emerged from the isolation ward on lagging feet and entered a decontamination room to shed his mask and gloves. Even to his tired ears, the hall outside seemed hushed: doctors and attendants, moving on cautious tiptoe, had long since found excuses to avoid this sector of Manhattan Central. His chin lifted at the approach of Eric Stowe, clip-board under arm and eyes alert. The immunologist had been in constant motion that afternoon —checking the statistics of his own domain, keeping in constant touch with the staff workers he had sent into all corners of Manhattan Island. Aware that the news on that clip-board would be bad, the medical chief could not help detaining him.

"What's the latest figure, Doctor?"

Eric glanced at him sharply. Weaver knew he had caught the note of despair under the question.

"We've tripled our morning's admissions."

"You don't seem discouraged," said Weaver. "May I ask why?"

"Contagions often climb sharply at the early stages. The fact's particularly true in plague."

"Do you really think we're ahead of this thing?"

"Just barely, as of now," the immunologist admitted. "Remember, the disease has had a wide-open field since Saturday midnight: *that* crop of victims is now being harvested. Beginning tonight—or tomorrow, at the latest—the bug should hit the wall of resistance we've built up in sensitive areas. If my experience means anything, it will start bouncing back——"

"Suppose you built that wall too late?"

"I'd share your pessimism, Dr. Weaver, if we hadn't caught those first cases when we did. You're right, of course, on one major count. Everything hinges on whether or not their contacts are now firmly pocketed. If the answer's yes, we can finish the job with tomorrow's mass procedure."

"Let me be sure I have the picture." The medical chief was still forcing himself to speak calmly. "Everything we've done so far depends on two suppositions. First, that this outbreak has been sealed off with massive doses of vaccine and streptomycin. Second, that the sulfamerazine you'll administer tomorrow, on a borough-wide basis, will cut off secondary outbreaks, even if the disease has hedgehopped a few barriers——"

"You've stated our case exactly, Dr. Weaver."

"What if those suppositions fail? Suppose the bug has gained more momentum than we realize? What if sulfamerazine won't do a wrap-up job?"

Again Weaver realized that Eric had given him a keen-eyed look. "What's behind these queries, Doctor? Don't hold back."

"I don't like the last three patients admitted to this floor. And there's a fourth case on the outside casualty list that puzzles me for the same reason."

"The policeman who jumped from the Triborough?"

"How did you know?"

Eric checked a name on his clip-board. "A naked man dives in the East River. A Sutton Place beauty walks out of her apartment starko. A professor of physics strips in the manuscript room of the Public Library. A model at the Knitwear Convention does likewise, before a thousand buyers. Are *those* the four you can't understand, Dr. Weaver?"

"Maybe I understand them too well," said the medical chief. "Didn't this happen often in medieval epidemics?"

"It's a matter of record."

"How do you explain the phenomenon?"

"Probably it was the intensity of the fever," said Eric. "Hysteria's a natural side-effect in such cases, like the dancing mania so characteristic of the Dark Ages. At one time, doctors thought plague was caused by tarantuala bites. At least that's the origin of the Italian dance called the *tarantella*."

Weaver knew he was staring; this time he made no attempt to cover his agitation. *The man's a block of ice,* he thought. *How can he speak of word origins at a time like this?* In the same breath, he knew the criticism was unjust. Eric was only striving to look at his task rationally, to remind an associate that he had observed their dilemma from every angle.

"Doesn't this characteristic trouble you a little?"

"I know what you mean, Dr. Weaver. It *is* ominous to find a side-effect turning up again, after a lapse of centuries."

"Couldn't it mean the bacillus is gaining in virulence? Perhaps even returning to a more primitive stage of its history?"

"Because of total lack of immunity in the early stages?"

"Isn't it a reasonable possibility?"

"Yesterday I'd have said no." Eric's voice was grave now. "Today I can only say God help us if you're right."

"When will we know for sure?"

"After the mass prophylaxis tomorrow."

"How long after?"

"Forty-eight hours, Dr. Weaver. If sulfamerazine holds the line, if there are no cases outside present areas, we can assume we've won." Eric smiled again, and resumed his brisk progress down the corridor. "If not, we'll have one consolation—we've done all we can."

5.

In the Merton mansion (the fortress from yesterday that still outfaced every apartment giant around it) *Pasteurella pestis* was fighting an antagonist whose capacity to resist—considering his age and frailty—passed all bounds. That Wednesday the battle was almost won, but the fifth richest man in America had refused to concede.

When he rose from his bed that morning, Jasper Merton had known he was desperately ill. He had turned his back on that knowledge while he drove his secretary through a rigorous vacuum cleaning in his baronial living room. Later, he had browbeaten his lawyers in a series of phone calls that grew more heated as the day advanced.

Shortly after noon, a senior partner from the law firm arrived with papers dissolving the Merton Project and a hastily prepared report of means available to divert funds from the support of Manhattan Central Hospital. The lawyer ventured to remind Merton that such action would be contested in court. Refusing to hear a word, the old man had ripped the papers to bits, and ordered that a new severance be drawn in even stronger terms.

Merton had insisted the new documents be delivered by morning. The lawyer had refused to make such a promise. His office, he explained, had only a skeleton staff, and it was being said that all business would cease tomorrow, by order of City Hall. The lawyer himself intended to retire to his home in Far Hills, where he would sit out the emergency now confronting New York. He strongly advised the philanthropist to do likewise.

All that morning, Merton had fumed helplessly at his failure to reach Selden Grove. When the director of Manhattan Central appeared in person (a half-hour after the lawyer's departure) Merton had regained his sense of proportion. No lawyer, he admitted sourly, could accomplish miracles; the actual severance could wait. Meanwhile he could tell Grove the axe was falling. Once he had reached this decision, he settled in his throne-chair and waved his favorite antagonist to a seat. Despite a throbbing head, he expected to enjoy the next few minutes thoroughly.

"It's time for my midday whisky, Boles," he barked. "Bring the siphon and leave us. Will you join me, Doctor?"

"Alcohol won't mix with the afternoon I'm facing."

Merton shot a malevolent look at the visitor. Grove seemed on the brink of exhaustion. The blow he was about to administer, he reflected, would be all the more shattering.

"Why don't you answer your phone?" he demanded. "I've been trying to reach you since breakfast."

"If you've kept up with the news, sir, you'll know I've been a fairly busy man."

The philanthropist downed a two-ounce glass of scotch, and poured another. It was a jolt his brain needed badly.

"Do I have to remind you my calls take precedence over other duties?"

"Mr. Merton, New York is in the throes of an epidemic. Hasn't the fact sunk home?"

"Of course it has. Yesterday I said the medical profession was responsible. Now I'm repeating the charge. As one of the bellwethers of your trade, you should pay the penalty."

The director got to his feet, resting both hands on the desk. "I'm not here to take your abuse," he said heavily. "It's time I can ill afford—even in your welfare."

"Since when has my welfare concerned you?"

"It's my duty. After all, my hospital owes you a great deal——"

"I'm glad you realize *that* at last."

"Stop baiting me and listen! Beginning at eight tonight, the mayor is cutting Manhattan off from the mainland. The announcement will be made after the commuter rush is over. It seemed only fair to give you warning. I've asked your chauffeur to stand by, in case you wish to leave at once."

"I've never been sick in my life, Grove. Besides, plague's a poor man's disease. How can it reach me?"

"Cases have been reported all over the city. I've brought a special permit. Once you've had medical clearance, you can go at any time."

"I've no intention of leaving New York until I've settled a certain matter with my lawyers."

"Believe me, tomorrow will be too late."

"Are you suggesting a pipsqueak politician like John Newman can coop me on Manhattan Island?"

"If you insist, you may stay on—and submit to inoculation, like any other citizen. Considering your age and infirmity, you'd be wiser to go now."

"I'm neither aged nor infirm." Jasper Merton's frail fist had banged the desk top as he spoke. "What's your game, doctor? To keep me from dying until you've milked my last dollar? We're parting company, the moment my numbskull lawyers file the papers. Not only am I scrapping the Merton Project, I'm withdrawing our funds from the hospital."

"May I ask your reasons?"

"I expect my bequests to show results. For six months, the project's been stalled by hooligans. Now you say a pestilence is threatening the whole city. A man who lets such things happen to New York doesn't rate a dime in philanthropy."

"Do you call that a fair estimate?"

Merton continued to study the hospital head wrathfully. He had expected cringing, or a flash of anger—anything but aloof calm.

"Is this all you have to say? Your record's on the line, man. Defend it!"

"My record will stand up to any inquiry from your trustees," said Selden Grove. "I won't deny your money is your own——"

"You're damned right it's mine. If I like, I can have it buried with me."

"Not if it's Foundation money, and your board thinks differently. Even if you're blind enough to wreck the project, Manhattan Central won't be allowed to go under. Not when it's proved its worth in this epidemic——"

"I'll do as I like, damn you. Don't think I'll take advice from my own board."

"They won't permit you to welsh. When you're rational again, you'll remember your duty to this city—and the country it serves."

"So I'm out of my head today. Is that what you're hinting?"

"I think you're an extremely sick man," said Selden Grove. "Unfortunately, I can hardly treat you against your will. Besides, I've other patients to think about."

The director of Manhattan Central departed with that pronouncement, leaving Merton fixed behind the desk. Something in their meeting had gone awry. His reeling brain could not pin down the cause of his failure.

He opened his mouth to bellow, but only a creak emerged as he fell back in his chair. Selden Grove had called him infirm to his face. Was his mind really failing, along with his body? Could his double-damned trustees declare him incompetent at last?

The pressure behind his eyes was intolerable, until he soothed it with another double whisky. When his secretary ghosted into the room with a final paper to sign, he scrawled his name across the neatly typed sheet without even glancing at the insulting dance of the words. Boles, he reflected, was a perfect amanuensis. There was no need to peruse what he had apparently dictated in a mental hiatus.

"That quack says I'm ill. Is he right for once?"

"If you'll remember, Mr. Merton, I suggested you see a doctor yesterday."

"Doctors are all fakes, Boles. I never trusted one of 'em." The old man dashed a hand across his eyes, to dispel a fast-rising mist. "Still, I *could* stand a checkup. Call my regular man. I'll let him examine me."

"I'm afraid you're a bit beyond doctors," said the secretary.

"Get on that phone! D'you want me to die?"

"Why not?" said Boles. "You've outlived your usefulness."

Secretary and employer faced one another for an oddly impassive moment. Groping for the remnants of his anger, Jasper Merton found it no longer existed. Once the incredible words were out, Boles's remark seemed quite reasonable.

"You've always hated me, haven't you?"

"Indeed yes, sir. Haven't you deserved it?"

"Never mind the doctor," said Merton thickly. "I'll cure myself, once I've left this damned town. Is Jenkins parked outside?"

Boles was standing before the desk, an impassive caricature of the secretary, hands folded on his notebook, eyes modestly lowered. Merton stared hard to bring the fellow into focus. Perhaps he had only imagined those last words.

"Answer me, you blockhead!"

"Jenkins is parked at the curb, sir."

"Get my hat. I'm leaving now. You can follow later with my things."

Boles had not stirred, but his lackey's manner was still beyond reproach. "I'm afraid leaving is out of the question, Mr. Merton."

"Who'd dare to stop me? Grove said I could go when I liked."

"Not without a doctor's permit," said the secretary, with the same reverent politeness. "Dr. Grove was prepared to examine you himself. It was the purpose of his visit. Naturally he realized he couldn't pass you—"

"Why not?"

"Because you're dying—of bubonic plague."

Jasper Merton rose from his chair, flailing one arm in an imperial gesture of dismissal. Never before had the flick of his hand failed to banish all arguments. Today his secretary was in his path when he tried to leave the desk. Without quite knowing how, Merton realized that Boles had shoved him back into the throne-chair.

The philanthropist made other attempts to rise in the next quarter-hour. Each effort was feebler than the last. Even now, he could not believe the obstacle was real; Boles would surely vanish when he made his next try for the door . . . His lassitude ended as abruptly as it had bemused him. Lifting his voice in a great shout, Jasper Merton swayed free of the desk, with both fists raised to strike. As he had expected, the secretary had disappeared.

Three strides would have taken him to the hall. Instead, he found himself falling into a sea of cotton wool. With the first immersion, he knew he would never rise again.

6.

Boles, who had withdrawn to the far wall, stepped forward calmly after his master had tumbled to the carpet. Without haste, he sat down in the throne-chair to reread the last paper Jasper Merton had signed. It was a note to his lawyer (presumably dictated to his faithful secretary) apologizing for a burst of bad temper he blamed on illness. It also advised the lawyer of a change of heart. The schedule of donations to both Manhattan Central and the Merton Project were to be maintained, according to the present wishes of the Foundation.

Boles, chuckling at a joke he could share with no one, folded the note into an envelope and left the library. At the curb outside, he wakened Merton's dozing chauffeur, ordered the man to deliver the note to the lawyer's office, then dismissed him for the day.

When he returned to the house, he moved slowly, as though he relished each cat-quiet footfall. Back in the library, he seized his employer's knee and shoulder and rolled him on his back. Death, he saw, had struck with lightning force. He resented the efficiency of the rod-shaped bacillus; he would have enjoyed prolonging the game.

In the end, he contented himself with transferring Merton's black-pearl stickpin to his own modest cravat. Almost as an after-thought, he removed most of the ten thousand dollars his employer always carried in his wallet, and slipped the best of his rings on his own finger. Then he picked up the phone to call Selden Grove.

## 7.

Just after seven-thirty, John Newman sat down in the tower studio of New York's own television station. He had arrived well in advance of the broadcast, to rehearse the mechanics of the program, which required split-second timing for its pickups. Now he had snatched these few moments to meditate alone.

A last-minute medical summary lay on the microphone table beside the manuscript of his broadcast; despite his promise of complete candor, he could hardly read those numbing statistics to the people of Manhattan. So far, Eric and his teams had identified al-most a thousand cases of plague. More than nine hundred doubtfuls were thought to be an early form of the disease. These were under observation, but not yet completely diagnosed.

This vast increase of patients—building like wildfire during the day—was graphic proof of the impact of *Pasteurella pestis*. Eric had said the disease was at its crest, that it would ebb tomorrow if tonight's sabotage could be held to a minimum. What if Eric was mistaken?

These patients, at least, were safely out of circulation, in dozens of hospital and overflow wards. A still unknown factor was the number who harbored the germ at this moment, with only minor symptoms. Such carriers were the real danger. They above all were the ones Eric hoped to catch with mass prophylaxis.

The city's present supply of sulfamerazine—the drug that had finally been chosen for tomorrow's distribution—had been barely enough to furnish outgoing commuters with their required dosages. By midnight, there would be almost none of it in the city. A few cartons might arrive by truck or plane. No real quantity would be available until the docking of the *Admiral Beattie*.

It had been a hard decision, the mayor reflected, to package current stock for the commuters, and to rely on the freighter's cargo for tomorrow. Yet Eric had insisted all departing workers be protected, and the order had been sound. With its unequaled hospital facilities, its fine public health and police departments, Manhattan could discover cases and treat them far more decisively than any of its outlying communities. It would have been just short of murder to release tonight's commuting army without such help, even if only a few had become unwitting hosts. Future office seekers would learn of the decision and use it against him, but John Newman did not care.

He lifted from his musings to look down on his city. The studio had a picture window in its south wall; his spirits lifted, as always, at that heart-stopping view of New York. Dusk was falling in the canyons below him. Trouble would come there with dark, as he well knew; it was all that other, no less malignant enemy needed to resume his work . . . Perhaps, with his last order given, he was already celebrating the triumph he so confidently expected.

A desk phone rang softly. It was the final report from police and Health Department details in charge of the commuter program. The mayor had suspected no serious trouble in that quarter, and the report confirmed his judgment.

The lemming-like migrations to and from the city were conditioned by tribal habits far stronger than mere catastrophe. Even with the staggering of trains and car pools, the slowdowns at terminals and bridges (where the booths had been set up to dispense the three-dose program of sulfamerazine), there had been no major dislocations. Now with the clock ticking toward eight, the tide was outward bound.

Since noon the broadcasts had hammered at the fact an important announcement from the mayor would come at this hour. By now, even the more remote suburbanites would be home, save for tipplers in the station bars. (There would be few such inbibers tonight. Long before morning, every tavern on Manhattan would be closed by the police.)

Inevitably, there had been flare-ups of violence. Fearful cliff dwellers (who had read disaster in the sky, and sought to escape in their own cars) had been turned back by the hundreds once their license plates identified them. Carloads of hoodlums, also masquerading as commuters, had been arrested at bridge and tunnel, with trunkloads of aspirin tablets labeled as sulfamerazine and streptomycin.

Similar arrests had been made at other points, as the city's criminal element sought to cash in on evil rumors. They had been unexpected dividends of the epidemic.

Downtown, where the privileged had ways of hearing news in advance, word had gone out that the Stock Exchange would be closed tomorrow. After the death of Russell Harrington, there had been a steady migration of Wall Street personnel, forcing the Port Authority Heliport to triple its scheduled flights.

Families starting on long-planned vacations had found themselves in a strange dilemma. It was already said that holiday spots were looking with jaundiced eyes on visitors from New York. Many had canceled reservations outright. Now, with their means of transport throttled, most would-be vacationers had bowed to their lot. New Yorkers had always had confidence in the effectiveness of their medical facilities. Accepting their pills, most holiday families had gone back to their apartments, prepared to sit out the emergency—and to await the mayor's broadcast.

Leafing through the manuscript of that broadcast, John Newman looked down again on the familiar pattern of city lights. He knew this town and its people. Had the buildings below him been transparent, he could not have visualized their occupants more clearly. . . .

On Grand Street, an old Jew would be rocking before his television. (The man could have been Newman's father, a Talmudic scholar who had endured his trials, like his poverty, with quiet courage.) In his youth, he had seen plague in ghettos abroad; unlike many troubled souls tonight, he could picture its horrors clearly. Here in New York, he'd been told, there was now a way of stopping this ancient sickness, a way the mayor and the doctors were about to review for the people. For himself, he was not too concerned (death can be a friend at eighty, a companion for one's last long journey). He would listen to the eight o'clock broadcast for the children's sake. He would insist they obey the doctors' orders; in this land you obeyed those who served you.

His daughter had been almost hysterical when she called from Stamford, telling of the tablets given to her husband at the gates in Grand Central. She had urged her sister, grandfather, and the children to join her in Connecticut, but the old man had refused to budge. He had always felt safe in New York, even at the beginning, when life had been hardest. In fifty years, he'd been outside the city just once, to attend the *bar mitzvah* of his first grandson. He wasn't leaving tonight, not when Mayor Newman was about to appear on TV.

In tenement flats, in furnished rooms, in apartments filled with the world's loot, still other listeners waited at their screens. Earlier broadcasts had said the mayor's speech would give them an assurance that would destroy the urge to flee. Aware of his terrible responsibility John Newman felt a sudden resentment at its weight. It was too much to ask of any man. Not even the people who had elected him had the right to demand he assume it. Yet even as his temper flared, he knew he could not shift his burden.

His anger receded along with his icy apprehension when he moved to the window for a closer view of those lights. New Yorkers had stood up to other threats and survived. They'd do it again. The response to the measures he had taken so far had proved their courage. There must be no surrender with that other adversary at large.

The studio door opened, to admit the program director. A battery of lights had begun to wink on in the control room.

"Five minutes to air time, Mr. Mayor."

"I'm ready if you are."

"If you'll just sit at the desk, sir, we'll check the line-up of the cameras."

John Newman settled in the converging glare of floodlights, and turned the first page of the manuscript. He was completely calm now, serene in the knowledge that his people trusted him. He would be worthy of that trust.

"One minute to air time, Mr. Mayor. The first take will be Camera One, right in front of you."

Newman nodded. The sweep hand of the clock over the glass-walled control booth seemed to move with glacial slowness. On the monitors below the booth, he could see his multiple image as he sat at the desk, but it was nothing like seeing one's self in a mirror. In a few seconds, millions of television and radio sets, from the core of Manhattan to the far reaches of exurbia, would pick up his image, his voice, or both.

The director's hand swept down as the light on Camera One blinked red.

"Fellow New Yorkers, this is your mayor——"

Newman heard his voice as if from a distance. On the monitor screens, his own likeness waited sternly—a dark-haired, unhandsome man whose eyes burned with purpose. There was no hesitation in his tone after that first pause.

"Tonight, our homeward-bound commuters were given packets of drugs to protect them against plague. The disease, as you already know, has invaded New York. It is still firmly controlled. However, the first purpose of this broadcast, which is beamed to reach every commuting town that serves Manhattan Island, is to order commuters *not* to return unless their work belongs in vital categories which I will outline later.

"This order is issued for their protection, and for the protection of those living on Manhattan Island. Until further notice, it has become necessary to isolate that island, not only from the other boroughs of New York, but from this country and the world. Our quarantine is part of the procedure we have called Operation Epidemic.

"Yesterday, I told you that Dr. Eric Stowe had been placed in complete charge of this program. He is a world authority on the disease we are fighting. From the first sign of the outbreak, he has taken stern measures to control it. Dr. Stowe is now in his laboratory at Manhattan Central Hospital. He will identify our enemy, and explain its weaknesses and its strengths."

Camera One winked out for the hospital pickup. With no visible hiatus, Eric appeared on the monitor screen before Newman's desk. The immunologist was seated at his work table in pathology. In the background, the viewer could see the controlled bustle of the laboratory.

"Your mayor has just told you of the threat we all are facing," said Eric. He spoke in measured terms, with the obvious certainty that his message would be accepted—and understood. "To save you and our city we must attack this germ with every weapon at our disposal. The major weapon is not in the test tubes before me. Nor will you find it in the great hospital of which my laboratory is a part. The weapon that will destroy the bacillus of plague is truth.

"It is true that New York has been attacked by a malignant sickness rarely seen in this part of the world. It is true that its inroads have been serious—though I am confident the case-load has passed its peak. It is *not* true, as some would have you believe, that we are helpless before it.

"Plague is a disease whose symptoms and course are well known. It is caused by a germ that can easily be identified. This bacillus is transferred from person to person in two ways. One is by direct contact—breathed out from the lungs of those infected. This form of plague closely resembles pneumonia.

"The other form of plague is transmitted by means of fleas, harbored on rats dying from the disease. We are fighting it by destroying both vectors. Our rat-control program will be described to you in a moment by Health Commissioner Thurlow.

"Let me repeat: we are facing a sickness whose cause, whose manner of spread, and whose cure are all well known. I have fought such epidemics in other parts of the world. I give you my absolute assurance that, if you obey instructions, the present epidemic can be turned back in New York—probably within forty-eight hours.

"Vaccines against plague do not always protect in present conditions. Therefore you cannot rely absolutely on such protection, even though you may have been vaccinated for travel in the Far East. We plan to use vaccine mainly to safeguard those who will be continuing our rat-control program in the next several weeks, to guard against any possible flare-up. For the same reason, it has been given to all hospital and city-service personnel.

"Unfortunately it takes time for immunity to develop after the injection of vaccine. Frankly, we cannot afford to wait. Tomorrow, therefore, we are instituting a somewhat different program, which will afford immediate protection to all of you.

"Plague can be treated effectively with some of the so-called 'wonder drugs.' It can also be prevented by a few doses of a special sulfa drug, called sulfamerazine, which is widely available. By midnight tomorrow, everyone on the island of Manhattan will be given this drug in sufficient quantity to complete the protective treatment or prophylaxis.

"Your Health Department is setting up dispensaries for this drug all over Manhattan; tomorrow, a shipload is arriving at a North River pier. Starting in the early evening, you will line up at these dispensaries, under police protection, to obtain it. Until that time, we are asking you to follow certain basic precautions to hold further infection to a minimum:

"If you have no legitimate reason to be out, remain in your homes until it is time to proceed to the station nearest you.

"Do not heed rumors. What I have told you is the truth.

"If you must go into the streets, wear a mask covering nose and mouth. The handkerchief variety will do.

"Stay away from all public places—unless you are engaged in an essential occupation, which the mayor will list for you. In such cases, provision will be made for you to receive the drug when you report for work.

"If you develop a fever, a cough, or an unusual swelling about your body, consult a physician or go to a hospital clinic at once. Emergency hospital facilities await you. If you are really ill, you will receive prompt treatment.

"Finally, remember that you have been told the truth about this danger and how it is being fought. Panic will only hamper us all. Panic that gets out of hand could prove fatal to our whole program. Have faith in authority: do as you are told."

The director in the studio had given John Newman his signal. He was ready when the red light winked on again.

"You have heard Dr. Stowe identify the disease we are fighting and his techniques for controlling it. Our health commissioner, Dr. Thurlow, will now discuss the functions of his department in this program."

Dr. Thurlow's rotund visage beamed with confidence on the monitor, as he described the rat-catching program and his method of isolating and protecting all contacts with known cases. He repeated Eric's warning against public assembly. From him, the scene switched to Police Commissioner Decker, who promised that his department would forestall any attempt to subvert tomorrow's drug distribution. Citizens were warned again to ignore rumors, to stand firm against mass fear, and to make no attempt to leave the city without authorization.

As Decker's face vanished from the monitor, Camera One picked up John Newman for his summary. His voice was solemn as he hammered home his final warnings.

"You who live on Manhattan Island are better off in your present abodes. It would be infinitely more risky to attempt to leave and fall ill among strangers. Here you will receive proven medication against plague. If you are already ill, you have the best of care. Nothing will be gained by attempted flight. You will only be turned back, unless you have a good and sufficient reason for departing.

"Beginning at this moment, only certain vehicles will be allowed to enter or leave Manhattan. These include trucks, trains, cars, and buses bringing medical personnel or necessary supplies, physicians, and all diplomatic staffs at the United Nations. Such persons have already been immunized—including UN personnel.

"As Dr. Stowe has told you, all vital categories in our work force will be asked to report for assignment tomorrow. Others will be granted a holiday until further notice. The police have a list of these categories. If you belong to one of them, you may leave your homes—and if need be, Manhattan Island as well—but only after you have received necessary protection.

"Among such workers are processors and distributors in our food centers, local food merchants, radio and television personnel, newspaper employees, surface-transportation drivers and maintenance men, hotel staffs and Red Cross staffs and volunteers.

"In order that you may know where to obtain protection tomorrow evening, I am listing the principal distribution centers for each section of Manhattan. They will be repeated on hourly broadcasts. Newspapers will carry maps, so please report to your proper station. Only in this way can we avoid confusion and overcrowding.

"Battery Park will serve our new apartment units downtown. Washington Square will handle Greenwich Village and its environs. Union Square and Times Square will be centers for midtown Manhattan. Central Park's Sheep Meadow and Carl Schurz Park will serve both East and West Sides. Booths will be set up on the campuses of Columbia and City Colleges for Morningside and Washington Heights. Mount Morris Park and the Polo Grounds will serve Harlem and Northeast Manhattan. Each of these centers, of course, will have its own substations. Proceed to the one nearest your home. Police will be on hand at all intersections to save you steps——"

John Newman had been marking out the various spots on a wall map of Manhattan. Now he turned to face the camera:

"No one of you need walk more than a few blocks to find his proper dispensary. In the circumstances, we can permit no traffic on the streets tomorrow, save for police cars and ambulances. No one will be left out. There will be ample time for distribution, and ample supplies. Later, you will be notified when it will be safe to return to your usual places of employment. We hope to have our subways running again by the weekend."

The mayor moved to his desk and seated himself before the center microphone. "All of us are proud that New York can claim to be the most modern city in the world. This is our chance to prove that New York also has character, a stern purpose, and the basic solidity to justify that claim. Those who serve the city have already risen to the challenge. Now it is your turn to show that you can help, no less courageously, to complete Operation Epidemic.

"Citizens of Manhattan Island, you have received your marching orders. Whether this battle succeeds or fails depends on you and you alone."

The red light winked off, and Newman felt himself slump in his place. While he was on the air, he had forgotten his weariness. The need to reach his audience, to make the emergency real, had driven him outside himself. Now it was over, he scarcely had the strength to move.

His eyes lifted when the program director appeared at his elbow with a scalding cup of coffee.

"A great broadcast, Mr. Mayor. It's bound to send them."

Newman found he was smiling through his exhaustion. It was like this high priest of television to think in his special argot, while the fate of a city hung in the balance.

"I hope you're right," he said. "Remember you're to repeat those instructions every hour."

"We'll do better than that, sir. I video-taped the whole show while it was going out——"

The director looked up quickly, as an unaccustomed sound reached them from the street below. At this height, it resembled the spiteful chatter of firecrackers. Even before the louder, deeper *whoom* of an exploding bomb drifted skyward, John Newman knew it was gunfire.

"Operation Saboteur is sharp on cue tonight," he said. He moved to the window and threw it wide, just as the first gush of red lifted like a banner against the sky.

# 6.  Thursday

DETECTIVE-Inspector Dalton had roamed the battle lines all night long, to test the city's pulse. By midnight he had felt the balance shifting, but it was after dawn before he risked using his car radiophone to reach the mayor.

"I've just talked with the commissioner," said John Newman. His voice, Pete noted, was tired but resolute. "Thanks for a hard night's work."

"You have the latest news, then?"

"Just about. I gather all fires are in control."

"Since four o'clock, John. There were nine gutted tenements. The same for the First Avenue car barns and the Midtown lofts. The rest was more smoke than damage."

"What about looting?"

"This time we were ready. They broke up fast, when they saw they were outnumbered."

"Any arrests that make sense?"

Dalton sighed: he was prepared for the question. "The usual psychos, of course. A few old pros—the sort who heave bricks for a price. Nothing that adds up."

"They won't name names?"

"They *can't*, John. Let's cover that angle when we meet."

"I'm heading for Manhattan Central now," said the mayor. "Suppose we meet there and settle things with Eric."

Pete Dalton felt his heart leap. "Does this mean you'll back me?"

"Wouldn't you say it's time?"

The inspector had called from Central Park, where he had been checking arrests. Instructing his driver to proceed slowly, he opened the car radio on the six o'clock newscast. Despite the knowledge that John Newman would support the ruse he had planned for tonight, he was not quite prepared to face Eric Stowe.

The announcer's voice was assured. Listening with divided attention, Pete knew the report he was making to millions of fearful citizens was entirely accurate.

The riots that had swept the borough last night (said the announcer) were now firmly checked. So were the fires that had lighted the night-long turmoil. Several tenements had been destroyed, but most of the occupants had escaped in time. Elsewhere the arsonists had done their work in storage lofts and buildings marked for razing; each blaze had been part of a pattern, designed to stir terror at the bottom of the city's economic ladder. Less than a dozen lives had been lost in this phase of Operation Saboteur. Most casualties had been confined to the Fire Department, whose performance had been outstanding.

Most of the rioting had occurred in slum areas: in every case, the overriding motive was flight. At first the uproar had seemed spontaneous. Later the police had proved beyond question that those human stampedes had been led by rumormongers. Except for a scattering of habitual criminals, the rioters had been ill-armed, but casualties on the field of battle (it was not too strong a term, said the announcer) had been heavy. Total fatalities were over fifty—actual figures would be given when the dead were counted. Nearly all the casualties were dupes of the agitators, who had faded from the scene when the odds turned against them.

An hour before midnight, it had seemed possible that a few thousand crazed tenement dwellers, convinced the air they breathed was poison, would lead a wholesale exodus from the city. In the end, not one of the rioters had reached bridge or tunnel. By early morning, each fainthearted group had been fragmented by the police. Finally they had hearkened to the loud-speakers repeating the mayor's proclamation from each street-corner. By dawn, sober second counsels had prevailed. Most of the would-be escapees had now returned to their homes.

This morning—said the announcer, with a new note of cheer— the Canadian freighter *Admiral Beattie* (diverted from her voyage to the Orient) would dock at her North River pier, with a full cargo of drugs and vaccines—more than enough to fulfil the mayor's promised program of borough-wide prophylaxis. A schedule of distribution would be announced on the eight o'clock newscast, and repeated at hourly intervals thereafter. Last night's rioters, as well as the good citizens who had stayed behind locked doors, were counseled to remain at home, until they received their instructions.

## 2.

The detective cut off his radio. The broadcast had been a model of its kind. No gloss had been applied to stark fact, nor had the announcer pretended the situation was less than perilous. There had been one significant omission. The mind behind last night's terror had gone unmentioned, since the police themselves had yet to name it.

The basic story remained a true one. Since the demolition of the power stations, organized violence had stalked the streets by dark; New Yorkers were now aware of its presence in their midst. Last night, with a few thousand crazed exceptions, the people had held their ground. Would they stand firm when the enemy struck again?

"Park a minute," said the detective. "Let me finish my notes."

It was pure subterfuge, but he continued to write busily in his book after the prowl car had halted on Forty-second Street. The gamble he contemplated was stupendous; a city's life would be the pawn. It was a plan he could never capture in notes. How could he find words to sell it to Eric Stowe?

Pete lifted his eyes from his jottings when he realized the young sergeant at the wheel was studying him covertly. The scene outside the car window, he told himself, suited his mood of indecision. Forty-second Street had always been blank-faced at dawn. This morning, stained by the smog that had followed the borough-wide fires, it seemed dead beyond recall.

Here and there on Manhattan Island, the detective knew, presses still turned, milk trucks discharged their freight, and ambulances sped on their errands of mercy. From this viewpoint, the city seemed barren as a lunar landscape, filled with the same hypnotic charm. Its worst features, at this moment, were its absolute silence, the total absence of motion. The dance of papers above a litter basket—a witches' saraband in the faint morning breeze—was the only counterfeit of life.

"Tell me, Ed. Does this remind you of anything?"

"Can't say it does, Inspector."

"I'm thinking of a movie called *On the Beach*," said Pete. "It was quite a hit, back in '60 or thereabouts. Don't pretend you're too young to remember."

"What was it about, sir?"

"The end of the world. Man had just breathed his last in atomic fallout. The finale showed what was left. It wasn't too different from now."

"Only *we're* still holding the fort, aren't we?"

"We held it last night, Ed. This is another day."

"Won't folks stop rampaging when they get their pills?"

"I wish I knew," said Pete Dalton, and snapped his notebook shut. "Hit the Drive, will you? I've a date with the mayor."

At the hospital, Inspector Dalton learned that Newman had closeted himself in the director's office, to talk long-distance with Washington. The argument had grown hectic, to judge by the voice behind the sanctum door. Pete knew the mayor was still refusing to ask for disaster status.

Selden Grove's secretary, still poised after a sleepless night, had greeted the visitor with her usual smile.

"How does it feel to know you're still alive, Inspector?"

"Right now I wouldn't risk an answer," said Pete. "Is Dr. Stowe available?"

"He's in O. R. Seven, but you'll have to wait outside. The patient has plague."

"And they're *operating?*"

"It's the weirdest thing you ever heard of. An old Japanese art dealer who knew enough to recognize the disease—and decided to commit hara-kiri. Actually it's only a mild case of bubonic. They hope to pull him through."

"Can Dr. Stowe assist in surgery?"

"Dr. Trent is conducting the operation, Inspector. Dr. Stowe was anxious to study side-effects inside the body. He's gone up to watch them repair the damage."

Pete sighed deeply. "If Dr. Trent doesn't mind, I'll watch too. It's just what I need to begin my day."

Though he had spoken lightly, the words were true enough; Pete Dalton was a layman whose curiosity about surgical processes was intense. He could hardly admit to the director's secretary that he was also a veteran observer of the ways of suicide. Secretly, he was wondering what a hara-kiri victim looked like, after he failed to complete that act of self-destruction.

When Pete settled in the last tier of the observation gallery, the scene behind the glass partition was proof that the art of healing was still practiced, despite last night's savagery. Bob Trent seemed totally engrossed in the work before him. The slender figure at his elbow was Eve Bronson. Eric, also in full surgical costume, was acting as second assistant. Even Dalton's untutored eyes could see the reason for his presence. Here, after all, was another face of the enemy he was fighting.

Operative techniques were routine, so there were no other spectators in the gallery. The microphone still hung low above the table. By straining his ears Pete could pick up the low-voiced comments as the work neared completion.

"Another inch, and he'd have severed the main mesenteric branch."

"Is it safe to look around a bit?"

"Explore all you like," said Bob. "I've caught the hemorrhage, and we're flooding him with tetracyclines. He's getting the best possible chance."

"Let's check the color of the liver."

A retractor shifted in the massive wound, giving Pete a glimpse of a blue, shiny organ high up in the incision.

"Vessels and ducts are a bit discolored," said Bob. "Nothing too serious, so far——"

The retractor moved down the extensive transverse cut. The watcher in the gallery (leaning far forward to understand what he could) saw that the surgeon had followed the hara-kiri wound in making his own incision. He had read that it was traditional to open the abdomen in this drastic fashion.

"Spleen's in much the same condition," said Bob. "Did you expect nodules?"

"Not really. Most deaths are toxic in this form of plague. Can we check the abdominal lymph nodes?"

"Service with a smile, Dr. Stowe," said Bob. The retractor moved again. "*They're* enlarged, all right. You'd expect that, I gather—with a tendency toward buboes?"

"Adenopathy is usually general—except in fulminating pneumonic cases."

"Want to go still lower?"

"No, Bob. I'll return to my service, if I'm not needed for the closure. Thanks for the view."

"Thanks for assisting," said the surgical chief. "For a public-health man, you did right well."

"I'll accept the accolade," said Eric. "I try to keep my hand in."

He broke free of the circle with the words, to vanish through the door to the scrub room. The observer in the gallery—sorting the jargon he had heard—found he had grasped the essential meaning. A life had been saved as he watched, and a footnote had been added to the record of man's endless search for knowledge. While his understanding lasted, Detective-Inspector Dalton found he was envying these men in white with all his heart.

"Shall we talk now, Pete, or wait for Eric?"

Dalton turned from the scene below. With no real surprise, he saw that the mayor had settled on a bench in the next row.

"I'd rather wait—unless you want the story twice."

"*We're* in agreement," said the mayor. "This is Eric's decision, not ours. He's in charge, remember?"

"All too well," said Pete. "The argument's academic. Here he comes now."

The immunologist had just entered the gallery by the stair reserved for hospital personnel. In a freshly laundered lab coat, he seemed oddly aloof from the operation Dalton had just witnessed.

"I *thought* we had an audience," said Eric. "Sorry I couldn't be sure—we'd have given a sharper performance."

"Can we talk here?" asked Newman.

"The terrace is better; this gallery will be jammed with interns in another moment. I'm told something serious is moving in."

"Even today?"

"Medical science is a continuing process—and interns are made, not born. They learn when and where they can."

Thanks to the gentle breeze, the smog that blanketed midtown Manhattan had missed the hospital cliffs. For a moment, the three men moved to the terrace rail without speaking. From this vantage point, it was hard for Pete to believe the city's very existence had been in jeopardy last midnight.

The mayor spoke first; his voice was constrained, as though he disliked the silence, yet was reluctant to break it.

"Have you caught the late bulletins, Eric?"

"I heard the essentials."

"Here's a recap, for the record," said Pete. "Last night was touch and go, but we held our own. Whoever blew the whistle thought we'd panic in depth after the mayor's eight o'clock broadcast. The hope failed, because that broadcast made sense to most good citizens. *They* stayed at home, and waited for their orders. Do we agree so far?"

"Of course," said Eric. His eyes were still on the downtown towers.

"Suppose Operation Saboteur really goes into high gear tonight? Would you kill it if you could?"

"Need you ask?"

"I think we can stop them, Eric. With luck, we may even collar their leader. Unfortunately, it's a job I can't finish alone. I'll need your help too."

"What more can the hospital do, Pete?"

"You've worked behind the Curtains—Iron and Bamboo." The detective was warming to his theme. "You know how this sort of cabal operates. The setup's old as the first spy ring. A head man calls the signals. He has perfect cover, and takes no part in the sabotage. Except for a few key operators, the chain of command doesn't even know his name. To his shock troops, he's only a paymaster to offer big wages. That's why the street bullies we've nailed so far can tell us nothing."

"Where does young Lemayo stand in the chain?"

"I'd call him key man for his group."

"Is he under observation?"

"We've lost his trail completely." Pete held up a detaining palm. "I'm blaming no one for that. The Dukes are old hands at lying doggo. My guess is they're waiting for the big push tonight."

"Do you think Juan could name his leader?"

"Yes, Eric. We all agree, I take it, that such a man exists?"

"I believed that from the start, Pete."

"D'you see why he's forced to hit us again, before you can distribute your drugs? Cornering Lemayo isn't a solution; even if he can identify his boss, he won't talk. Somehow, I've got to anticipate this last big strike and smother it."

"Suppose they raid the *Admiral Beattie* after she docks?"

"They'd like nothing better, if they could swing it—but I don't think they'll go all-out at the pier. Their head man isn't that stupid: he knows we'll be defending that freighter in depth. Naturally, he'll try hit-and-run tactics——"

Eric turned to Newman. "Are you going to let people assemble on the water front?"

"The whole borough has been told we're unloading drugs and vaccine," said the mayor. "We've got to let them see we aren't lying about that shipment. How else can we set the stage for tonight?"

"Set the stage?"

Pete cut in quickly. "Let's assume I'm right, all down the line. Let's say they threaten us at the pier, and pull back, when they see we'll hold our lines. For my money, that means the all-out blow will come tonight. When our defenses are spread thin, to cover drug depots all over Manhattan——"

"Are you suggesting we *invite* attacks on those booths?"

"We already have, Eric. With your own Times Square command post the number one target."

"Do you expect me to use medical personnel as decoys?"

"At this late date, can you back down?"

Eric did not speak for a moment. When he did, Pete saw he had won his argument—simply by stressing the alternative.

"Just what is your strategy?"

"I'm passing the word that we'll need every man to guard the streets tonight. With his pipelines, the enemy's bound to pick up the order. The subways are dead. We'll pull out trackwalkers and platform guards—make them a perfect short cut to Times Square and other key points. Meanwhile, I'll ghost in plainclothesmen everywhere. By six tonight, I'll have three thousand men waiting. We'll be ready for infiltration, when the lines form at the booths—"

Eric broke in heatedly. "It's risky enough, having people assemble for mass medication. I'm taking that risk because our situation's desperate. Now you're asking both patients and doctors to serve as sitting ducks, so you can crack a gang of terrorists. It's a pretty tall order."

"It isn't an order," said the detective patiently. "It's a logical battle plan. If you called off your program now—or even changed its timing—you'd stir up genuine panic. The sort of chain reaction we'd never control."

"Do you endorse this scheme, John?"

"I'm afraid it's the only way," said the mayor. "If we succeed, we'll stamp out two plagues at once."

"Suppose the story gets around—and we have only a fractional turnout?"

"Man will always risk his life to save it," said Newman. "You'll get your patients. How many do you expect?"

"Close to a million for the whole borough. It's a conservative estimate—counting family heads and people who live alone, and leaving out the thousands of contacts we've already protected. We'll be handling at least sixty thousand in Times Square itself."

"I've seen bigger crowds there on New Year's Eve."

"The whole area will be packed for hours, no matter how fast we process the lines."

"This won't be the first time you've worked under fire, will it?" said Pete.

The immunologist looked hard at both Pete and Newman—then, with a last reluctant shrug, took each hand in turn. "I've bought your trap," he said. "Don't make me sound like a hero." He left the terrace abruptly when a nurse signaled from the door.

"I don't know how you feel, John," said the detective, "but that's quite a man."

"Did you think he'd refuse?"

"If that mob gets out of hand tonight, he'll be trampled too."

"He'll still keep the bargain," said the mayor. He was gone in turn, moving with the quick step of a general whose time is rationed.

A little shaken by his victory, Pete was still anchored at the terrace rail when he saw a stir of white in the doorframe. Thinking it was Eric, he turned to ask pardon for his browbeating. When the figure moved into the light, he saw it was Bob Trent. Eve was close behind. Both nurse and surgeon seemed to be sleepwalking. Wondering if they had been operating round the clock, the detective could guess the answer.

"Are we intruding, Inspector?" Eve asked.

"You're practically alone right now. I'm on my way."

Bob had already moved forward, to put a detaining hand on his arm. "I think we've the right to know if your news was good or bad."

Pete smiled wanly. "Do I resemble a bearer of tidings?"

"The grapevine says you stopped to talk with Dr. Stowe and the mayor. Is the rioting over?"

"I wish I could say yes. Actually, I'm no wiser than you." Pete hesitated, then went on firmly. "If you want a professional estimate, I'd suggest you both stay close to that operating room. I think we can guarantee you a full schedule."

Bob glanced pointedly at Eve. "You heard the inspector, Miss Bronson. Sure you won't change your mind?"

"No, Bob. I'm going to be in the front line tonight. You'll do nicely here without me."

Pete had expected the declaration. "Does this mean you'll be helping Eric?"

"In Booth One, in Times Square," said Eve.

"Can't you dissuade her, Dr. Trent?"

"Miss Bronson doesn't dissuade easily, Inspector."

"Let's hope that's a good omen," said Pete, and departed hastily before he said too much. The weight of tonight's decision seemed heavier, now that Eve Bronson would be part of it; yet it was hardly news that she would refuse to turn her back on danger.

In the prowl car again, he slept fitfully as the sergeant sped down empty streets. Ten minutes later, wakening in the shadow of St. Patrick's Cathedral, he frowned at the driver.

"What are we doing uptown again, Ed?"

"Don't you remember, sir? If Dr. Stowe said yes, you wanted to burn a candle to St. Christopher."

"How'd you guess the answer?"

"It wasn't hard, Inspector. You were humming in your sleep."

"Some men sing to keep up their courage."

"Will things be worse tonight, sir?"

"I wish I knew, Ed. Park where you are. I'll be right out."

Inspector Dalton's manner belied his gloomy words. His step was almost jaunty as he turned in the church door to lift his face to a sliver of sun that had cut through sooty clouds. *Let's hope they take the bait,* he told himself. *There's no other way to close the case.*

It seemed a reasonable favor to ask of St. Christopher. He would handle the rest on his own.

### 3.

The shard of sunlight that had graced Inspector Dalton's act of piety was soon muffled in rain. By midmorning, the squall had drenched most of Manhattan. It still hung dank above the harbor when the freighter *Admiral Beattie,* Amos Duncan master, cleared her berth at quarantine and began a cautious approach to her North River pier.

In the Upper Bay, she hooted a mournful greeting as the cliff-like mass of the *Queen Mary* glided by. Captain Duncan, tilting a verdigris-green bridge cap, squinted up at the Cunarder's flying bridge.

"My radio said you were holding up all traffic, Dr. Stowe. How come she's putting to sea?"

"The *Mary* was given a clean bill of health last midnight, Captain Duncan," said Eric. "So will you, once you've unloaded."

Two hours ago, the immunologist had come out to quarantine by helicopter for the all-important business of cargo check. He had roved the *Admiral Beattie* from bridge to keelson, rejoicing at the neat mountains of drug cartons that towered beneath each hatchway, the refrigerator compartments packed with vials of vaccine. He had gone topside only a few moments ago, in time to watch the North River piers take shape in the wrack ahead.

"I've seen better berths in my time," said the skipper.

"New York has had a rough night, Captain. Don't judge her by her complexion at this moment."

"Smog's a by-product of our century, Dr. Stowe. What bothers me is your stink. Sorry I can't think of a kinder word."

Eric felt his fists tighten on the rail at the man's all too natural re-action. The miasma that had drenched the Upper Bay this morning seemed thick enough to cut—a blended echo of the garbage strike and the stench of smudge pots massed by the hundreds during the wholesale rat hunt. A yellow-brown vapor, it was part of the foggy rain that seemed to ooze rather than fall from low-lying clouds. Eric's nostrils, trained to measure such exhalations, told him the New York water front was on the mend, after its week of near-collapse. Sight unseen, he could hardly ask Captain Amos Duncan to accept his verdict.

"Believe me, you've a proper berth for the ship," he said. "Of course you'll have special clearance, the moment we've unloaded those drug crates."

He stole an anxious glance at the captain; the whole future of his program could depend on the man's ship-handling in the next half-hour. So far he had seemed prepared to obey the orders of the Port Authority—which meant fulfilment of the contract his company had signed in Quebec. Still, he would be within his rights if he refused to touch land today, on the sound premise that a visible threat of plague outweighed other commitments.

The captain had made no objection when Eric asked for paid vol-unteers among the crew to speed the unloading. A score of willing hands had worked at top speed in the last hour, transferring drug cartons from hatchways to ship's waist. The move would save pre-cious minutes when the actual unloading began—assuming Duncan had made up his mind to dock.

Before he had taken the helicopter, Eric had verified the promise that a full complement of longshoremen stood ready on the pier. The dockers' strike had long since been broken. Shaken by the virtual stoppage of their employment (now that most incoming vessels had

been diverted to other harbors) they had been eager to repair their
shattered prestige. Ken Busch, the once militant union boss, would
carry the first carton of sulfamerazine ashore. Dr. Thurlow would
follow with a crate of vaccine. Both acts would be picked up by television cameras mounted on the pier. It was vital that all New Yorkers (glued to their screens at home) should witness the delivery.

Even at this distance Eric could hear the boom of a sound truck,
broadcasting a tape of the mayor's latest announcement. John Newman's voice reached him fitfully, blanketed in a deeper rumble he
could not at once identify; in that blend of rain and smog, it was difficult to orient sounds clearly. Eric glanced again at Duncan, taking
what comfort he could from the man's nonchalance. The captain had
already opened his public-address system, to facilitate verbal contact with the nearer of two tugs that had taken form in the mist.

"What goes on ashore?"

"Hope you like to perform for a crowd, skipper," bawled the tug-
boat captain. "You got a right smart audience for this berthing."

Moving at a cautious crawl, the *Admiral Beattie* was within two
ship's lengths of the pier. At that moment, a gust of wind, lifting the
skirts of fog, revealed the actual shore line, and the ramps of the
West Side Highway above it. Eric saw that every foot of the space
was packed with people. It was the growl of the mob that had obscured the mayor's voice and given Duncan cause for his doubting.

In that uncertain light, it seemed the crowd had swallowed the
water front. Save for those occasional, deep-throated rumbles, it
hung there in strange immobility—a dark wall that seemed ready to
close on the pier at any moment. Eric knew these people had been
gathering since dawn; they might need only a whisper to go berserk.
The fact that the silent watchers wore improvised masks was a
final, grotesque overtone, giving the whole human mass the look of
surrealist bandits.

Actually, the threat was more apparent than real. The police had
promised an iron guard around the pier, and Commissioner Decker
had fulfilled the assignment. It was unfortunate that Captain Duncan could not see the blue-helmeted figures that stood between
warehouse doors and street.

"If you ask me, Doctor," said the master of the *Admiral Beattie*,
"that's quite a reception committee. Suppose they mob us?"

It was a question that required a truthful answer. Eric forced himself to reply steadily.

"In my opinion, the police line will hold. If I were you, I'd take the chance."

"My first duty is to my ship. Couldn't we unload elsewhere?"

"There simply isn't time. Besides, we must convince the city we mean business. If we back away now, they'll think the drugs we promised them aren't aboard."

Duncan addressed the tug that was nuzzling his bow. *"You're* fresh from land, mister. Is that boat slip safe?"

"Safe as church, skipper. The health commissioner's there to welcome you. What more d'you want?"

"I don't mean the rats, damn it! What about that reception committee? Will it stay put?"

"The cops can handle 'em," bellowed the captain of the second tug. "Come in fast, or we'll lose the ebb."

"Maybe he's *afraid* to come in, Joe. He's looking mighty white round the gills."

Stung by the taunt, Duncan flailed his right arm downward. His first officer signaled the engine room for half-speed ahead.

"Hit me, you swabs! I'm going to tie up."

The tugs pressed expertly at the flanks of the *Admiral Beattie*. Once her commitment was announced, the freighter approached the dock in short order. The first command was bawled to toss a line ashore: the crowd on the water front waited in stony silence when it fell short. The second toss from the bow was caught and whipped over a bollard. When the stern line was secured, the whine of winches told Eric that the gangways would soon be lowered.

He clung to his place on deck, unwilling to quit the bridge ahead of Duncan. Now the freighter was in her slip, his presence had been noted at the captain's side. The proximity had a certain value, until ship and land were fully joined.

"No Yankee can call Amos Duncan a coward," said the skipper with a last, hostile look at the retreating tugs. "Just get me back to sea pronto, Doctor."

Eric roused himself to action, moving to the bridge wing, which commanded a view of the pier itself. Intent on the temper of the crowd outside, he had forgotten that his program was still functioning smoothly within.

Forty work trucks were in clear view, parked cheek by jowl with some twenty ambulances. All were aligned as precisely as a wartime car pool: a driver sat at each wheel, and helmeted patrolmen waited at the running boards. Ken Busch's stalwarts stood at uneasy parade rest along the stringpiece, while they waited for the lashing of the gangways. Busch himself, flamboyant in whipcord breeches and lumberjack's shirt, faced Dr. Thurlow in the roped-off area below the *Admiral Beattie*'s waist.

The tableau (grotesquely solemn at first view) took on meaning when the mooring was complete and Eric could take in the vista at the wide-open doors of the pier shed. A double file of police stood here with linked arms, facing down the surge of bodies in the street. On a platform just inside the portal, a phalanx of TV cameras, flanked by floodlights, waited to record the unloading.

It was an impressive tableau, awaiting the opening of the first gangway to give it meaning. The lights picked up stars on a captain's crash helmet and splintered on Dr. Thurlow's horn rims. The stocky health commissioner, flanked by uniformed attendants, seemed to have eyes for everything in this last-minute survey of equipment and personnel. There was nothing hurried in his movements—and his pontifical calm, when he turned to answer questions at a commentator's microphone, was a powerful antidote for the slow-boiling hysteria outside.

"Are you going ashore, Doctor? Or can they run the show without you?"

Even from the bridge wing, Eric could sense the appeal in Ken Busch's eyes. The bull-necked strong man of the Dockers' Union, (who had done his part to throttle the city only yesterday) seemed almost childishly eager to make his gesture of atonement. Aware of the expectant audience in both street and warehouse, Eric glanced at the waist of the freighter and nodded to the boatswain who would serve as foreman of the hands aboard.

A carton of sulfamerazine was lifted from its place beside the hatch and passed swiftly to the forward gangway. Busch took the box from a crewman's hand and trudged toward the nearest waiting ambulance: on the TV platform, floodlights and cameras swiveled to follow his progress. The sweep was repeated as Dr. Thurlow received his first burden. Then the lead camera lifted to the *Admiral Beattie*'s bridge. Hearing the commentator's well-modulated voice identify him (and the part he would play) Eric yielded to a theatrical impulse of his own and held out his hand to Captain Amos Duncan.

It was a gesture of thanks, no less fervent because it was wordless.

Once the unloading was under way, the crowd accepted it with no visible emotion, besides an occasional uneasy murmur. When Eric moved to join the long line of stevedores, and the murmur changed to grudging applause, he felt his spirits lift a trifle. It was still too soon to hope the deliveries would proceed without incident. Twice in the next hour, the mob mood just escaped exploding into naked violence.

The first real testing came when the lead ambulance (springs sagging under its precious freight) nosed from pier to street, to negotiate the rain-slick highway ramp. The crowd had parted slowly to let it pass; a pair of anonymous hands, thrust from the roiling sea of bodies, snatched a carton from the tail gate and tossed it skyward like a huge brown football. Passed from hand to hand in the crowd, wrestled over at the curb, it exploded with a sickening impact against a pillar, dribbling its contents into the North River gutters.

The watchers behind the police cordon held their collective breaths until the ambulance gained the highway without further depredation. The second attempted theft (made a half-hour later, after a score of vehicles had butted their way to safety without incident) had a more fortunate outcome. This time both driver and guards dove into the melee with fists flying, to snatch back the carton and restore it to its place. When other fists in the crowd were used on the driver's side, Eric could tell himself that enemy agitators (outnumbered, for the moment, by the advocates of common sense) would hold their fire. For all its beast-rumble, the crowd was still human.

It was almost two when the last ambulance was loaded. By this time, Eric was staggering with weariness and refusing to admit he was approaching the end of his endurance. He had planned to ride with the last driver to Manhattan Central. He was still checking the load when the television commentator swooped upon him with a portable microphone.

"You're just in time for our hourly roundup, Dr. Stowe. May we have a statement?"

Eric stared dazedly at the street outside. For the past hour, intent on the mechanical chores of loading, he had not paused to look beyond the police line. To his amazement, he saw the street was now almost empty. The once sullen crowd, aware at last that the unloadings had been made in its welfare, had seeped away. Save for a few knots of spectators at street corners, the water front had resumed its normal aspect.

"I'm afraid we no longer have an audience."

"Forget those no-accounts outside, Doctor. They've gone about their business, now they've realized self-medication is impractical. How about a word for the *good* New Yorkers—who listened to John Newman and stayed home?"

Eric blinked back his weariness and faced the camera that had swung his way: the preliminary exchange, he saw, was already part of the broadcast. He had forgotten the vast body of law-abiding citizens, who at this very moment were waiting at their living-room screens. Obviously, he owed them what assurance he could offer.

"You have been watching the preparations for the borough-wide distribution of a drug cargo," he said. "As you are no doubt aware, it was en route to India—until it was diverted here by your Port Authority, to help solve the emergency all of us are facing. It is the most tangible evidence we can offer that we are sparing no effort for your protection.

"By now it will hardly be news to you that we are fighting an epidemic of plague, whose threat has been almost entirely confined to the island of Manhattan. A century ago, we would have had no way to subdue this menace. Today we have an absolute means—through what are sometimes called miracle drugs—to eradicate it. To that end, your mayor has asked for your wholehearted obedience to the authorities, who have no thought except to achieve the greatest good for the greatest number.

"The protective drugs we have just unloaded will be made available to each one of you, whether sick or well, no later than tonight. If you will take them as directed, we are confident that the plague will be safely controlled and our present epidemic status ended no later than tomorrow. The trucks you saw leaving the docks are en route to our distribution stations. Providing we have your complete co-operation, these drugs will be given to every man, woman and child in this borough, sometime before midnight. Only you will be to blame if you do not get your share.

"In the next city broadcast, you will see the first drugs and equipment arriving at Number One Booth in Times Square, which will serve as the pilot point for our program. On radio, television, and in the newspapers you will learn just where you must go to obtain your medication. Please follow all instructions exactly. Nothing must keep you from your assigned station—no rumor, no threat to your safety, no false assumption that you can escape.

"Treatment is available for all. You have only to take it."

When the announcer had intoned his thanks and moved on, Eric felt no emotion beyond a profound relief that this phase of the program was ended. A moment later, climbing to the jump seat at the tail gate of the ambulance, he was aware of the presence of Dr. Thurlow. The health commissioner, thrusting his head into the carton-jammed interior, was beaming like a contented tabby.

"Thanks for that final word, Doctor. It's just what the moment needed."

"I'm glad you think so," said Eric. Already he had forgotten what he had said on the broadcast. His whole being was concentrated on this return to the hospital, the seclusion of his room in the Residents' Wing, the scalding shower that would precede his first real sleep since the examination of Willoughby Fellowes.

"See you at Father Duffy's statue, in just four hours."

"It's a date, Doctor."

At noon the first vehicles to leave the pier had moved like argosies in a frozen sea. Now, save for the screen of police along the curbs, the roadway below the ramps was empty; the motorcycles that preceded each convoy gained the highway in a single swoop, where the riders paused in impatient Vs, until the lumbering, overloaded trucks and ambulances could follow. Riding the last ambulance in a waking trance, Eric remembered to hook his arm through the strap on the jump seat and lapsed into an unashamed doze. It was a trick he had learned as an intern, when there were no patients inside. . . .

When he wakened, the jolting nap had not really refreshed his tired body. The other members of the convoy had long since branched off to their respective stations. His own ambulance was traversing the usual side streets Manhattan Central drivers followed in their runs for the emergency platform. Even when his drowsiness faded, the sense of waking nightmare persisted. The iron shutters of the warehouses lining the bypass were part of that evil trauma.

In a flash, he knew this was the alley where the Dukes had ambushed his car. Today there was no barrier to halt the arrow-swift rush toward the hospital. There was no sign of life in the shallow street—until a warehouse window opened, revealing the face of Juan Lemayo, behind the barrel of the Skoda automatic which lay level on the sill.

In that moment of confrontation, Eric felt sure the gun was aimed at his heart. Thorough as his planning had been, he had not reminded his drivers that a clever enemy (familiar with their routes) might choose to strike at such a point, rather than risk arrest on the water front. It was too late to seek shelter now, if his life was forfeit for that neglect. He lifted his head and stared up at Juan as the youth opened fire.

There were three shots from the warehouse before the guards on the driver's seat, alert as terriers, leaned out to return the fire. A sitting target on the tail gate, Eric felt his flesh cringe from the expected thud of the bullet—until he realized Juan had aimed at the ambulance wheels.

Only one of the shots found its mark, thanks to their tearing pace. When the right rear tire blew, the tail gate gave a sickening lurch toward the curb. At that same moment, Eric saw Juan reel back from the window with a stain of red at one shoulder. Then, as the ambulance bumper crashed against the platform ahead, he felt his head make contact with the frame of the door so violently that the scene was lost in starry blackness. . . .

The oblivion was soon over. Disengaging his arm from the riding strap, rubbing a considerable swelling at his temple, Eric found himself facing one of the two police guards. The man stood on the pavement with his service revolver drawn in search of other antagonists. There was no sound in the alley, save for the hiss of steam from the ambulance's cracked radiator. In the warehouse window, the second patrolman had just put out his head, making a thumbs-down signal as he did so.

"We winged him, Doctor. Not so bad he couldn't run."

"Is our driver hurt?"

"Conked out like you. He knows his job; even with a blowout, you didn't lose a carton. It's have been another story, if that punk had hit both tires."

"Did you know it was Juan Lemayo?"

"Is *that* his name, now? Inspector Dalton will be sorry to hear he's still above ground."

Eric moved groggily to the interior of the ambulance, to check the tiered crates of drugs. Until he had verified the report with his own hands, he would not believe the load had arrived safely on the hospital threshold. *Pete was right,* he thought, *their shock-troops are still at large, and we've yet to outsmart them.*

"Tell me one thing, Officer," he said. "Don't they ever stop pushing?"

"Who are *they,* Doctor?"

"I wish I knew. It'd make tonight a lot easier for us all."

4.

Eve had arrived at Times Square on the dot of six; since that moment, she had been kept far too busy to think. Now, with the routine of distribution set to the last detail, she could survey her group's work and call it good.

All through the late afternoon, television cameras had featured this focal point of Operation Epidemic. The arrival of the drug cartons had been duly recorded; so had the appearance of hospital personnel and the precise routine they had followed at Booth One. It had been a pilot scene for a hundred similar centers in all parts of the borough, a living proof to New Yorkers that their government, and their health authorities, could back their promises.

Physically, the structure was not impressive, with its makeshift green plywood and flat roof that would serve Eric as an observation post. Within, shelves were stacked with thousands of ready-made packets of sulfamerazine. Thousands more were waiting outside, where a whole convoy of trucks had been parked on the concrete island between Broadway and Seventh Avenue. Sturdy partitions to separate the crowds that would soon be pouring through, and a half-dozen tables stacked with the first batches of the drug, completed the basic pattern.

The routine that Eric had worked out seemed both admirable and simple. As the lines entered, each person would be asked to give his name and address to a stenotype operator. Family heads, when possible, had been asked to bring wife and older children. Those under twelve, the sick and the aged, would be served by supplementary packets. No other record would be kept, Eric had decided; there was no time. Once inside the booth, each applicant would be handed two tablets of sulfamerazine and a paper cup of water—and watched by the admitting nurse until the tablets were swallowed. At the next table, he would receive drug packet and instruction sheet, covering the routine of self-medication. Once the second nurse was sure he understood its use, he would be ushered out, and shunted expertly on his homeward route.

Inevitably, there would be lying at the stenotypes, as professional chiselers picked up unlawful packets for resale later. For the most part, Eric argued, the collections would be honest, responding, as they must, to man's basic need to save himself.

Dr. Norris Weaver (who would serve as Eric's assistant in Booth One) came in from the square with his usual air of efficiency. Eve saw that his quick glance had missed nothing. His nod of acceptance, and the way he offered a cigarette as he settled at his table, told her that Booth One, at least, had passed muster.

"Light up, Miss Bronson," said the medical chief. "It's probably your last chance until midnight."

"Are we in business, Doctor?"

"Times Square's as ready as it'll ever be. So is the borough—with a few exceptions, which we anticipated. Dr. Stowe will be here in a few more moments. He's just sent a rush squad to Washington Square. We've had a fight on our hands there."

"I hope our side won."

"Eventually—with an assist from the police."

"Was that the only trouble?"

"A few trucks were hijacked during delivery—not enough to slow us down. For once, we have medication to spare."

Eve met the medical chief's eyes across the dispensary table. "Will we be attacked here, Doctor?"

"I won't risk an answer, Miss Bronson."

"What's your opinion, then?"

"In their place—whoever they may be—I'd take that gamble. If they won, we'd have the stampede of the century."

"With Booth One in the middle?"

"Put it that way, if you insist," said Weaver. He looked up as George Peters ambled into the room—a tall, gangling figure in his whites, who seemed utterly at home in this new milieu.

"Don't look so startled, Eve," said the resident. "I'll get back to Bob, long before the evening rush begins. They asked me to lend a hand outside, until things get under way. I'm on a kind of roving assignment. Dr. Weaver and I are checking the lines for doubt-fuls——"

"Incipient plague cases, you mean?"

"We're sure to turn up a few, on the law of averages. Our job is to make a snap diagnosis, and send 'em to a night club in the next block. We've converted it into an emergency ward, just in case."

"Dr. Stowe has thought of everything, it seems."

"It's his job," said the resident. "I'll admit he's good at it. Want a pigeon's eye view of the theater, before the show begins?"

Eve glanced at the medical chief, who nodded his permission. The young doctor's eyes were already on his wrist watch. His ear seemed tuned for the rumble of an approaching bombardment.

During air-raid drills, when she had served as hospital liaison with a Civil Defense unit, Eve had seen this crossroads of the world devoid of humanity. Tonight, it had the same bareness, and the bath of floodlights, mounted on a dozen marquees, only heightened the effect. So did the patrolmen at each side-street entrance, and the lone squad car roaming the sidewalks in a final check of padlocked shops and closed lobbies. Times Square, in its day, had taken war and peace in stride—the blare of horns at New Year's Eve, the frenzy of V-J day. Tonight it seemed like the flight deck of some monster battleship stripped for action.

"Up you go, Eve," said Peters. "Don't let the desert-island look depress you. We'll be chockablock full soon enough."

A makeshift stair, formed by two firemen's ladders anchored to a police truck, led to the top of the dispensary: Eve was glad of the resident's hand as she scaled this elevation. Two hours ago, hurrying to her work, she had not paused to review geography. She saw now that Booth One stood at the extreme northern terminus of this long, rectangular canyon—the portion New Yorkers called Duffy Square, because of the statue of the soldier-priest that dominated it. The booth had been erected in Father Duffy's shadow.

Like the statue behind it, the pilot dispensary dominated the square. It was matched, to the south, by two squat structures—the Armed Forces' recruiting station and the city information center. Both had been converted for medical use this evening. Behind them, the tall wedge of the Times Building, its lighted news-strip repeating a message of reassurance, made a striking contrast to the blind-windowed buildings and darkened theaters that faced it.

These three booths, Eve knew, would handle the major traffic. Other dispensaries (identical with Booth One, but slightly smaller) stood at the mouths of every cross street debouching on the square. At each entrance, the police had taped out lines on the asphalt. The familiar gray-white crosstrees, aligned precisely before the doors, were intended to slow the streams of humanity to manageable trickles, before individuals were admitted to the booths themselves. There could be no visible tensions, no sense of pressure from behind, while first-comers swallowed their doses of sulfamerazine and accepted their drug packets.

Eric and his roving staff had timed the processing at several booths. Allowing ten seconds for each dispensation, and estimating a maximum turnover of sixty thousand patients in Times Square alone, the immunologist had calculated the program would end in a

little over three hours. It had seemed a reasonable estimate when
Eve had gone through the routine with the others. Now, with the
real test impending, she could wonder if Eric's timetable had taken
too much for granted.

Her eyes moved to the mouth of the nearest cross street. Since
yesterday, the city broadcasts had stated repeatedly that distribution could not begin until eight o'clock this Thursday evening. The
mayor, Dr. Thurlow, and Eric had added their exhortations, reminding citizens of New York that an earlier appearance would
only prolong their time of waiting. Naturally, the advice had fallen
on deaf ears. Two hours ago, when Eve's contingent had arrived
from Manhattan Central, the streets leading to the square had been
jammed as far as the eye could reach.

The compulsion to be first in line had been anticipated. The police
had opposed good-natured bodies to the press, diverting the crowds
into adjacent streets, promising the drug on a first-come-first-served
basis, and keeping arterial approaches open for the still arriving
trucks of supplies. Eric had insisted the dispensaries be amply
stocked before a single applicant set foot in Times Square. Operation Epidemic would collapse in a shambles if the supply ran short.

In that last, taut half-hour, the crowds had been held at a firm distance. Entertainers from darkened theaters—some of them world-
famous—had done yeomen's service to keep those waiting thousands
occupied, capering as gaily as buskers in a London queue with no
rewards but spatters of applause and increasingly hostile stares.
Now, while she continued to watch from the roof of Booth One, Eve
realized the last singing voice had stilled. In the nearest side street
(the only approach she could view clearly) the barriers had been
moved flush with the eastern sidewalks of the square. The crowd,
penned only a moment ago in a long double line on Sixth Avenue,
had begun to flow toward that barrier, as implacably as a lava river.

"Are you going to let them in now, George?"

"Not quite," said the resident. "We're hoping a direct view of
their destination will soothe 'em a little longer."

"Perhaps I should get back to my station."

"I saw Eric when I was crossing the square. He wanted a word
with you—away from the others. He's in that police car now, with
Dalton."

The green Ford, describing a final arc on the gleaming asphalt
desert, braked at the barrier that flanked Booth One. When Eric
stepped out, a low murmur ran down the line across the way: most

of that waiting crowd (hanging on its screens all day long) had heard his statement from the water front. Eve could feel herself withdraw into Father Duffy's shadow while the immunologist ran nimbly up the ladder. Guessing why he had planned this rendezvous, she was braced for his words.

"You'll find three patients in the Paramount Theater lobby, George," said Eric. His tone was casual; knowing how harried he must be, Eve could only marvel at his poise. "Could be some cracked ribs. They'll be walking wounded, so you can handle them there."

George Peters moved to the fireman's ladder. "How soon do we begin?"

"Ten minutes, at the latest. You'll still have time to take a look and get back." Eric moved to assist the resident's descent. His back was turned to Eve when he spoke again: she knew he had made the move deliberately. "How are things below, Miss Bronson?"

"We've been ready since half-past, Doctor."

"I thought you would be," he said, with that same glacial formality. "Dr. Weaver's a good man at organization. Tonight, our weak sister was Booth Three—the information bureau fronting the Times Building. With all that glass in the walls, we found we needed plywood barriers." He turned abruptly—and she saw the tortures of unuttered fears in his eyes. "Let's stop pretending, Eve. You've guessed why I'm here."

"Tell me anyway."

"I want you to leave this cul-de-sac at once."

"Don't you think I know my job?"

"I'm not questioning your competence, or your courage. Just take my word you're in mortal danger, and go quietly."

"I've yet to run out on a job, Eric."

The immunologist turned to stare blankly at the still empty square. Incredulously, she realized this was the first time his poise had deserted him. When he spoke, his voice was as broken as his manner.

"It's no excuse to say I've had a whole city on my mind, Eve. I should have realized you'd volunteer for this work, and prevented it."

"Surely I've the right to do my part."

"I want you alive this time tomorrow. For Bob's sake, if not for mine. Must I tell you why?"

"No, Eric," she said gently. "I realize you're in love with me. The fact doesn't excuse me from my duty."

"I can't bear to see you harmed. Will you go while there's time—
if I tell you the reason?"

She did not interrupt while he described his meeting with Pete
and the mayor, and the ambush Pete had planned. When he finished, she dared to put a hand on his arm. Knowing they were the
target of a thousand eyes, she could hardly do more.

"I suspected most of what you've said," she whispered. "What are
you calling it? The Battle of Times Square?"

"It could be the worst we ever fought."

"Do you expect to lose?"

"We're prepared to repel boarders—but the crowd may still run
wild at the first shot. If enough saboteurs get above ground, they
could turn the whole square into an abattoir. We've no way to measure their strength, or their strategy."

"I'm one of the nurses in Booth One, Eric. I'll take my chances
there."

"Suppose I order you to leave in that squad car?"

"You can't, without breaking up your team downstairs. *They'd*
refuse to go, if you told them what you've just told me. Don't think
you've the exclusive rights to martyrdom."

There was the sound of a foot on the ladder; when Eric turned
toward the interruption, she knew he had yielded. There was even
time to wonder why she had not been more deeply stirred by his concern. When Pete Dalton stepped up to the roof, the chance for self-
analysis was gone. The detective's presence told her she could not
linger a second more.

"Thanks for your candor, Dr. Stowe," she said. "Believe me, I'm
where I belong."

Eric held her glance briefly, then put out a hand to help her down
the ladder. "As you wish," he said, with the same careful formality.
"Forgive me if I've taken too much on myself."


5.


"Did you really think you could frighten her?" asked Pete.

"I felt I should do my best," said Eric. "Do you find that strange?"

"Far from it. Every man in love has the urge to play Galahad."

"Since when have you been an authority on love?"

"In my trade, you see all kinds," said the detective. "That girl's a
first-rate Amazon. *She* doesn't want a knight-errant standing be-

tween her and life. What's more, she'd never be happy on a pedestal. If that's the future you've planned for her, I'd advise you to back up and start over."

"So far, I've planned no future for either of us."

"Come off that pose," said Pete. "You'd marry her tomorrow, if she'd have you."

"I won't deny the thought has crossed my mind."

"Then you must share your world with her. Especially when the going is roughest. She won't have you otherwise."

"This is no time to discuss my matrimonial problems, Pete."

"Perhaps you're right, Dr. Stowe. I'm aware you've a job to do here. I was only trying to distract you until it began."

"It's beginning now," said Eric—and leaned forward to study the vanguard of the crowd moving toward Booth One.

The tide of humanity, Pete noted, had begun moving on schedule, led by two outsize patrolmen who had been chosen as bellwethers. The lines seemed eager to obey orders—pausing at the first saw-horses, dividing into neat columns along the side walls of the booth. Still guided by the two tall policemen, the leaders in each line passed through the wide doorway—to swallow the first tablets, receive the first drug packs, and move on.

"Ten seconds flat," said Eric. "Let's hope we can hold the average."

*To you they're statistics,* thought Pete. *Potential breeders of pestilence, to the last man. Blockbusters that can destroy a city unless they've visited your pill factory.* Not that he could censure Eric Stowe for that incredible detachment. A doctor with sixty thousand patients to process in a space of hours could hardly stop to look into faces—even if most of them had not been masked to the eyes.

Detective-Inspector Dalton (whose business was faces, and the evil behind them) needed a closer scrutiny. Yet he could not stir from this rooftop now. There was no other way to check the whole square. He could trust his plainclothesmen to separate black sheep from white.

Troublemakers at the moment were surprisingly few. Here and there in the still docile lines, Pete could sense telltale mutters—all of them a little too strident to be genuine. He was happy to note that most of the complainers had been told off by their neighbors; there were more cheers than boos when the police moved in swiftly, to take each false prophet into custody. So far, these were citizens intent on a single objective—the dark-green temple of healing that had already swallowed them by hundreds. . . .

Measured against the vast surge of bodies that had begun to jam the square, such disturbances were only ripples on the flood—but Pete continued to check each threat narrowly. These were only tentative overtures, meant to test the crowd's temper. Already it was evident that the real menace, whatever its nature, must erupt from below. It would come soon, unless the enemy was prepared to concede defeat.

Steadying himself with a hand on Eric's shoulder, Pete leaned above the doorframe to study each entering face as best he could. The district Booth One was serving tonight was a mixed bag. Save for the impromptu masks, the unnatural stolidity, the people in these lines seemed no different from the multitudes that filled Times Square at curtain time.

Luxury apartments had sent their quotas of dowagers and demimondaines; city housing developments had disgorged their own crowd of clerks and typists. Tonight they inched forward side by side with pensioners from decaying brownstones, whey-faced men from airless basements, bronzed Thespians from straw-hat circuits.

Here were denizens of the new Bohemia, the men who resembled women, the short-haired girls who could have passed for boys. Both sexes wore spindle-legged jeans and sneakers. All of them murmured their own jargon, and stared with naked scorn at the everyday citizens they elbowed.

Here (awaiting his turn as calmly as the rest) was a producer Pete recognized instantly, a famous esthete who resembled a truck driver. Beside him was an actress famous on two continents, arm in arm with a poet-playwright.

Here were the out-of-town visitors trapped in hotels, and the staffs of those same hotels, caught with their guests by the mayor's quarantine.

Here were the players in a tennis round robin, stranded in their quarters at the Astor.

Here were the bakers from a Chinese noodle factory on Ninth Avenue. . . .

Here, in short, was the American melting pot in action, a rich amalgam whose living whole far exceeded the sum of its parts. Would it survive the testing that was now imminent? Or would it dissolve under this final attack, prey to the blind terror that has stunted man's growth since the Stone Age?

The first warning reached Pete's ear, just after he drew back from his fruitless scrutiny. It was a low, pulsing sound, not too different from the rumble of a train on the still dead tracks below. In less than a moment, it had grown to a sullen roar. When it was joined by the dry-stick rattle of gunfire, he knew the underground battle was joined. The enemy had risen to the bait.

"Hear that, Eric?"

"I'm surprised it didn't come sooner. What's our next cue?"

"To keep those lines moving. We've lost if they break."

The Battle of Times Square (which was really a war of the subways) was a booby trap of Dalton's own fashioning. He could see its beginnings in his mind's eye as clearly as though that whole vast rectangle of asphalt had rolled back to expose the tracks beneath.

In the square itself, his men had moved in from the moment the first lines snaked toward their booths. They had mingled quietly, eyes shaded by panama hats and summer fedoras, quiet business suits cut loose to conceal the bulge of service holsters. At first they had done no more than close in on trouble spots, and help George Peters and his staff to head off suspected fever cases. Now, responding to another wordless signal from Booth One, most of them drifted toward the subway kiosks.

The moves had been routine, the automatic control of the enemy aboveground, before those other makers of chaos below could surge toward fresh air. In the subways themselves the main battle had been largely decided. The fusillades Pete had just heard had been fired by the police, massed in depth behind stalled trains, in nooks known only to the trackwalkers and platform guards who served as captains of each squad. Strategy had been elementary. The saboteurs had been boxed in enfilading fire and shot down without mercy when they began their rush for the exits.

Pete knew that not even the best of booby traps functioned perfectly. The bulk of the enemy had been stopped in their tracks or arrested by other ambushed units when they turned tail and fled. Here and there, units of Operation Saboteur attained their objective: to burst from the kiosks with faces streaming sweat, eyes glazed with the same panic they had meant to create. Clubbed down by the waiting plainclothesmen, not more than a dozen die-hards reached the square itself before they were brought to earth.

Meanwhile the lines moved on.

There were still enemies in the crowd itself, patient masqueraders who had held their tongues until this moment, when they had hoped to join forces with the enemy from below. Now they burst into belated action. Gunfire cracked from every line as a dozen fists fights erupted. Pete, marking each outbreak of violence, saw that it had been contained promptly. Scattered screams now had the tempo of hysteria, but the files before each booth held firm.

He needed a moment more to realize that New York was insisting, with its own fists, on the right to survive. Tormented by days of nameless horror, shaken by the paralysis that had invaded its streets, the citizens of America's greatest city had refused to be cowed now that the enemy had dared to show his face.

Inspector Dalton (choking down an irrational impulse to cheer) had time to note that the producer had broken the jaw of a would-be assailant with a roundhouse right. The poet-playwright had seized two men by the scruff, to bash their heads together with the efficiency of a housewife cracking eggs. The Chinese noodle-makers, flinging themselves upon a quartet of goons with teeth and toenails, had routed the hoodlums in a storm of good Cantonese cursing.

Already the kaleidoscope of violence had taken a pattern Pete could measure clearly. The still nameless enemy, relying on the same shock values that had won victories all over the world, had met his match tonight. It was true that the initial trap had been baited and sprung by expert hands. The nemesis might still have prevailed —without the city's readiness to match blow for blow.

There was a last flurry of fists in the line before Booth One. A tall man in a raincoat burst free of the melee—a wild-eyed, vulture-faced man with a grenade nested in his palm. The mask that had covered his maniac visage had been ripped aside. Long before the arm went back (in an odd burlesque of a pitcher's windup) Pete recognized Emile Karam, an *agent provocateur*, wanted in a dozen capitals for most crimes on the docket.

A detective, hard on Karam's trail, knocked down the grenade before it could leave his hand. A second booted the missile down a manhole, where it detonated harmlessly. Karam made no move to resist while he was handcuffed. Then his head bobbed turtlewise into the flaring collar of his raincoat.

Even from the roof, Pete could hear the crunch of glass. The man's eyes stared up at him like dying embers; he laughed wildly as the cyanide took effect.

"Was he the leader?" asked Eric.

The detective shook his head sadly. "Karam was a killer, not a brain. *This* kind of leader has a way of fading from the picture once he's beaten."

"We've won, then?"

"Hands down, in the square," said Pete, but his voice was still muted. "We haven't won the war, though. Not while the man who planned it is still at large."

# 7. Friday

Eric had been optimistic in estimating the duration of his program. It was close to midnight when the booths dispensed their last packets of sulfamerazine, and though a maximum crowd of sixty thousand had been expected in the area, over eighty thousand units of the drug had been distributed.

Operation Epidemic, judged by its Times Square performance, had been a sellout. Reports from other centers were uniform. Every booth on Manhattan Island had exceeded its quota; the police had suppressed violence with the same ruthless skill.

Eve Bronson, caught up in split-second routine, had found herself responding mindlessly to the needs of those never ending lines. The queries and the fears had seemed endless too, but she had soon trained herself to answer every question with the same smiling patience, to soothe away doubts before they could take form in troubled minds. . . .

At eleven, she had stood with Eric and the Booth One staff to accept the mayor's thanks—a moment staged for television cameras, a final assurance to the people of New York that their protection was now as complete as science could devise. A little later the immunologist had called her briefly from her duties to add his own thanks.

"Do you understand *now* why I wanted you out of this?"

"Of course, Eric. Aren't you glad I didn't go?"

"You've been invaluable, my dear—but I'm still reproaching myself for letting you remain. Did you have too many bad moments?"

"I'm afraid I was much too busy." Eve knew she was laughing at the reproach in his tone. "I *had* to be part of this thing, Eric. Can't you see why?"

"Karam might have killed the lot of you."

"So he might. Don't accuse me of posing as Florence Nightingale. I just didn't have time to be afraid."

Remembering that brief exchange now (with Booth One closed at last and the hands of the Paramount clock on midnight) Eve could not regret her candor. If she had teased Eric a little, she felt he deserved the raillery. It was still hard to believe that he had almost refused to let her share his danger.

When the battle of Times Square was really ended, she sat at her distribution table a moment more, while Dr. Weaver and the others hastened to close up shop. The pharmacist's book before her was evidence that Booth One had done its share; she had been asked to deliver it to Eric, who had long since returned to the hospital to correlate the total immunization figures. Curiously enough, now the ordeal was ended, she was in no hurry to present the proof of her diligence.

Twenty minutes later Eve dropped out of her ambulance unit on the driveway of Manhattan Central, but she did not turn at once to the portals of the laboratory. Eric, she knew, would be at his work table in pathology; in another moment she would add her ledger to the stack before him. Meanwhile, obeying an urge she understood perfectly, she entered the corridor of the accident ward, where a line of stretchers still awaited their turns in surgery. It was the aftermath of Operation Saboteur—a cogent reminder the battle might have had a far different ending.

The need to volunteer was strong, but Eve resisted it. She had been on continuous duty for over eighteen hours; even if the surgical chief would have permitted it, she was in no condition to assist. At the admissions desk the intern on duty gave her a welcoming grin.

"Aren't you working for Dr. Stowe tonight, Miss Bronson?"

"I'm on my way to his office now. Where's Dr. Trent at the moment?"

"Operating in Number Two. He's been there since midnight. They just brought him a dilly from across the street. A Mrs. Lemayo."

"Did you say Lemayo?"

The intern consulted his admissions book. "It's her second time here, I see. Dr. Trent pulled her through before. He may not be so lucky tonight. Ambulance reports she had both legs shattered and internal injuries besides."

"How did it happen?"

"Bomb blast. Someone tossed a pineapple into her apartment from the fire-escape. Blew the place sky-high."

Eve did not wait to hear more. O. R. Two was at the end of the corridor, a compact surgical suite used mainly for emergency work. Before she could reach the door to the anteroom, she saw that she was too late to witness the battle for Rita Lemayo's life. There was no mistaking the import of the wheeled stretcher that had just come through the portal, and the inert, sheeted form upon it.

George Peters, still in his operating suit, had come into the hall to speak to the orderly who would take the body to the morgue. When he saw Eve, he hurried forward to steady her.

"What's wrong? You're white as paper."

"I still can't believe the report, Doctor."

The resident glanced at the wheeled stretcher, as it vanished in the waiting lift. "It was a bad one, all right. We've got others waiting." He led Eve gently to the nurses' room just outside the ward. "We did what we could for her, but it was hopeless from the start. Bob tried every surgical trick in the book, including guillotine amputations——"

"You knew she was murdered, didn't you?"

"Yes, Eve."

"Did the killer get away?"

"I'm afraid so."

Eve nodded slowly, without trusting herself to speak. At Booth One tonight, there had been a police cordon to deflect Emile Karam's grenade-toss. With Juan afield, there had been no protection for Rita Lemayo . . . The admissions intern was waiting at the door of the nurses' room, ready to steer the resident to a new case. Eve knew she had no right to detain him longer.

"Bob's in the scrub room upstairs," said George. "He can give you more details."

"I've heard enough for now, I think."

Eve sat unstirring after the resident had hastened on. The need to seek out Bob Trent was strong, but she knew she would not yield. At this moment (while he prepared for his next battle to save a life), she could never break the iron wall of his concentration.

"Telephone, Miss Bronson."

She looked up from her musings to find herself facing a harried orderly.

"Who is it?"

"A man who won't give his name. He tried to get you before. Take it on the extension, please."

The orderly was gone instantly, responding to a shouted order from admissions. When Eve picked up the phone, she recognized the voice at once, though she could not understand the language.

"Speak English, Juan. Where are you?"

"*Perdone, señorita.*" The boy's voice was a hoarse whisper. "I am at a pay phone nearby. Tell me what they do to *la madre*—" Again, he slipped into his native tongue.

"English, Juan! Did you know your apartment was bombed?"

"I watch it happen, *señorita*. From the warehouse loft. I see your ambulance take her away. Did they save her?"

"I'm afraid not. Dr. Trent did his best."

"She is *muerto?*"

"She died on the table, Juan. Can you tell me why?"

"Yes, Miss Bronson. I tell you now—gladly." Once he had taken the blow, Juan's voice had steadied. "We use my room to hide our guns—" The boy faltered badly; for an instant, Eve felt sure the connection had been broken.

"Are you there, Juan?"

"*Si, señorita.* My breath is hard to come by——"

"You're wounded, aren't you? The police said——"

"I am not hurt too badly." Again the voice had steadied: only its singsong lack of syntax betrayed the weakness beneath. "I hide in loft, to watch our street. All day long, I see the Dukes are turning chicken. *Amigos* I trusted, climbing the stair to my room to hide their guns, before they hide themselves. Since I am not there, they refuse to fight for the *Jefe*. You would say the Leader."

"What leader?"

"I tell you that too, Miss Bronson. Tonight he knows he will be found out. Before he runs away, he strikes again. Not only to—how you say—destroy the evidence. To punish me for failing him."

"Will you tell this to Inspector Dalton?"

"I do not talk to *policía*, Miss Bronson. I do not give myself up. If they want me, let them track me down."

"Come to the emergency room. Let them dress your wound——"

"No, *señorita*. We cannot meet again. But I tell you the *Jefe's* name before I die. He has made a lie of all he promised. He too deserves death—" The voice failed briefly, then rose to a reckless shout. "Tell the *policía* the man they want is Charles Tully!"

Staring at the phone, Eve felt her vision cloud. While the blurred detachment lasted, she could not credit her own hearing.

"Say that again, Juan."

"Charles Tully, the man at Merton House. It is what you call his cover. So is the desk he keeps in your hospital—" The voice faded from the phone, though the line remained open. Eve heard the shots clearly—and a nearer shot that seemed loud enough to shatter the earpiece. Juan Lemayo, it seemed, had given his message in his last moment on earth.

When the line remained dead, Eve replaced the receiver and got to her feet. The pharmacist's ledger was still clutched in one hand. Remembering that Eric was awaiting her in pathology, she turned down the corridor, forcing her steps to a hurried walk, and praying she would not encounter Charles Tully en route.

2.

Eric sat quietly at his desk while Eve gasped out her story.

The gooseneck lamp was bent low above the blotter. With a mechanical gesture, he took the ledger from her hand, and added it to the stack before him. The move gave him a second more to think. Until his mind could fasten on a plan, he could only reach for his phone and dial Pete Dalton's private number.

As he had feared, it was a desk sergeant at headquarters who answered. At the moment, it seemed, Inspector Dalton was somewhere in the network of subways beneath Times Square: he would return Dr. Stowe's call the moment he could be reached. Eric hung up. Somehow, he could not bring himself to give Eve's news to a desk man in uniform—even if the sergeant would have believed him.

"Where's Tully at the moment?"

"With Irene, I suppose. He called me from her apartment to wish us luck."

"She's his accomplice. She has to be."

"Probably she took the gun from Dr. Keller's locker. I've seen her use that hallway as a short cut." Eric struck the blotter with both fists and bounded to his feet. The moment cried out for action, not for a fumbling recital of the enemy's past. "This is getting us nowhere, Eve——"

"What are you going to do?"

"I don't know. We can hardly ask for their arrest, on the word of a dying hoodlum."

"There must be proof somewhere."

"Let's start with Tully's desk."

It was a relief to be in motion, futile though the action seemed. Standing aside to let Eve precede him, Eric turned off the gooseneck lamp. The flick of the switch plunged the lab into darkness, save for the red glow of the fire exits; moving on tiptoe by instinct, they took the short corridor leading to Tully's cubicle. Eric would recall these precautions soon enough, and rejoice in them. . . .

Tully's desk was padlocked, as he had expected. He heard the footfalls outside, a second after he knelt to test the hasp. There was just time to draw Eve into the only available hiding place, the steel filing cabinet that held Irene's case histories. A flashlight was already probing the glass walls of the cubicle. In another moment a gloved hand turned the knob softly.

Even in the gloom, Eric saw the man was impeccably dressed, in one of those dark silk suits that are cut only by Roman tailors. The homburg on his brow was set at the classic diplomat's angle, and the compact brief case in his free hand completed the picture. So did the woman who followed him into the office with her flashlight's beam turned downward. The *trottoir* she was wearing would have graced a fashion plate; so would the traveling hat and veil. They suggested the diplomat's wife—or the diplomat's mistress. The man's gloved hand had unlocked the desk before Eric could quite realize this was Tully and Irene. Tonight their protective coloration fitted them both like second skins.

Tully's intent was obvious, once he had opened his desk drawer and extracted his diary. During the summer, Eric had often seen him bent above that same leather-bound volume. At the time he had assumed the social worker was recording the achievements of Merton House, and the troubled history of the Merton Project. Even at this moment, he needed a mental wrench to recall that Tully (by his very nature) had always been the project's enemy.

Now, of course, the man was closing shop and moving on—with his secretary-companion as his faithful satellite. Their quick, confident whispers, as they emptied both desks and transferred the papers to the brief case, established that motive beyond question. So did the unaccented French they were both speaking; the sibilant exchanges fitted the moment perfectly.

The veneer of calm broke as the last paper vanished into the brief case and Tully's whisper rose to a high, keening note of anger. Irene's flashlight outlined his face for a moment, as he continued to stand his ground in the cubicle. Then with a shrug he swallowed his fury and followed her from office to corridor. The flashlight winked among the work tables in the lab before the two bogus diplomats vanished through a fire door.

"What were they saying?"

Eric stepped from his hiding place, rejoicing in Eve's ignorance of foreign tongues. Tully, assuming that he was still en route to the hospital, had meant to lie in wait here, to murder him in cold blood when he entered the laboratory. He could hardly tell Eve that they had both missed death by a few second's margin. Or that those manic bursts of French (no less than the glimpse of Tully's face in the flashlight's beam) had convinced him the man was mad. The madness was still controlled. But it was real enough, even though Irene had persuaded him to depart while his immunity lasted.

The discovery, stunning though it was, gave Eric no choice of action. He knew he must bring this madman to earth, now his true nature was revealed. If Tully escaped tonight, the defeat of Operation Saboteur would be only an empty triumph.

The decision, and the means to implement it, crossed Eric's mind in a flash. Already he was moving toward the elevator, wishing he could find the words to put Eve off, and aware (even as they dropped to the basement garage) that he must tell her everything.

"They have a car downstairs. It's parked in the service alley. The moment the driveway's clear of ambulances, they're heading for Idlewild."

"Surely we can stop them."

"How? They have diplomatic passports and a clean slate. Who'll come forward to accuse them, now Juan is dead?"

"Can't you swear out a warrant?"

"Not without proof, Eve. Not unless Pete can help—" There was no time for more; the elevator's automatic doors had clanged open at basement level. Eric went to his car on the run, and dropped beneath the wheel.

"Why can't we go to Pete now?" Eve asked.

"There isn't time. And stop saying *we*. This is a one-man job."

Eve slipped into the bucket seat beside him, and spoke above the revving of the motor. "Not if you mean to follow them."

"I *can't* let you come with me——"

"You can't prevent it, Eric." Her voice, like her level eyes, matched his in firmness.

"Have you lost your mind?"

"Tell me your plan."

"I'm riding a hunch—and the sort of luck that won't come our way again. Tully knows the Ferrari by sight. Once he sees I'm on his taillight, he's bound to suspect the worst. I can still stop him, if I can make him lose his head."

"In that case," said Eve, "you'd best put this car in gear. Otherwise he'll be home free."

"Suppose I told you I mean to draw his fire, to have an excuse for arresting him?"

"Two targets are better than one," said Eve. "Take the ramp to emergency: we can follow him faster."

Eric permitted himself a single, blistering oath, then zoomed up the incline that led to open air.

"You realize this is completely mad, don't you?"

"Not half so mad as you'd be to go alone."

The tunneled entrance to the emergency room, like the service alley, opened to the esplanade of Manhattan Central. Nosing a cautious bumper into the night, Eric saw that Eve's advice had been sound. The last of the long file of ambulances had just pulled free. After the briefest of waits, Tully's car moved from its parking place.

It was a diplomat's limousine, hearse-black and purring like an earthbound jet. Once it gained the street, it settled into a correct city speed. It was meticulous in its observance of traffic signals while it approached the access to the East River Drive. Eric resisted the urge to ram the enemy to the curb and rely on his fists to bring the police. Tully had not yet observed him; he had been careful to hold well back in this first cautious pursuit. It was important to make sure of the man's present intentions before joining battle openly.

He glanced at the girl beside him. Eve's eyes were on the gleaming license plate ahead, and the plaque identifying the privileged registration of a *corps diplomatique*. He did not speak until both cars had swung into the empty uptown lanes of the Drive.

"You can still drop out at the toll gate."

"Pick up your speed a little, or you'll really lose him," said Eve.

"Did you hear my last remark?"

"Sorry—it didn't register. Isn't there some way to have him stopped on the Triborough?"

"Not with his license plate, and the credentials he's carrying. United Nations immunity's a hard nut to crack."

"You're right, of course. He'd end by having *us* arrested if we created a scene at the toll gate."

"The best we can do is report his number, and ask them to contact Pete. He'll have ways to pick up our trail—I hope."

"Suppose Tully heads straight into Idlewild, and doesn't mind being followed?"

"Once we're on the parkway, I'll make him mind. Promise to keep your head down when I hug his taillight."

As Eric had expected, the diplomat's car was stopped in the file of empty toll booths just long enough to record license and destination. His heart sank when Tully jumped from the gate at top speed. He roared into the same slot, to face the impassive eye of the attendant.

"Got business on the island, Doctor?"

"I'm going to Idlewild. Where is that black car bound?"

"Idlewild too. He's rushing to catch a plane."

"I'm Dr. Eric Stowe. That man and woman are wanted by the police. Their real names are Charles Tully and Irene Lusk. Write them down."

"Sure thing, Doc. They *said* they were UN——"

"Call Inspector Dalton—and have us followed."

Eric had spoken in staccato bursts. There was no time for more, with Tully's lights vanishing on the sweep of the Long Island Triborough.

It was a strange feeling to enter the Grand Central Parkway at a speed just under seventy—to realize, as the gap between Ferrari and limousine narrowed, that he could conceal his identity no longer. Again he wrestled with the temptation to crowd the enemy from the left-hand lane, to lock bumpers in a panic stop. Even here Eric knew he must play a waiting game. The first act of aggression must come from Tully himself.

The moon, obscured by rainy cloud rack, burst briefly into view, to bathe the six-lane highway in cold radiance. A moment later, the limousine cut its speed—so sharply that its pursuer was forced to brake sharply to avoid collision. The maneuver brought an exultant shout to Eric's lips, since it proved his strategy had paid its first dividends. Intent on his objective (and positive he was in the clear) Tully must have already visioned himself airborne—until the Ferrari took shape in his rear-view mirror.

Tully's cut in speed, Eric observed, was only a temporary ruse. While it lasted, he could half-believe the man was prepared to join battle on the spot. The hope was brief: a maintenance car, blinking red cruising lights as it drifted by, was warning enough that a moon-blanched superhighway was no place for a showdown. So was the police helicopter, crisscrossing the Grand Central one more

time before it churned from view above the roofs of Queens. When
Tully gunned his motor to streak east, Eric answered the challenge
—until he was hugging the enemy bumper, in the same dogged
effort to force his hand.

"He's spotted us, Eve! He knows why we're tailing him!"

What was Tully thinking at this moment—assuming that clouded
mind was rational? The success of Eric's plan would depend on the
answer. Did he fear that his pursuer had chapter-and-verse proof of
his crimes and waited only for their arrival at Idlewild to order his
detention? Did he suspect that the white meteor behind him was a
decoy, to give Dalton time to organize his pursuit from New York?
Or was Eric's first premise valid—namely, that Charles Tully (a
world citizen whose mask of virtue remained intact) was merely
teasing him, confident that no power on earth could keep him from
his waiting plane?

Pondering these estimates, Eric responded automatically when
the limousine swept into an exit some miles from the Idlewild
turnoff. Almost without transition, they entered a two-lane road
that led south, between silent blocks of suburbia. Tully had already
resumed his parkway speed. At this velocity, he could hardly
swerve again without overturning. Eric cut his own speed a trifle,
permitting the limousine to draw ahead by a dozen car lengths; it
was a routine precaution to guard against sudden enemy moves.

He could not repress a sense of fate converging when the two
cars raced into yet another world—a row of cemeteries that lay like
a great white wedge beneath the midnight sky and seemed at first
view to sweep on as endlessly as the road itself. Eric had observed
the district before on flights from Idlewild. Now, a trifle tardily, he
saw why Tully had chosen this particular route. The wedge of
cemeteries lay athwart Brooklyn and Queens, a necropolis that
made a natural no man's land between the boroughs. He had just
time to guess Tully's strategy when he heard the scream of brakes
ahead, the slurring complaint of tires on asphalt.

The guess became a certainty when the limousine, held in control despite its skid, careened to a stop astride both lanes of the
highway. Tully, finding the pursuit intolerable, had finally risen to
the challenge. His sudden blocking play gave his pursuer two
choices. There was still time to brake in turn and reverse course, a
move that would make the Ferrari a slow-moving target in this
city of the dead. Or the pursuer could hold his course, for the head-
on collision he had hoped for secretly since the enemy's flight

began. In either event, Tully would have a second chance to turn from hunted to hunter.

"Jump when I give the word," said Eric. "Make for the wall on your left."

Eve nodded, and her hands locked with his on the wheel as he trod on the gas. Ahead, the dead-black car seemed to rise out of the road with ghastly swiftness. Two jets of flame burst from its front window. The shots went wild; Tully, it appeared, was less than shockproof after all.

The Ferrari rammed the limousine before he could fire again—with enough force to cant the larger vehicle on its mudguards. Hearing Irene Lusk's scream, Eric saw that she had been pinned to the floor by the impact. Tully had already popped through a doorframe, like a jack-in-a-box: the brief case on the seat beside him, (governed by the same blind law of physics) jetted into space to drape across the Ferrari's bleeding radiator. Eric risked another shot to snatch up this windfall the second after he leaped free.

The collision had come too fast for thought, but he saw their luck had held. Eve had leaped on order, to roll harmlessly on the grassy shoulder of the road. She was on her feet at once, to make a fast, crouching run for the cemetery wall to the left. Eric followed, jamming the brief case inside his white hospital coat, and buttoning the garment to his chin.

Later he would realize that only seconds had intervened between that leap for safety and the appearance of Charles Tully from the shadow of the canted limousine. At the time (flattened at Eve's side behind the wall) the wait seemed hours long. While it lasted, he could almost hope that the architect of Operation Saboteur had collapsed beside Irene, who continued to moan faintly from the tonneau.

Tully's appearance banished such wishful thinking; so did the blunt-nosed gun he carried. The man was still a trifle groggy, but there was no mistaking his intent as he stood in the moon-blanched road. Luck (and good timing) had given Eric and Eve a brief advantage. Now it was obvious that one of the two cemetery walls concealed them—or at best, one of the first tiers of gravestones. Should they break cover, Tully could shoot them down at leisure. Should they cling to their meager shelter, he had only to mount to the roof of the wrecked car to seek them out.

Nature conspired briefly in their favor when drifting clouds began to obscure the moon, turning the twin wastelands beside the road to ghost-white blurs. When Tully moved to scan the far wall, Eric risked rising to his knees, to lob a stone into the cemetery. The impromptu missile made a devil's clatter as it fell among the graves, a good hundred feet from the pavement. Tully responded alertly to the decoy.

"Kick off your shoes and run, Eve."

Side by side, the hunted pair raced down the first alley between the headstones, tending toward higher ground within the cemetery where a cluster of mausoleums promised shelter. Safety depended on the chance that Tully (still exploring the far graveyard) would turn too late to discover them. The hope vanished when Irene shouted a warning from the wrecked car. There was just time to catch Eve in a flying tackle before Tully opened fire.

"Stay down, Eve, and make for high ground."

A second shot, like the first, was wasted on thin air. Tully did not waste another as he began to stalk them. Even in that white pattern of eternity, he could guess the precise spot where they had come to earth.

Progress on all fours, Eric soon realized, was a losing game. Their chances were lessened by a roving beacon from LaGuardia Field. Unnoticed in the bath of moonlight, the searchlight now became Tully's ally, brushing the gravestones like a questing white finger and pinning them to earth until it swung past. Already Eric could hear their enemy's panting breath on the slope below them. In another moment, he would mark their fumbling advance by sight as well as hearing. . . .

"We'll have to run, or we're lost," he said quietly. "Cut through the headstones on a diagonal. He'll have a better chance to miss."

Again Eve took his advice with no show of fear. This time, he let her lead their final, heart-bursting dash for the knoll, where a cluster of pseudo-Greek temples stood out clearly against the sky. Twice more they were forced to lie flat until the beacon had swept across their chosen path.

Tully was firing as he ran. Irene continued to shout directions from the road. She had forgotten her embassy French, in favor of a dialect Eric recognized as a *lingua franca* for all Central Asia. It seemed the proper obbligato for a deadly game of touch tag.

Just below the crest, he stumbled over a neglected grave. His fingers closed on a chunk of marble; it was a poor substitute for a Skoda automatic, but better than none. With Eve's hand in his, he dashed toward the shadow of the nearest tomb. Tully had lost their track for the moment in the snarl of graveled paths below.

The situation on the hilltop was no less desperate. The mausoleums were widely spaced, each with its sweep of lawn and knee-high privet hedge. There was no escaping the probe of the beacon. Once Tully had located them, they would be ideal silhouettes against those white backdrops.

"This door is *open*, Eric!"

He turned toward Eve's whisper. She was in the porch of the largest tomb and the bronze gate had swung wide at her touch. He had read of eccentrics whose wills specified such aboveground internment, complete with escape for Judgment Day. Tully (a careful hunter among the meaner graves below) had yet to mark their presence. Obeying an urge that transcended logic, Eric stepped boldly inside the tomb and drew Eve in beside him.

Once he had closed the gate, he realized his mistake. Tully (responding to a final shout from Irene) was tardily aware that they had vanished among these marble cenotaphs. Even if Irene had not marked their actual hiding place, he could now seek them out at leisure. Once he had found them, there was no way of excluding him. Heavy though it was, the gate would open at a touch; by its very nature, it could not be secured from within.

"We're cornered, aren't we?" It was a small, lost question, but Eve uttered it steadily enough.

"I'm afraid it's the end of the road," he said quietly. "We should have kept on somehow."

"Don't blame yourself, Eric. He was too close behind."

Even here the roving beacon sought them out, making the cramped shelter seem bright as day as it touched the grille work of the gate. At the first sweep, Eric could see their plight clearly. Four bronze caskets occupied the marble walls and projected into the mausoleum itself. Because of their massive bulk, there was barely room to stand between them. The fact that he had entered first placed Eve directly in the doorframe—which meant that her body, not his, would stop enemy gunfire. He was still damning his bad generalship when he heard the expected footfall outside.

Once the beacon swept their way again, Tully would see that the gate had neither hasp nor lock. The fragment of marble in Eric's hand had the rough shape of a baseball. Should he risk everything in a single attempt to brain their pursuer? He lifted his arm, then

leaned in despair against the gelid wall. The space was too confined for a full-armed throw.

"Drop to your knees," he whispered. "I'll tackle him when the door
opens."

"I can't budge, Eric. There isn't room."

Eve's tone had not wavered as the gun muzzle showed at the
gate, which had come ajar at its touch. Tully was still too cautious
to show himself. He spoke from the porch of the tomb, letting the
snout of the automatic advertise his presence.

"Toss out my brief case, Doctor, if you please." The voice had the
same comradely timbre the social worker had used in their hospital
encounters. *This is the moment he planned,* thought Eric. *He risked
everything to pin us down. Already he's savoring what's to follow.*

"Come and get your diary, Tully, if you want it that badly." The
dare was deliberate, and he was glad to note that his voice was as
detached as the enemy's.

"Let's not argue over trifles," said Tully. "I'll spare Miss Bronson,
if the contents of that brief case are in order. Sorry I can't do as
much for you."

"Am I that important?"

"Damnably important, Doctor, in our scheme of things. Men like
yourself have a way of spoiling our best-laid schemes. The power I
represent can't abide meddlers."

"It can abide failure even less, Tully."

"If it hadn't been for you—and that shipload of drugs—I'd have
succeeded brilliantly."

"Sorry to be a spoilsport. With your record, is it wise to go back?"

"Are you testing my courage, Dr. Stowe?" It's most unwise. My
guarantee for Miss Bronson won't last forever."

The sadist's game, Eric thought, had gone on beyond all reason.
Did Tully fear he was armed? He explored the suspicion cautiously.

"You must see you can't get away now."

"It's true I've paid a high price to dispose of you," said Tully.
"There's a short-wave set in my car; it picked up the police call
from the toll gate. Fortunately I've a refuge nearby. It's much
more secure than the one you've chosen. I'm nursing Irene there,
until she's able to travel——"

*"Stop your baiting, Tully!"*

"Why should I, when I'm enjoying each word of it?"

"I've asked you once to shoot it out."

"If you carried a gun, Doctor, you'd have used it long since. My desire to save Miss Bronson from your folly is quite genuine—but my patience won't last forever. I'll give you just twenty seconds to return my property."

"This time he means it," Eric told Eve in a whisper. "Take the brief case and go out. Run for your life when he starts in after me."

To his surprise, Eve made no objection. As she left the mausoleum, he flattened hard against the wall to await his moment. He was totally unprepared for the sudden scuffle outside, for Tully's bellow of rage. The sound was all he needed to send him charging into fresh air.

Eve, he saw, had approached the enemy with the brief case held before her like a shield. Her hand and Tully's were locked at the handle; her free hand clutched at Tully's right wrist, sweeping the gun away from the mausoleum door. In the uncertain light, her antagonist seemed twice her size, but he was held immobile for the moment. *Pete called her an Amazon,* he thought dazedly. *She's earned the title tonight.*

The beacon swung their way again, making the panting tableau real. Joining the unequal contest with no pause for thought, he lifted the chunk of marble to smash at Tully's skull. The man staggered from the blow, just as he broke free of Eve. The shot, delivered as his knees crumpled, struck home dully. . . .

It was followed by a rush of feet, converging from two sides on the tomb. Watching his man go down, aware that Eve had thrust her body between them as the Skoda automatic belched flame, Eric was only half-conscious of the keening sirens on the road. All that mattered was the fact that Eve had stopped the bullet meant for him, that the man who had fired it still lived.

While his red rage lasted, he did not even turn to see how badly she was hurt. His whole being was fixed on Charles Tully, on the blood-flecked stone that had felled him and would now avenge this last attempt at murder.

He was still astride his fallen enemy, with one arm raised for a deathblow, when a hand closed on his wrist.

"Leave him lie, Doctor."

The red haze lifted. Eric found himself staring into a pair of friendly eyes beneath a visored cap. Other blue-clad figures crowded the grass around him. Abandoning Tully to willing hands, he staggered to his feet.

"Who are you?"

"Sergeant Finch, sir. The inspector's driver. Seems we got here just in time."

Finch put both arms around Eric's shoulders as the immunologist turned with a great, strangled cry to the spot where Eve had fallen. "We're taking Miss Bronson to an ambulance now, Doctor. You can ride back with her."

### 3.

When a man operates for eight straight hours, Bob Trent reflected, his techniques grow automatic. There was no other defense against fatigue.

He had always known how far he could push his store of knowledge, how near exhaustion his nerves could take him. This morning, an hour before dawn, when he was told that his next case would be a bullet wound of the spleen, he did not question the intern about details. Compared with other crises he'd met tonight, a splenectomy seemed an almost simple procedure.

It was only when he crossed the sill of the emergency theatre—and found George Peters donning a gown—that he sensed the note of tension.

"Why are you assisting, George? You have cases of your own."

"One of the assistants will take them," said the resident. "They're no real problem."

"Neither is my next job, unless I've forgotten my surgical anatomy. Is the patient still hemorrhaging?"

"We've replaced the blood loss and brought her out of immediate shock," said Peters. "At the moment, she's in good shape."

"Then why the sudden concern? Afraid *I'll* collapse?"

"Dr. Stowe thought I should be with you. Your patient's Eve Bronson."

Bob stiffened and passed a hand across his eyes. "How did it happen?"

"I didn't get all the details. Apparently the shot was aimed at Stowe—and she stopped the bullet."

"Where is she now?"

"In the anesthetic room: Hank's looking after her." The resident gave Bob a searching glance. "You've got your first team, Bob. Sure you want to do the job yourself?"

The question was all the surgical chief needed to clear his brain. "Of course I'll do the job. Let's have a look at her."

At the table in the anesthetic room, the feel of Eve's pulse beneath Bob's fingers confirmed the resident's report: it was full and steady, and only a little above normal. A transfusion was working in the anterior vein of the left foot and the level of the blood-pressure chart was satisfactory. Eve herself was sleeping under her premedication, and her color was excellent.

"Start prepping," said Bob. "I'll be with you as soon as I've scrubbed."

"Dr. Stowe's outside," said Proctor.

"I'll talk to him later, Hank. I want this job behind me."

Aware that both doctors were frankly staring, he walked into the scrub room without meeting their eyes. His mind had closed in on the task before him: there was no need for further questions now. At the moment, he was not even curious to learn what twist of fate had brought Eve Bronson here. The fact that she had gone out with Eric to face mortal danger, the still more revealing fact that she had used her body to save him, was quite enough.

The operation was over in thirty minutes. Neither weariness nor the knowledge that the woman he loved was dependent on him for survival could affect Bob Trent's skill. The damaged spleen (blasted into a dozen sections by the explosive force of the bullet) had been removed and the sutures placed. Now, with the closure finished, Bob was dimly aware of Eric's presence as he followed the wheeled stretcher to the recovery room.

The immunologist was talking rapidly, Bob noted: the words registered, after a fashion. A story of flight and pursuit in a cemetery, a bizarre finale among the tombs . . . He found he could accept it without a flicker of surprise. George Peters had already told him the only facts that mattered.

He was sure now that Eve would live—and just as sure that he had lost her.

# 8.   Friday

ALL that week Eve had been a hospital heroine. From the moment Bob allowed visitors, the parade of well-wishers had been constant.

The visitors had come from every service in Manhattan Central; their thanksgiving for her recovery had sprung from their hearts. With their work-load close to normal once more, with the menace of *Pasteurella pestis* fading, she had put the final seal on their victory. Sulfamerazine had been another hero of that anxious week: the capture of Tully and Irene had given the first victory its imprimatur.

This morning, seven days after her emergency operation, Eve was well enough to sit on the terrace outside her room: an hour of fresh air and sunshine was part of her doctor's regimen. The fact that she could take the prescription a few feet from her hospital bed was Selden Grove's doing. He had insisted on these quarters, in the tower of the private wing.

Grove had made a point of daily visits—whenever he could steal time from the aftermaths of what, after all, had been a nine-day alert. He was standing beside her wheel chair now, having just removed it to the terrace rail, so they might look down together at the once empty plain of the Merton Project.

It was the third day of the power shovels. Already, between the taped-out building lines, one could sense the shape of things to come, as swarms of tin-hatted workmen atoned for lost time in the dust clouds. Only yesterday, the mayor and the governor had honored the ground-breaking with their presence. Selden Grove (as the moving spirit) had sealed the traditional time capsule into the project's first cornerstone.

When the director of Manhattan Central spoke, his voice was muted, Eve knew he was reliving that high moment in memory. "I still can't believe those shovels are real," he said. "To my dying day, I won't grasp Jasper Merton's change of heart."

"Perhaps he saw that *he* was dying," said Eve. "He must have wanted a better monument than oil derricks."

"It's a pious thought, my dear. I'm glad to accept it—and so were the project trustees." Selden Grove continued to stare down at the roiling dust cloud, with the air of a man reprieved. *He looks ten years younger today,* thought Eve. *It's easy to see why.*

"When will the first housing unit be ready?"

"By next fall," said Grove. "We're paying extra to make them keep that promise."

"I'm glad there are New Yorkers left to fill it."

"Thanks to you and Eric," said the director. "Did you know this is the second day since a new case of plague has been reported?"

"Thank Eric for that, not me. *I* did no more than a hundred others on your staff."

"Do you deny you risked your life to save him?"

"So would anyone who'd known him, Doctor. This won't be the last battle with plague—or the men who paid Charles Tully."

Selden Grove smiled. "If I were a French general," he said, "I'd kiss you on both cheeks. Heroines are rare enough. A heroine who refuses to wear her laurels is rarer still."

Eve was still on the terrace when a soft knock sounded on the hall door. Inspector Peter Dalton (looking a shade more rested than usual) slipped in at her call, with his familiar air of a harried bookkeeper on the prowl.

"Sorry I couldn't visit you sooner, Miss Bronson," he said. "I hope the flowers atoned for my neglect."

"I've read the papers, Inspector. Congratulations on your promotion."

The detective moved to the terrace rail and perched there precariously, with his eyes on the growing excavation below. *"You'd* get that promotion, if you'd consent to join my department," he said. "Not that you wouldn't need training. Next time you pursue an international bandit, promise you'll use a squad car, not a snow-white roadster."

Eve smiled. "Does it matter now? The Ferrari was insured."

"Your lives weren't," said Pete. "Not for their full value, at any rate. Didn't you realize we had every parkway covered, for just such a getaway? Or that both cars were spotted by 'copter, the moment they left the Triborough?"

"Sorry, Inspector. As you say, I've a great deal to learn."

"You were followed five minutes after you made that turnoff," said Pete. "We'd have nailed Tully and his girl, with time to spare. Couldn't you have stayed in that tomb a little longer?"

"I'll answer your question with another," said Eve. "Could you have arrested Tully if he'd reached Idlewild on schedule?"

The detective did not answer for a moment. When he turned, his grin matched Eve's. "All right, Miss Bronson. I admit you saved us a great deal by stopping that bullet."

"And keeping Tully's brief case," said Eve. "Don't forget that."

They exchanged a still broader smile. During the return by ambulance, both Pete and Eric had tried in vain to loosen Eve's grip on that square of bloodstained leather. Her fingers had relaxed only when they reached the emergency room at Manhattan Central, and George Peters had administered preoperative sedation.

"Thanks to his brief case," said Pete, "we hardly needed to put Tully on the grill. He spelled out his intentions in that diary. As thoroughly as the mad paperhanger in *Mein Kampf*."

"Enough to convict him?"

"More than enough. It pin-points every act of sabotage. And names every victim, including Rita Lemayo. Strange, isn't it, how such men insist on blueprinting their conquests—and how good citizens refuse to believe them?"

Pete left his perch, and looked down again at the excavation Selden Grove had surveyed with such loving care. The detective's glance, though it seemed cursory, was quite as inclusive.

"In my youth," he said, "I lived in one of those cesspools we're destroying now. So did John Newman—and your hospital director. With luck, our grandchildren may go to the history books to learn what 'slum' means."

"Only if we can stop other Tullys," said Eve.

"Blue chips win card games, Miss Bronson—including world-poker. At the moment, the free world's dealing. If those builders finish their work, I think our grandchildren can handle the next big card party."

"I trust you aren't an optimist, Inspector."

Pete Dalton shrugged, and moved to the door of the hospital room. On the threshold, he lifted one hand in a solemn gesture of benediction.

"A man in my trade has no time for philosophy," he said. "He has still less for romantic pictures of tomorrow. As a good Catholic, may I ask all the saints to guard your future?"

The immunologist came to the terrace a few minutes after the law's departure. Eve had been anticipating his arrival all that morning—and dreading it a little. Somehow her glimpse of the airplane satchel he carried made her feel easier.

"Is this really good-by Eric?"

"Apparently you've read about the outbreak of Q fever in Ghana. I'm flying there tonight, now my job is over in New York."

"I'd give a great deal to join you," said Eve.

"I wish you could."

"Don't be *too* resigned about it," she warned him. "It's hardly gallant."

"May I ask just one question before I go?"

"Of course. I try to answer truthfully."

"That night in the cemetery—when it was your life or mine. Why did you save me?"

Eve had expected the question since she opened her eyes in the recovery room. Knowing just where it would lead, she was careful to speak without emotion.

"I had to fight Tully. There was no choice."

"You could have given up his brief case so easily. Why did you try that suicide wrestle?"

"Because I don't believe in surrender," said Eve.

"Was that your only reason?"

"Of course not. I meant to save your life, if I could. I'm glad I succeeded."

"It wasn't because you love me."

"Men like you are in short supply, Eric. There'll always be enough nurses."

"Bob doesn't think so."

"When did you find out for sure—about Bob and me?"

"In the ambulance," he said ruefully. "You mentioned his name several times while you were in shock. *Mine* didn't come up once."

It was the last hurdle: Eve faced it squarely before she soared above it.

"Would you take me to Ghana if I asked?"

"Only if you'd promise to stay above the battle."

"Do you think I'd be content on the sidelines, while you were saving lives?"

"I love you, Eve—whether or not you love me. Don't you see I'd have to spare you all I could?"

"Even when I don't want to be spared?"

He took her hand in his. She kept her counsel to the end, knowing she could still change his whole life with a word.

"Thanks again, Eric," she whispered.

"For what, my dear?"

"For making tomorrow's miracle come true today."

He was still smiling around the sadness of losing her. She made no effort to help him. Someday, she felt sure, he would find a partner to share his loneliness: it was hardly her fault she could not volunteer.

"Don't praise me for Operation Epidemic," he said. "It's the job I was trained for. If I've succeeded, that's reward enough."

"Who else could have saved New York from plague?"

"Who else could have saved us from Tully?"

He had kissed her with the words: the kiss was a form of homage. Then he left her. She was fighting tears when she heard Bob's step in the door—but the smile she offered him glowed with happiness.